WEB OF LIES

BOOK TWO
OF
THE HUNDRED HALLS

THOMAS K. CARPENTER

Web of Lies

Book Two of The Hundred Halls

by Thomas K. Carpenter

Published by Black Moon Books

Cover design by Ravven
www.ravven.com

Discover other titles by this author on:
www.thomaskcarpenter.com

ISBN-13: 978-1539733874

ISBN-10: 1539733874

Also by Thomas K. Carpenter

ALEXANDRIAN SAGA
Fires of Alexandria
Heirs of Alexandria
Legacy of Alexandria
Warmachines of Alexandria
Empire of Alexandria
Voyage of Alexandria
Goddess of Alexandria

THE DASHKOVA MEMOIRS
Revolutionary Magic
A Cauldron of Secrets
Birds of Prophecy
The Franklin Deception
Nightfell Games
The Queen of Dreams
Dragons of Siberia
Shadows of an Empire

THE DIGITAL SEA TRILOGY
The Digital Sea
The Godhead Machine
Neochrome Aurora

GAMERS TRILOGY
GAMERS
FRAGS
CODERS

THE HUNDRED HALLS
Trials of Magic
Web of Lies
Alchemy of Souls
Gathering of Shadows
City of Sorcery

All courses of action are risky, so prudence is not in avoiding danger—it's impossible—but calculating risk and acting decisively. Make mistakes of ambition and not mistakes of sloth. Develop the strength to do bold things, not the strength to suffer.

–Niccolo Machiavelli, *The Prince*

WEB OF LIES

1

Sometimes keys opened portals into other worlds. Other times, they had the mark of secrecy, locking away things that should never be seen. Keys could do all sorts of things, but the one thing they couldn't do was lie about what they were used for.

The key in Aurelia Silverthorne's hand cleaved to the high-grade lock on the old building in the Enochian District like a long-lost friend. The door solid, not rattly like the one in Aurie's old apartment in the thirteenth ward. The former historical district had deep bones in the city, good brick walls, and doors that couldn't be picked with a coat hanger.

The shelves and counters inside were covered in dust, and water stains covered the back wall, but a quick inspection revealed no rat droppings, which was a relief. When Aurie had purchased it at the property auction, she was prepared to fix things, but she didn't want any rats, or spiders. The building had other features she couldn't quite understand, like a row of large cubbies along the west wall and a pile of mannequins in the back room.

A deeper inspection revealed that she'd gotten lucky. The

price had been virtually free—the city wanted the property off their records and back to earning taxes. She hadn't entirely planned on purchasing a property, but a freak storm had kept attendance at the auction to a minimum, and she was able to purchase it with the money she had in her purse. The only reason no one had outbid her was because the only other person in the room had stepped out for a cigarette, and he'd already bought two dozen properties.

The clerk had asked why a smart-looking young woman wanted a building in *their* area, but Aurie had just smiled and ignored him. While she didn't know any non-humans, she wasn't going to judge them en masse, and what was the point of opening a clinic if it wasn't in the area that people needed it the most?

Aurie had also checked into the legality of the clinic, but found nothing keeping her from the idea. The city of Invictus had loose laws surrounding magic, assuming you were not violating norms by committing crimes like murder, or assault. The only reason she couldn't practice magic at Golden Willow was due to hospital rules. While she loved interacting with the kids and helping out on the floor, she didn't feel as useful as she thought she should be.

Opening her own clinic seemed kind of crazy—she hadn't even told her sister Pi about it—but once she'd seen the property auction on a flyer at the Supermagic Market, she couldn't shake the idea.

Once she'd surveyed the property, Aurie carried the box of cleaning supplies from the light blue Corolla she'd borrowed from Xi into the building. Then she drove the car back to Arcanium, and came back to the eleventh ward on the Red Line.

When she returned, a man in a baggy lime green sweater approached from the row of brownstones across the street past the empty dragon fountain in the middle of the square. A woman holding a toddler by the hand stood at their front door, watching.

"You can't be here," said the man in a squeaky voice before he'd reached her. His frayed corduroy pants whisked together as he walked. He was shorter and smaller than her, with a shaggy head of hair and an elongated nose indicating he was a non-human. The loose-fitting clothes seemed to be hiding other differences.

"I bought this place," Aurie said, jabbing her thumb at the building behind her.

His nose wriggled with what she could only assume was disgust.

"I'm Aurie," she said, holding out her hand in greeting.

After giving the air a testing sniff, he scooted forward until he barely touched her fingertips with his hand, then backed away as if she might be contagious. "Nezumi," he said, eventually.

"It's nice to meet you, Nezumi. Is that your wife and child over there?" she asked.

Nezumi's black eyes rounded with excitement. "Yes. Best wife. Best child. Now we have good house. Warm bed. Happy family."

"Congratulations," she said. "I'm happy for you."

He eyed her carefully as if he didn't believe her, but she was happy, even if it came with a twinge of jealousy. Would that ever get better? Would that ever change? Or would she always look at families and wonder how hers might have been?

"Not many live here," she said, trying to make small talk.

"Maybe good. House cheap, so Nezumi can afford. Otherwise, live under bridge or in Undercity," he said.

He kept glancing around as if he expected an ambush at any moment. Life in the Undercity had probably engrained that. She could tell he had a gentle soul.

"What do you do, Nezumi?" she asked.

He puffed up his chest. "I am assistant librarian. Head librarian lets me sniff books, find the mold, so we can keep the books safe. Lets me read when no books to sniff. Maybe someday I will be a regular librarian and get to work counter."

"I love books, too! I want to help you," said Aurie, a bubbling joy forming in her chest. To help someone like him carve out a little more civilization within the crowded city was exactly why she'd come to the district. She knew in her mind that she had unreasonable expectations of how quickly she could accomplish it, but that wasn't going to stop her.

"You do?" asked Nezumi suspiciously.

He kneaded his hands together. His jacket was threadbare. She could tell he was barely keeping things together.

"I'm opening a clinic," she said, trying to sound confident, yet to her ears she felt like a child telling their parents they wanted to be an astronaut or a fireman.

"Clique? We don't need clique here, whatever that is," he said, nose twitching furiously. He glanced at his wife anxiously as if they were late for an appointment.

"No. A clin-ic. I'm a mage. I can help people," she said.

He recoiled from her as if slime had poured from her nose and ears. He scurried to her side and started pushing her.

"No-no-no. No mages. You can't be here," he said. "Nezumi say go."

"What's wrong with mages?" she asked, genuinely curious.

"Mages okay, but not here," he said, nearly to tears. "Big problems."

She outweighed him considerably, but didn't want to hurt him, so she let him push, even though he wasn't budging her. "I'm not leaving. I came here to help. This place needs public services."

"We okay on own," squeaked Nezumi. "Magic brings the wakers from the darkness. Gives them life. So you must go. No mages. Always trouble. Trouble they are. Shoo, mage, shoo."

She sighed and gently removed his hands from her, pushing him towards his wife and child on the other side of the street.

"It'll be fine," said Aurie. "I know what I'm doing."

He turned away, but the last look on his face said otherwise. It was disappointed, and worried, and almost to tears.

Once he was out of hearing range, she added, "I hope," and went into her building. The first thing Aurie did was remove the boards on the front windows, letting in the afternoon light, and revealing the previous shop name: Enchanting Apparel. The name explained the cubbies and mannequins.

She didn't know any spells to remove sign lettering from windows, so she used a variation of truth magic, whispering to the letters that they really didn't want to stick to the glass. After a few pokes with a scraper, the letters fell off.

Next, she spent a few hours sweeping, mopping, scrubbing, and generally sanitizing the room. She could have removed the grime with a spell, but she knew from her work at the hospital that it was more satisfying to do it by hand.

As daylight faded, Aurie turned on the portable lamp she'd brought, since the electricity hadn't been turned back on, and kept cleaning. On previous visits to the Enochian District, she'd made herself scarce at night, but she decided that if she was going to serve the community, she needed to get over her fears.

Aurie was cleaning a counter when she saw movement outside the window, felt eyes watching her. She didn't think it was Nezumi, since the figure was much larger. Despite her heartbeat doubling, she kept cleaning as if nothing was wrong.

A single thump of a fist against the window made her drop the soapy sponge back into the bucket. Nezumi's words about wakers in the darkness trickled back into her mind.

Magic brings the wakers from the darkness. Gives them life.

Aurie moved to the window and pressed her face against it to see past the glare. No one was out there, at least that she could see. Probably some kids pulling a prank. She knew they wouldn't want her here at first.

She kept cleaning, and after a while, she forgot about what had made the noise. Then something hit the door hard enough to rattle the bell.

When she couldn't see anyone in the immediate vicinity, she unlocked the door and slipped outside.

"Hello?"

The night swallowed her greeting. The street lights in the Enochian District had been knocked out, except for a pair further down the street.

Aurie was prepared to go back inside when a figure moved to the edge of the light from her clinic.

"Hello, friend," she said.

The person stood awkwardly, one shoulder lower than the other. On a scale of zero to creepy he was somewhere around vaguely nightmarish.

"You shouldn't stand like that. Bad for posture," she joked, hoping to break the mood if it was just some kid trying to get a rise out of her. There was no response, not even a twitch.

Aurie was aware he was only a few strides away, and could be on her before she could muster a single spell, but she didn't want to get off on the wrong foot with a resident of the district.

Aurie stood her ground and said in as calm a voice as

she could muster, "I'm opening a clinic to help those in need. You can pay what you can afford. I'll be here Tuesday and Thursday evenings, and Sunday afternoons."

The last part she'd made up on the spot. She hoped that would work with her classes, since they started in a week, but she didn't think it'd be a problem.

When he didn't respond, Aurie decided to get a closer look. She touched her earrings to summon the light that was contained within. The figure recoiled from the lumination and, rather than return to its nearly comatose state, started pawing at the air as if it were waking. She'd caught a brief glimpse of the man; he looked like a mindless drug addict, or a well-dressed zombie without the rotting flesh.

On the far end of the street near the dragon fountain, Aurie detected more movement, a couple of shapes milling around. A tangy metallic scent filled the air, making her nose itch.

"Goodbye," she said, then dispelled the light and returned inside. She checked the lock twice before resuming her cleaning.

A minute later something heavy hit the window like a rock or a balled fist. The lantern reflected against the window, making seeing outside impossible, so she switched it off. After her eyes adjusted, she saw a figure slumped against the glass. Probably the same guy who wouldn't leave her alone.

The urge to run out the back and abandon the clinic for another night nearly overwhelmed her, but she knew if she left now, she'd never come back. Sure, the Enochian district was filled with non-humans, but they were essentially people, mostly.

But also like people, some of them had less than savory motives. Annoyed by the constant attempts to turn her cleaning into a horror movie, Aurie moved outside, this time ready to use magical force if necessary.

The person was leaning against the glass at what appeared to be a painful angle, almost as if they didn't have a working spine.

"You need to leave now," she said.

The person pulled away from the glass in a grotesque undulation, then took a shambling step towards her. She didn't like the way the creature held its arms, a little too grabby for her tastes.

"If you don't say something, make me a little less nervous about you, I'm going to knock you on your ass," she said.

The figure lurched towards her, arms rising. The distant streetlights revealed a slack expression, which could mean any number of creatures, none of them promising.

When it made a grab for her, she knocked it back with a force bolt. This only incensed the creature, and as soon as it regained its feet, it doubled the effort.

"Get back," she said, hitting it again.

After the second force bolt, interested grunts from the other side of the square moved in her direction. Not wanting to further enrage it, she slipped back into the building and locked the door.

The creature, acting like a zombie minus the rotting flesh, pressed against the glass, banging his fist. Aurie backed into the middle of the room, regretting taking the wooden boards off the front. Shapes moved towards the shop, while the creature rattled her door.

A half dozen of the creatures milled about the front. Some of them pressed against the window as if they could sense her, while the one at the door continued trying to turn the handle. A good rock and they would overrun the front.

Then something attracted their attention. They moved away like a school of fish. Aurie silently cheered until she realized they could be going after someone else.

She slipped out the front door. The creatures were headed directly across the street towards a house with faint illumination peeking through a gap in the curtains. It was the brownstone that she'd seen Nezumi and his family enter.

Magic brings the wakers from the darkness. Gives them life.

Aurie silently cursed. He'd warned her, but she hadn't listened close enough. Some creatures fed on faez, or were attracted to it, which made using magic around them dangerous. She was fine with putting herself in danger, but not another person, especially with a young one in the house. And she really liked Nezumi, even if he hadn't liked her.

She jumped into action as soon as she heard glass shattering. Aurie ran across the street. One of the creatures was pushing through the broken glass on the front door while more were headed towards the house. Nezumi's silhouette appeared in the doorway. He was using a baseball bat to knock the creature back, squeaking loudly each time he swung.

The distant streetlights made seeing difficult, and Aurie ran into one of the creatures. It clutched at her arm. The strength surprised her. She pushed and pulled to no avail, fearing to use magic while surrounded by them. It wasn't trying to bite her like a zombie, but it wasn't letting go either, squeezing tighter by the second. Another one swiped at her arm, so she spun around, using the one latched onto her as a shield. There were a half dozen of them closing in.

Nezumi battled the creature in his doorway, squeaking curses at it as he swung the baseball bat, but the creature knocked him away and marched inside. Screams from his wife, followed by a child crying, put an ache in Aurie's chest.

"Greased!" she yelled, hoping to convince the cobblestones around her that they had been lathered in lubricating oils.

The effect was immediate. The creatures slipped and fell, looking like drunks on roller skates. The one latched onto her went down, dragging her with it, but she was able to kick it off.

More grunts and calls went up from further down the street. Each use of magic seemed to be drawing out more and more of them, but she had no choice. Aurie cast a sticky spell on the soles of her boots and scrambled past reaching hands to Nezumi's doorway. The creature inside the house was reaching towards Nezumi's wife, a petite woman who had features similar to his. Aurie blasted it with force magic and, while it was stunned, launched it through the open door.

Nezumi clutched his bat, shaking with fear, beady black eyes smoldering. "Told you. Go away, mage. Go away. Ruin everything."

He had tears in his eyes. The concern for his family was evident in his quivering lip.

"Do you have anything to block this door with?" she asked.

"No matter," he said, shaking his head. "Thralls come, and come, and come, woke by magic, drawn by light in the darkness. Now we must leave, never come back. Home ruined."

Aurie's heart broke in two while Nezumi checked on his wife, who was calm despite the danger. The little girl in pigtails standing at his wife's side had big wide eyes as she stared at the open door. She also had a thick hairless tail sticking out her dress.

She slapped the door in frustration. It was never easy, was it? It would have been better had she never had this clinic idea. But it was too late to turn back, she'd already ruined things.

"What are they?" Aurie asked, keeping an eye out the front for the next batch of thralls. The ones in front were still trying to gain their feet.

"*His* thralls," said Nezumi. "Coming soon, I bet. Woke by magic. Now we all dead."

Aurie looked past Nezumi. His wife had white hair, an elongated nose, and a reddish tint to her eyes. She held their daughter to her side, looking ready to fend off an army to protect her.

"Is there a way out back?" asked Aurie.

Nezumi shook his head. "Alleyway. Thralls catch us there. Keep us for him."

Aurie looked back out the front. The thralls were recovering, making their way to the door. She knew what she had to do, even if it wasn't the best option.

"I'm going to lead them away," she said. "Once they come after me, then you can escape."

"But where? Home ruined," said Nezumi, jowls quivering with sobs.

"I'm sorry, Nezumi. I just wanted to help," she said.

He grew angry and hissed at her, revealing a mouth full of sharp teeth. "You bad mage. Bring this on us. You humans all bad. Ruin everything."

Aurie had run out of time if she was going to get away. "I'll make up for this somehow, I swear," she said, before leaping past a thrall about to make the steps. As soon as she landed, Aurie clicked the light on her earrings on. She almost regretted doing so, as there were more thralls than she expected. The street was crawling with nearly a hundred, and now they were focused on her.

A thrall tried to grab her, so she used a force bolt to knock it back. Bad idea. It was like each use of magic turned them up. They came on stronger. She tried to break out, make it to the open street so she could get to the train station, but a group of thralls cut her off. She dodged around the first two, but realizing she was cut off had to make a beeline for her shop.

As she ran, the sensation of wings passing overhead spiked her heart. The presence of something older, more dangerous woke a primal fear. The hair on the back of her neck was at full attention.

She made the clinic, closing and locking the door behind her. The thralls slammed against the window on the door, rattling the bell again.

A fist broke the window. Shards of glass flew through the air, some sticking in her hair. She was cut. Blood flowed from her arm.

She unleashed a jet of flame, powerful enough to char the chest of the first row. This threw them back, but others smashed through the picture window.

Aurie had no time to worry about what else was out there as the crowd flowed into the front room, ignoring the jagged glass as if it were merely cardboard.

There were too many to fight, so Aurie retreated towards the back. A thrall flanked her and grabbed her wounded arm. She blasted fire into his face, but he held on. Only when she yanked her arm away did it come free, helped by the slick blood.

Aurie threw herself into the back room with the mannequins, locking the door behind her. Fists pounded on the door. She could hear glass breaking as more marched into her clinic.

While the front door that she'd come through had been made of iron, the door between the two rooms was flimsy wood that bulged as the creatures pressed against it. It wasn't going to hold, and she didn't want to rush out the back, or the other thing in the darkness might get her.

Aurie whispered to the door that it was strong and could withstand a battering ram if needed. This helped the door, but she knew it wouldn't hold forever. There were too many of them.

She looked around the room for things she might use for spells. She always kept a few reagents in her purse, but it was in the other room. The only things in her pockets were the keys and a tube of superglue. The room was empty save for a pile of coat hangers and the dozen mannequins lying in a pile like a plastic pyre. It wasn't a lot to go on, but she couldn't be picky in an emergency. She'd make do with what she had.

Aurie grabbed a mannequin, a female model missing an arm, and set it near the door keeping the creatures out. She whispered to it, explaining that it wasn't really plastic, but flesh. She knew this wouldn't work for long, but she hoped to distract the creatures long enough to give her a head start.

She only got half the mannequins in place before the first hole was put in the wooden door. Aurie abandoned the rest and started working on the hangers. She unfolded a few into long wires and twisted them together to make a cube-like scaffold. Some creatures didn't like the touch of iron, and she hoped the winged creature was one of those.

As the undead bashed the door into bits, Aurie waited at the back with her hanger sculpture. She wanted them to come all the way in before she went running out, in hopes that the big one in back would be lured in by the thick scent of flesh.

When the first creature shambled into the room, ignoring the light from her earrings, it went straight for the nearest mannequin and started bashing its plastic head. Aurie caught the reflection of crazed eyes before she switched her earrings off.

As more shuffled in, falling upon the remaining mannequins, Aurie went out the back, taking the time to lock the door with her keys while simultaneously trying to ignore their rattling as her hand shook.

Distant city lights reflected off the upper portions of the building, giving Aurie a good idea of her running lane through the alley. She thought she'd gotten away until she broke into the street and she heard wings thrashing into the air from the front of the clinic.

With the coat hanger scaffolding suspended above her head, Aurie pumped her legs as fast as she could. It was a good half mile to the Red Line station. If the coat hangers didn't work, there was no way she was going to make it.

The horrible presence neared. She reflexively ducked as she ran, which probably saved her neck from getting snapped off when the creature flew over, snatching the coat hangers from her hands. A crumpled pile of hangers went bouncing past Aurie.

Shit.

The thing circled her from above. She zigged and zagged a few times, hoping to throw it off, but she had so far to run.

Then it was gone. She couldn't feel it above her. Aurie wondered if she'd passed some invisible barrier, then a heavy boot hit her in the back, throwing her forward to tumble into a pile.

The winged creature landed ten feet away. There was no mistaking the malevolence directed at her as it made a laughing sound so deep that it only registered as a rumbling in Aurie's chest.

She thought about running, but there was no way she'd get away now. She was feeling dizzy from the loss of blood, the fear-filled sprint, and getting knocked off her feet. She'd have to make a stand, here and now.

Aurie staggered to her feet and removed her earrings. She whispered to them, telling them how they were mini-suns, waiting to come out, to shine like the deep desert, when nothing could avoid their gaze. Then she pulled the tube of superglue out, performed a bit of delayed transference magic on it, and threw the earrings as she activated them. The sunburst was as bright as welding light. Even Aurie was temporarily blinded, but she sprinted ahead, brushing past the leathery wings of the creature.

The earrings stuck to the creature, which screamed in rage. Aurie pushed as hard as she could, glancing back occasionally to see it still fighting to remove the earrings. They didn't seem to be injuring it, but annoyed it enough that it was distracted.

By the time the earrings had been removed, Aurie was way down the street. She finally let the fear into her limbs, if only to go a little faster as she imagined it right behind her. She kept expecting to be lifted off the ground, to be carried high into the air in its deadly embrace.

She'd seen it briefly when the earrings had flown through the air. The image of a well-dressed human with leathery wings wasn't what she'd expected. The nature of its origin unknown to her, but she had no time to contemplate as she raced towards the train station.

Eventually her lungs and thighs burned so hot, she was forced to slow, especially when her boot ripped from the sole, giving her a partial flat tire. Salty sweat stung her eyes, and she recognized she'd lost too much blood. Between heaving breaths, Aurie patched her arm with a simple spell. It wasn't permanent, but she could worry about that later.

At last, she limped onto the train, throwing herself into a seat right across from the door. A mother and her two boys got up and moved when they saw her sweat-soaked hair glittering with broken glass and blood-soaked arm. Aurie watched the open door for the appearance of the creature, only allowing herself to relax when the doors finally closed and the train lurched into motion.

Aurie laid her head back and closed her eyes, relishing the feeling of being alive. That'd been too close.

When she opened them, the woman was still staring at her, holding her hands over her boys' eyes. They both squirmed to get a look at her.

Aurie heaved quietly, catching her breath, shame filling her chest at the disaster of her first night in the district. She hoped that Nezumi and his wife and child had gotten away, but even if they had, they had no place to go as she'd ruined their home. Why was trying to help people so hard? Aurie leaned her head against the cold glass and watched the lights turn into streaks.

2

The ethereal sounds of experimental jazz wafted into the back room of the Glass Cabaret, vibrating the picture frame in Pi's hands. She took a big breath and blew the dust off the rectangle, revealing a picture of Radoslav standing next to a mobster with a Tommy gun tucked under his arm. Except for the cut of his clothes and a slightly different haircut, Radoslav hadn't changed a bit.

Pi imagined a shiny picture frame and whispered to it. A halo of dust puffed away, coating her hands and cascading to the floor. She set it in the early 1900s pile and was digging through the box when she heard a purposeful foot scuff in the doorway.

Radoslav, the owner of the Glass Cabaret and a city fae, stood with his hands behind his back, his impeccably tailored suit and thin tie reminding her of Joseph Gordon-Levitt if he had chalky skin tones and eyes as gray as an Irish day.

When he didn't say anything, she shrugged and pulled out the next picture frame and blew the dust off.

"Preparing for a birthday party?" she cracked, letting a wry smile ghost her lips.

He stared at the brick wall on the other side as if it were a movie screen. A trickle of worry shivered down her spine.

"Radoslav?" she asked.

He blinked and looked back to her as if he'd forgotten she was in the room.

"Yes?" he asked, his voice making her want to spill her every secret. It was getting easier hearing him without getting all mush-brained, but she had to concentrate.

"Why do you have me doing this? I mean, isn't this a waste of my talents? Can't you have one of your employees clean this room out?" she asked.

He raised a lone eyebrow, a gesture honed to a priceless art form. After working for him for a year, she'd come to appreciate the language of that one motion. He could say a thousand things with it. In this case, it was both mocking and humor-filled.

"They might wonder about my history if they saw me standing next to Billy the Kid or Anastasia Romanov," he said.

"They don't know?" she asked.

"Deep down inside they do, but they choose to ignore it," he said. "Besides, they cannot enter this room and leave."

A chill passed through Pi. The room didn't seem remarkable. The walls were regular brick and mortar.

"It's a place of between," he added.

It must be her ability to wield faez that made it possible for her to leave, she decided; otherwise he would have never let her in.

Radoslav kept staring at the back wall.

"How come I haven't seen any pictures of your family?" asked Pi.

"We do not speak unless it is necessary," he said.

"How long has it been?" she asked.

He tilted his head. "One hundred and thirty-one years."

She didn't know much about the maetrie, but it tugged at her heart to think they were estranged.

"You should let them know how you're doing," she said. "I wish I had family to talk to. After my parents died, there was no one left, except my sister and I. I've checked online, but there's no one else. Supposedly my dad had a brother, but he ran away from home at a young age and disappeared somewhere in Russia. I'd give anything to learn about my family."

"Be glad you don't know the rest of your family. They might disappoint you. I know mine have," he said, glaring at the wall.

She checked over her shoulder. "Why do you keep looking over there?"

His nostrils flared almost imperceptibly. Disappointment. She knew that gesture well. He did that after just about every job she did for him. *Why is he disappointed...? Oh. Between.*

Fae magic required extensive mastery of linguistics, even more than Infernal. Many a historian thought Tolkien had used fae as a basis for his Middle Earth, except that he'd dumbed it down for ordinary readers.

Pi whispered a few phrases and cast a spell on her eyes so that she might see past the mortal structures that bound her world. Like ink being bleached by the sun, the brick room faded from view until she could see through the walls to the rain-slicked street. Spires twisted themselves into the sky, the tops hidden by the low clouds, ever-present giants watching with disapproval. Two figures moved towards them with impossibly slow grace.

"Are they coming to see you?" she asked.

His lip twitched, and his eyes turned black. "You've done enough today. Come back tomorrow and finish."

"Could I stay? You're the only maetrie I've met," she said.

"Be glad," he said, a little more forcefully.

"I promise I won't say anything," she said. "It'll be good for my education, which is good for you. My employer. Maybe I'll want to re-up at the end of my three years."

"Re-up?" he said, tasting the words like a fine wine. He seemed amused by her loyalty.

"I might need a favor down the road," she said.

To her surprise, he agreed. He blew out a puff of smoke that collected around her. It made her feel dizzy, like she'd been breathing in a bag for a minute.

"Say nothing, do nothing. My enchantment will obfuscate your presence. They will know you're here but think you're a leal guardian, or a summoned imp. You won't be worth their notice," he said.

Pi slipped into the corner, imagining herself as a mouse. The room no longer held boxes of old pictures. An obsidian cube sat in the middle of the room like a table. Power vibrated from the object, making the back of her teeth itch. She assumed it created a portal between realms, just like their runic switches had last year.

As the two figures neared, the vibration increased until Pi was squinting. Their features stayed blurry as if they were living watercolor paintings.

They stepped through the barrier as if it were a waterfall. Their details snapped into existence. Pi gasped, eliciting a flickering glance from the first maetrie. It was damning. Dismissive.

Pi hated herself for staying, until she remembered it was their inherent magic.

"Raddie, ya facking clank," said the first.

He wore a jet-black three-piece suit with a black tie. Reminded her of David Beckham if he had pale hair and sharper features. Could cut glass on his cheekbones.

"Slyvan," said Radoslav with a coldness that should have seen frost coming out his mouth, then to the second maetrie, "Bastone."

Bastone, she guessed, was the muscle, based on his size and imposing crossed arms. It took a moment for Pi to realize his arms were made of iron. The maetrie weren't as allergic as their forest cousins, but she couldn't imagine one having iron permanently attached to his body. It would make a fearsome weapon though.

"Now that you've seen me, you can kindly get the fuck out," said Radoslav in a level tone.

Slyvan adjusted his black tie. "Have a mind, Raddie. Have a keen mind. Her Ladyship don't like that you been ignoring her requests, that you been ignoring your obligations."

The thickness of his speech surprised Pi. It reminded her of a cockney Englishman trying to do a Russian accent.

"I've been busy," said Radoslav with as much effort as if he were brushing a piece of lint from his lapel.

"Her Ladyship don't give a fack about your busy. Be busy for her. She needs you," said Slyvan.

"I do appreciate the sentiment," said Radoslav. "But I must decline."

Bastone, who had been standing back, stepped to Slyvan's side, letting his iron arms swing.

Radoslav raised an eyebrow. It said: "Do you think I give two shits about you?"

Pi snorted softly in amusement, drawing another glance from Slyvan, this time more lingering. His forehead bunched.

Before anyone could do otherwise, Radoslav produced a dusty bottle from the inside of his jacket. He held it out like a magician performing a trick. Both the Ruby Queen's henchmen looked at it with apprehension. He unstoppered it. Three shot glasses appeared in his hand. Without spilling a drop, he filled them.

"You must be tired. I know how exhausting crossing the barrier can be. This'll knock the shine back into your hustle," he said.

Bastone reached out to receive a glass, but Slyvan knocked them out of Radoslav's hand. He'd moved so fast his hand had blurred. The glasses shattered into smoke; the liquid sizzled on the stone.

"She told us to take nothin' from him," said Slyvan, admonishing his partner.

Radoslav's nostrils flared. "Now you've been rude, so you may leave."

Her magic-enhanced eyes saw the nearly invisible smoke seep from his skin like hungry tendrils. By Pi's judgment, the two Ruby maetrie didn't even have a candle's worth of power compared to Radoslav's bonfire.

"I wouldn't do that if I were you," said Slyvan.

"I'm not you," said Radoslav, flexing his hand. The smoke formed into a spectral dagger.

Slyvan pulled a figurine from his jacket. It looked like a miniature Easter Island head, except the features were more square. The smoke around Radoslav evaporated when he saw the figure.

"How did you get that?" asked Radoslav, his voice as hard as stone.

"The only thing that matters is that you return to her Ladyship," said Slyvan as he pulled back his sleeves, revealing bone bracelets on each arm carved into a snake.

Radoslav wasted no time in answering. "No."

"What if we take a lil stroll into your bar and smash a few walls, maybe your bar? You'd be amazed at what Bastone can do with those things," said Slyvan, holding his tongue between his teeth.

"I'll build a new bar," said Radoslav.

Slyvan sighed and rolled the figurine over in his hands while Radoslav's gaze never left it. Pi caught a whiff of metal in the back of her throat. She wanted to examine the figurine.

"I didn't want to have to resort to this," said Slyvan. "Her Ladyship hoped you might come on your own. But it seems you cannot be persuaded by normal means. So how's this little morsel. If you don't come back, she'll kill your mother."

Radoslav's eyebrows didn't dip or furrow or twitch. They didn't round with delight, or crease with anger. They didn't do anything at all.

Within the invisibility spell, Pi shook. *They're going to kill his mother?* Heat rose in her chest. She wanted Radoslav to rage, to fight back. Why didn't he fight back?

If it were my mother, she thought, not even completing the words in her head for they were too terrible to consider.

Radoslav glanced her way as if he sensed her anger. His lip twitched.

She squeezed her hands into fists. *Why aren't you doing anything?*

Pi pushed through the spell.

"Don't let them," said Pi, then as their gazes fell upon her she added, "I can help if it's worth anything."

Radoslav put a hand over his face.

"Got yourself a mageling on retainer, how sweet," said Slyvan.

"You shouldn't have revealed yourself," said Radoslav without looking at her.

Slyvan strolled over. She could feel him trying to seduce her with his maetrie magic, but between practice with Radoslav, and her general dislike of the Ruby Court's representative, she resisted.

"Interesting," he said, tasting the word. "She could be of

use, you know."

"No," said Radoslav. "She wouldn't know what she would be agreeing to."

"Agreeing to what?" asked Pi.

"Radoslav don't want you to visit his old home. I mean, why would he, after what he did, but that's beside the point," said Slyvan. "But you, you're bound to him. His little loyal mageling. You could go as his representative."

"It's too dangerous. She doesn't know the rules," said Radoslav.

"Then teach her," said Slyvan harshly as he strolled around the room, his boots clicking loudly, heel to toe. "You don't have to come right away. There's plenty of time before the Reaping."

Radoslav's head snapped around. He glanced away, emotion threading through him like steel wires in his limbs were being pulled taut.

"I'll do it," said Pi, overwhelmed with sympathy.

"No," said Radoslav. "It's too dangerous."

Slyvan's lips were peeled back in an obscene grin. His eyes crackled with mirth. "How sweet that he cares for his mageling."

"You know I can handle it, and it sounds like you don't have any other options," said Pi.

Radoslav took a long look at her. The emotionless mask that he normally wore was missing. She saw an old soldier who'd seen far too many battles. He gave one brief nod.

"Excellent," said Slyvan, clapping his hands.

Before she could do anything else, Slyvan appeared at her side and plucked a hair from her head. With dizzying speed, he tied it into a tiny bow and blew on it. The hair hardened into silver.

"With this you promise to be Raddie's sweet little errand

girl for the Ruby Court," he said.

"I promise," she said, feeling a tug on her chest, the spell sinking its hook into her.

"She didn't even hesitate. Where did you find this one, Raddie, and are there any more like her? I'd like to get one myself," he said.

Pi concentrated, whispered the word *constrict*, and touched the bone bracelet on his wrist. Suddenly, the bone carving of a snake was squeezing his wrist. He started yelling and tugging on the bracelet, trying to get it off, but the snake squeezed tighter. Finally, he slammed his arm on the obsidian cube, breaking the carving and releasing his wrist from the bracelet.

His jolly attitude had evaporated to be replaced by searing anger. He pulled back his sleeves and advanced.

Before Pi could even summon her faez, Radoslav intoned, "This is still my fucking bar, so if you touch her, I'll rip Bastone's arms off and beat you with them myself."

Slyvan seemed ready to ignore Radoslav until he saw his face.

"Fine," said Slyvan, the anger disappearing behind a mask of indifference. "But it doesn't change what you promised, mageling. I'll see you in the Ruby Court later. You won't have Raddie to protect you."

The two maetrie disappeared into the portal. As soon as they were gone, the wall turned back to brick.

Radoslav faced her. "You shouldn't have done...well, any of it. Especially that bit with the bracelet, as amusing as it was."

"I didn't like him," she said.

"There's a lot of things I don't like in this world, but I don't go pissing them off, especially when I don't know the score. You may have talent and grit, but if you don't learn a little caution, you're going to have a short life span," he said.

Anger rose in her chest. "I got it. Hubris. Mages. We don't live long. But what about a little thanks? They were going to kill your mother!"

His gray eyes flickered black, then back to gray. "You'll learn soon enough."

"What does that mean?" she asked.

"I'll send for you when it's time to go over," he said.

"Out of curiosity, what would happen if I didn't go?" she asked.

"You'd become their slave for the rest of your short life," he said as he turned to leave.

With Radoslav gone, the room reverted to a storage area filled with cardboard boxes. The stacks of pictures waited.

Pi picked up a frame. The photo was obscured by a thin layer of dust. She couldn't shake the idea that she'd been tricked somehow. Why else would he have placed her in the room before the meeting and then allowed her to stay? Or maybe she was just a little salty from his lack of appreciation for her gesture.

After a while she decided she was just being paranoid. And helping him would be in her best long-term interest. She didn't know for what, but it was always useful to have powerful friends, especially when you didn't have much family.

3

A few days after the debacle in the Enochian District, Aurie was headed to Freeport Games. She'd tried to reach Nezumi, but he'd disappeared back into the Undercity, and scrying magic wouldn't penetrate the low-level faez that hovered in the background down there unless she had a specialized trinket like a crystal ball.

Desperate to atone for the disaster, she'd volunteered with Hannah to help out at Freeport Games. Hannah ran role-playing games for kids to help them with making friends. She had a special case she wanted Aurie's help on. When Pi and a few other Arcanium members had found out, they asked to be included. Besides supporting Hannah, Aurie was excited about going to the shop to play a game rather than work.

Aurie had agreed to meet Ernie, Hannah's friend, ahead of time and walk to the shop. Hannah had suggested that as a way to reduce his anxiety about meeting so many people. She'd warned her that his nickname was "Echo" and that he didn't like to be touched. He was supposed to meet her outside of Arcanium, while the rest of the group was waiting at Freeport Games.

Aurie really wasn't paying attention when she crossed the drawbridge leading to the street until a musky plum scent caught her nose.

"And this, my trendy little bitches, is where the magic happens, literally," said Violet Cardwell, eliciting a round of laughter from her pack of fashionable girls. At first Aurie thought they were friends of Violet's from high school, then she saw the Order of Honorable Alchemists pins on their lapels.

"Oh my," said Violet, holding her neon orange fingernails against her chest in faux indignation as she finally noticed Aurie, "this is one of those total blanks that I'm forced to endure in Arcanium."

Suddenly, Aurie was acutely aware of her ratty jeans, plain black T-shirt, and stained sneakers that she'd gotten at Goodwill.

"Excuse me," said Aurie, stepping around them and hoping that Ernie wasn't far behind. She really didn't want to have to linger near Violet any longer than necessary.

Violet spoke to her friends loud enough that Aurie was forced to hear.

"Arcanium is such a bore. There are musty, old, worthless books everywhere. Even the villa I stayed in on the Spanish coast was nicer than this Hall," said Violet, contempt dripping from her lips.

A million pithy insults sprang to Aurie's lips, but she held them back while she craned her head, looking for Ernie. The street was filled with tourists walking or driving by, holding their cell phones up for pictures. Souvenir carts with aggressive hawkers pestered the tourists with miniature plastic versions of Arcanium.

From the crowd on her left, Aurie heard someone mumbling excitedly, "I do not want. I do not want. I do not want."

She found Ernie trying to avoid a short, greasy looking

fellow. He was stepping side to side, while the salesman was matching his movements and trying to shove a plastic model into Ernie's hands.

"I suggest you let him past or I'm going to enchant your underwear to give you a permanent wedgie," said Aurie.

When the salesman turned, she could tell he hadn't believed her until his gaze fell upon the Arcanium pin on her T-shirt.

"That's right, asshole, go sell your crap somewhere else," she said.

He disappeared right away, a look of concern imprinted into his forehead.

Aurie held out her hand. "Hey, Ernie. I'm Aurie. Hannah told you about me, right?"

Ernie looked at her hand as if it were a venomous snake, so she let it fall by her side.

"Call me Echo. Call me Echo," he said, glancing nervously at the concrete sidewalk.

"Nice to meet you, Echo," she said, looking up into his chubby face.

He was taller than her, and thick in all his limbs, the kind of weight one gets from playing a lot of video games. He had dirty blond hair and a wolf shirt that most people wore ironically, but she didn't think that was the case for him, especially because he also had a colorful backpack with cartoon ponies on it. He was also around her age, which surprised her. She'd thought that Hannah's friend would be one of the younger kids that frequented the store.

"What is your class?" he asked while staring at his shoes.

"I'm...in Arcanium. We study a lot of things," she said.

Echo squeezed his eyes shut for a moment as if he were in pain. "What class? What class?"

"I...uhm...I don't know—oh wait, you mean in the game.

I don't know. I didn't have time to read the stuff Hannah sent me. What do you suggest?" she asked.

Echo brightened at the idea of picking for her. "Every party always needs a cleric. You could be a cleric."

"A cleric? Like I'm leading a congregation? Church thing?" she asked, not liking how it sounded.

He snuck a look up to her face, and smiled briefly. "Cleric like a doctor. Like Golden Willow. A healer."

"Did you know I worked there?" she asked.

He nodded, as if it were an important secret. "Hannah told me. I like Golden Willow."

Aurie took a second look at him. Had he been in the hospital when she worked there and didn't realize it? She didn't think so, or at least not on the Children's Floor for the Irrevocably Cursed, Magically Ailing, and Supernatural Virology.

"A cleric it is. Let's get moving. The rest of the group is at Freeport," she said.

The number of people in the area seemed to bother him based on his rapid eye movements. As he nodded and moved to follow, a voice interrupted them.

"Am I witnessing a date? Look at this, girls, we have a first date," said Violet.

Echo froze as the squad of girls approached, surrounding him. Aurie tugged on his arm, but the sudden and overwhelming direct interaction shut him down.

"This isn't the time for games, Violet," said Aurie.

Violet ignored Aurie and stepped to Echo. She put a finger under his chin and made him look at her. His lips writhed from her contact.

"Is something wrong with him?" asked Violet. "Are you so desperate to have a date that you'll pick someone who's this stupid?"

A kernel of anger formed in Aurie's chest, like a flame catching dry tinder in a rain-starved forest. It'd been a long summer, working unhealthy hours. This was the last thing she wanted to deal with, and it took a supreme effort to contain the wildfire she wanted to unleash.

"Violet. I know we haven't always gotten along. But please, step aside. This is my friend, and we're going to play some games," said Aurie, reaching out to pull Violet away.

Violet smacked her hand, and the Alchemist girls snickered. Aurie knew that look in her eyes. Violet was proving herself to her new friends. Aurie had been on the receiving end of this ritual at many a school and had learned to ignore it, but she knew Echo wasn't equipped for Violet's machinations. She needed to extricate Echo from the young socialite before something happened.

"What's your name?" asked Violet.

"His name is Ernie," said Aurie, trying to step between them, then under her breath to Violet, she said, "Please. Let this one go. We're leaving now."

Violet's long fingernails latched onto Aurie's arm. "Why should I? Last year, you tackled me, enchanted me with sleep, and after failing miserably in the *verum locus*, still got top grades in the class. I know your *kind*, and I know how you're getting by, and I won't stand for it."

Unleashing her rage would feel so good, and she nearly did, until she saw Echo's quivering lower lip and darting eyes. He looked ready to run.

Aurie lashed that anger down with steel ropes. It took every bit of her self-control. She calmly placed her hand on top of Violet's and tugged it off.

"We're leaving now," said Aurie.

A snicker, followed by a rubber stopper being popped from a vial, made Aurie spin around. The other girls had their hands behind their backs.

She suspected something was about to happen and moved to pull Echo away, but they cut her off. Their exaggerated smiling masks were caricatures of deceit.

While Aurie was still on the drawbridge, she was on Arcanium property, so she didn't think they would do anything too overt. But she also didn't want her hair turned to snakes or something like that.

After she caught a whiff of solvent, Aurie pointed at them. "Back the hell up, or I'm roasting the eyebrows off you skinny bitches."

The look of victory on Violet's face, followed by a sloppy wet sound, like a plunger in a toilet, gave Aurie only a moment's warning.

The books in Echo's backpack crashed onto the drawbridge in a pile of goop. His gaming books, loose papers, and other materials were covered in a green slime.

A horrible wail exited his lips as he fell to his knees. "Noooo! Noooo! Noooo!" He sounded like a warning siren.

Whatever control she had evaporated, seeing Echo crouched on his knees, his precious things ruined. The bevy of girls were laughing, pointing at Echo and her. The whole spectacle was heartbreaking. She'd been tasked with easing Echo into a social group as a favor, but Violet had destroyed that, destroyed the poor guy's fragile hold on the world.

Aurie wanted to lay into Violet and her friends, decimate them with a litany of insults, but a sudden rage gummed up her works, followed by a surge of faez, and as she looked at those perfect girls in their designer things and how they had been so callous and cruel, the only thing she said was: "Ragged!"

Later, Aurie recalled that she was thinking of how the bottom of Echo's backpack had been turned to slime. She'd wanted to enact petty revenge by making their purses or hemlines snap a few threads, or make the fabric shift, giving the clothing a thrift store look, ruining its value—not that they all couldn't afford it.

But that's not what happened.

After she said the word, she felt a sudden letdown from the intense usage of faez. She'd funneled far too much magic into the spell, which wasn't truth magic, but felt something akin.

When threads on the straps on a girl's purse just sort of jumped off, as if they were tiny worms springing to life, a collective gasp—Aurie included—went up. A few of the girls had devious grins, as if they thought some long-held grudge had been served in the chaos. At least until the threads fled from their purses in a spray of confetti.

But the initial threads had been the steam leaking out before the explosion. In an instant, the rest exploded off their clothing, like fibrous fireworks, tiny strands floating in the air afterwards as if a cloud of insects had descended.

The carnage set their expressions on kill. Aurie couldn't decide if she should grab Echo's hand and run, or flee back into Arcanium.

Sharp ozone burned her nostrils as magic filled the air, but before one spell could be cast, their clothes just fell off. Without the threads, the cloth, leather, polyester, or whatever they were wearing had nothing to bind them together. Their clothing fell away in sheets, like skin sloughing off a molting serpent, and then not one of them was worried about revenge, but covering themselves.

Aurie was vaguely aware that foot and automobile traffic had stopped. Tourists liked to walk or drive by Arcanium, and Aurie had gotten used to little hands pointing out of car windows at the building that was a cross between a monastery and Notre Dame, but now the throng was several deep with dozens of cell phones held high to record. Like naked birds taking flight, Violet and her pack of Alchemist friends fled down the street, the cell phones following them like sunflowers following the sun.

Aurie flipped Echo's backpack upside down and shoved the fallen books inside, ignoring the green goo clinging to her hands. Then she helped Echo up, being careful not to touch him too long.

"You're going to be okay, Echo. I'm so sorry. That's my fault they did that," she explained.

He seemed shaken, but willing to follow her to the subway. At least making the girls leave had reduced his anxiety, but the whole train ride he rocked in his seat. Aurie asked about the role-playing game, but he kept mumbling to himself the whole ride to the ninth ward.

When they reached the table at Freeport Games, Hannah was sliding back and forth on block skates while chatting with the group. She wore an "I Skate Like a Girl!" T-shirt. Her friend, Brian Travers, was seated to her right. The others at the table were Pi, Deshawn, Xi, and Daniel.

"I wasn't planning on any oozes today, but if you're really into role-playing it," said Hannah, nodding towards the trails of slime on her arms. Then she saw Echo's expression.

"Echo! Are you okay?" asked Hannah.

He sat in the chair and hugged his ruined backpack. Aurie felt like a total jerk for letting Echo get mixed up with Violet.

Not wanting him to have to relive the experience, Aurie said, "Violet."

The other Arcanium members nodded with understanding, while Hannah and Brian shared glances. They were members of the Royal Society of Illustrious Artificers, though everyone just called them Tinkerers.

"My character is ruined," said Echo, holding up a dripping piece of paper with the ink smudged.

Hannah smiled and produced a meticulously filled out character sheet from a folder. "It's okay, I always keep a few extras for emergencies."

"What about me? I never did get around to making one," said Aurie.

Hannah smirked, producing a second sheet and handing it over. Aurie frowned at the class listed in the box on the paper. "An assassin? That's really not my style. I was thinking about a healer. Right, Echo?" He smiled covertly. "Don't you have something like that back there?"

Hannah did a little spin on her roller stakes. "Nope. You'll be fine."

Aurie tried not to sink in her chair. She was grateful that Hannah was going to run a game for them, but she really didn't like the idea of playing an assassin.

"Alright, the rest of you hand in your backgrounds. Aurie, you can come up with one later."

Her stomach twisted a little. She hated the idea of creating a history for a character when she didn't even know her own.

"Whoa," said Hannah, when Pi handed her a stack at least twenty pages thick. "That's one serious background."

Pi blushed a little, and a timid smile formed on her lips. "I didn't mean to. I just, you know...it was fun to actually have a history."

Aurie shared a glance with her sister. They didn't know much about their parents' families, except that her father had been an orphan, and her mother had fled Iran with her parents before they died.

After a little time for Echo to recover and get acquainted with the others, Hannah weaved a tale on how the party had been hired from their respective guilds to put order to a fallen kingdom. The others threw themselves into the game in earnest, which helped Echo engage. He had moments where he seemed to burrow internally, but Hannah had a good eye on him, and threw the action his way to distract him.

But as the game went on, Aurie found herself distracted by thoughts about the conflict with Violet. She was worried about how the whole incident had been recorded on cell phones, but more importantly, how she'd completely lost control of her magic. She wasn't even sure what she'd done to make their clothing fall off. It wasn't truth magic, that much she knew.

"Aurie? Aurie?"

Everyone at the table was staring at her. "What?"

"It's your turn. Did you want to attack the kobold?" asked Brian.

"Uhm, yeah. Sorry," she said, then threw a twenty-sided die across the table.

The battle in the game went on. Aurie paid attention just enough to keep things moving, but she didn't have her heart in it. It didn't help that everything had gone wrong with Violet and that she was playing an assassin. Assassins killed people, murdered them for profit or political intrigue. It was the exact opposite of a healer, of helping people.

In between rolling, Aurie glanced around the room. She saw something small and black moving across the floor. At first, she thought someone had lost a die and she started to get up to retrieve it, but then she realized the small black object had legs. It was a spider.

Without moving her head, she watched it with her eyes. The little arachnid crouched beneath a table, watching. As Aurie turned her head to get a better look, it went scurrying away, repositioning itself beneath a different table. She might not have thought anything of it, except that it seemed to be avoiding her inspection.

Aurie excused herself to use the bathroom, but moved to a different location to get a glimpse of the spider. Something strange was going on. The spider, upon seeing her, made a tiny hopping motion as if it'd been caught, and went scurrying towards the back room, running beneath tables and chairs faster than she could keep up.

She weaved through the gaming area after the spider. She caught sight of it through the tables, before it sped into a hallway that led to a couple of storage rooms and the janitorial closet.

Not wanting the critter to get away, Aurie whisked open the closet to find a handsome guy with dark skin and webbing tattoos across his chest and arms standing in his boxer briefs, trying to shimmy into a pair of jeans.

The word "Speller" came tumbling out of her lips like an unformed mass. Part of her mind was saying hello, while the other part wanted to say spider.

"Speller?" he replied, arching an eyebrow.

He had ice blue eyes like a glacier. Yet, they weren't unkind.

"Spider or hello, or both, I guess," said Aurie. "I'm an idiot. I meant spider. I saw one come down this hall. I thought it might have run under the door."

"Spider?" he said, glancing down as if he expected one to be crawling up his leg. "I hope it didn't come in here."

"What about your web tattoos? Don't you like them?" she asked, also noting he had more muscles on his stomach that she could stare at in one glance.

He quirked a smile that made her heart pant for breath. "I just like the way they look."

The way he said it wasn't so much that he liked it, but more so that the ladies liked the way they looked, and Aurie had to agree.

"So...uhm, why are you in the closet with your clothes off?" she asked, scratching the back of her head while simultaneously trying not to stare at his stomach muscles.

He bit his lower lip, in that sideways style that said you-probably-won't-believe-this, then yanked up his pants and buttoned them before reaching down and grabbing a small medical bag on a shelf. He pulled a syringe out of the bag.

"Diabetic?" she asked.

He gave a curt nod. "Two shots a day leaves a lot of marks."

Suddenly, the web tattoos made more sense. He wasn't wearing them for how they looked, but for what they hid. Though she'd never known anyone to take off all their clothes for one shot, but something about the way he looked at her scrambled her thoughts.

"I'm...I didn't mean to..."

"Hey, don't feel sorry for me. Everyone has their burdens. This one is mine," he said as those glaciers burned bright.

The silence stretched between them, before Aurie remembered what she'd been doing in the first place.

"Once again, I'm an idiot. You're trying to put your clothes back on, and I'm just standing here with the door open. I'll leave you to it," she said, and started to close the door.

"What's your name?" he asked hopefully.

"Aurie," she said, pausing at the open door, feeling her cheeks warm.

"Zayn," he said.

"Nice to meet you, Zayn," she said, before she returned to the others.

When Aurie sat at the table, Pi gave her a look and mouthed the words, "Why are you blushing?"

Aurie waved her hand in front of her face like a fan and tugged on her shirt, indicating that it was hot. Her sister seemed to accept the answer.

For the rest of the afternoon, Aurie found it a little easier to enjoy the game, forgetting for a short, sweet while that Violet was sure to cause trouble later. Aurie decided that if Violet hadn't slimed Echo's backpack, she would have never been distracted enough to notice the spider, or find Zayn in the closet in his boxer briefs. So maybe, after all, the day hadn't been so terrible.

4

For second years, school at the Hundred Halls officially began a day after the first-year trials, but most came early to watch the parade of potential initiates on their way to the Spire. Half the second-year Arcanium class had camped at the Carnifex Cafe to watch the thousands of nervous students stream into the gondolas, wondering which ones would make it past the trials. Bets were placed on which ones they thought would succeed or if they would make it into Arcanium.

Aurie didn't feel comfortable making those kinds of judgments, especially when she'd just gone through it the previous year. For the others, the trials had been an exciting adventure that culminated in their acceptance. Every one of them had had more time to try again, or backup plans should they not get into the Hundred Halls. That hadn't been the case for Aurie, which left her feeling irritated each time a new gondola soared into the sky.

They met each day until the potentials had passed their trials to become the newest initiate class. Her classmates spent the time between gondolas telling stories of their summers and guessing about the second-year competition that would have them teaming up with other halls. No one said anything about the incident with Violet, though everyone knew about it, since it'd been all over the internet within hours.

Waiting had also given everyone a chance to meet Pi. As Aurie expected, everyone accepted her sister right away. That'd always been the case whenever they'd had to move schools, which simultaneously had been annoying and relieving, since constantly meeting new people wore Aurie out.

When it was their time, they entered the Spire through a special entrance in the lower part of the city. Their mood was light, unlike the nervous energy of the first years'.

A grassy grove in the shape of a bowl welcomed them in, a far cry from the hard gymnasium floor of the previous year. Students from the various Halls took up different quadrants. Coterie, Protectors, and Alchemists formed the largest classes, and naturally, they grouped on one side of the bowl. Aurie kept an eye out for the fourth hall of the Cabal, the Academy of the Subtle Arts, but she couldn't find sign of them.

Violet sat with the Alchemists, even though she was still a part of Arcanium. Thankfully, they were on the other side of the grassy bowl, so her dirty looks dissipated into nothing by the time they crossed the gulf. Aurie hoped she wouldn't get paired with anyone from that Hall.

Aurie found Hannah easily because of her outsized personality and rainbow headband. Though her hall class was only three people, including her, she already had everyone around her laughing as if they were longtime friends. After getting Hannah's attention, Aurie waved. It would have been lonely being a part of a small Hall, she decided.

Next, she found the Aura Healers, who wore white doctor jackets as long as robes, milling about as if they were on rounds at a hospital. While she was happy in Arcanium, especially since her sister had joined, Aurie had pangs of regret that she hadn't followed in her father's path.

At the center of the grassy bowl was a wooden platform with a pedestal. It appeared the pedestal could hold something, but it was currently empty. The other Arcanium students speculated on the meaning, but no one had any real ideas.

Aurie noticed Echo, Hannah's friend from Freeport Games, sitting alone. She was surprised that he was a mage, and wondered what Hall he was in. He was by himself, which suggested one of the smaller specialty Halls, but he wore no markings to give an indication.

She started to get up to invite him to join them when the grass parted and a set of stairs rose out of the ground, ending the nervous chatter. From the pit, Professor Delight strolled out in a yellow track suit. This year, no one made the mistake of catcalling, and when the professor reached the platform she gave a sassy hip shift.

"It seems my little second years have gotten smarter," she said with a wink.

Her comment brought laughter from the crowd. A girl from Stone Singers yelled out: "We love you, Professor Delight!"

"You only say that because you aren't one of my students. But enough about me—as much as I enjoy the subject, today we begin the choosing for your second-year projects. Some might call these competitions, but that would defeat Invictus' intended purpose. When the school first started, there was intrigue and infighting between the Halls. When the battles—and I do mean battles—threatened to destroy the school, Invictus created the second-year project to teach us how to work together. No one Hall can achieve their goals alone, and together we are stronger," she said, glancing meaningfully towards the three Cabal halls.

A wave of her hand and four students appeared from the stairs, each wearing fifth-year robes and carrying a long pole.

A huge rainbow-colored gem was suspended in a sling between them. Zayn, the guy she'd found in the closet at Freeport Games in his boxer briefs, was at the back left pole.

To Aurie's surprise, Pi elbowed her in the side, whispering, "I know that guy. I saw him last year when I turned in the third gallium coin. He's in the assassin's guild."

Her stomach twisted with disappointment.

"The Academy of the Subtle Arts, you mean," she whispered back, more forcefully than she intended.

Pi gave her a funny look. "What was that?"

Aurie knocked a piece of grass off her leg while she looked away. "Just pointing out they're not all assassins. Diplomats and negotiators, too."

"You've met him before, haven't you?" said Pi.

"Once," she said, hoping she wouldn't have to explain the awkward meeting.

Pi bit her lower lip playfully. "He's easy on the eyes. Too bad he's in assassins."

Aurie was saved from further discussion about Zayn when they placed the rainbow-colored gem on the pedestal.

Professor Delight said, "What you're about to see is a spell memory from our founder, Invictus. In the early years of the Halls, he addressed each incoming class, but as demands on his time became too great, he recorded this. Thankfully, for our sake, this was finished when it was because he died a few years later."

The professor placed her hands on the gem and mumbled a spell. When a massive figure appeared in the air, the whole crowd gasped.

Aurie had seen Invictus before. Everyone had. There was a famous picture of him creating a butterfly from a discarded gum wrapper for a little girl in a wheelchair who'd been bitten by a kitsune. He was crouched down, a wizened expression on his face, the butterfly perched on his fingertips, wings fluttering. The girl had an expression of wonder. The picture was famous because through the power of his magic, the gum-wrapper butterfly bred with normal ones, using ordinary trash to create their bodies. They called them Adelyne's Butterflies after the girl in the wheelchair.

Aurie had always imagined him as a kindly old grandfather who had a bowl full of treats in his study, but the whole crowd recoiled from this vision as if a madman had appeared in their midst. It took a moment to realize it really *was* Invictus. Even Professor Delight seemed disturbed.

"Power is both a gift and a curse," he said, booming his voice into the arena.

The first word to come into Aurie's mind was *ravaged*. His iconic wavy shoulder-length black hair was matted and filthy. His darker skin tones, which had always left his origins a mystery—some thought he'd come from the Mediterranean region, others from the Far East, some even thought he was Native American—had been either bleached white or burnt black, depending on the area of his skin, as if he'd been in a horrible chemical accident.

"When I created the Halls, I wanted to tame the power that floods through our mortal veins. We are not meant to wield such power freely. Too many wars and atrocities had their origins in the madness of faez. Too many well-meaning wizards bound themselves to supernatural beings in hopes of taming their power, only to find they had become slaves to a different master," said Invictus, his voice granite, but filled with cracks and fissures.

Pi touched her on the arm and whispered, "Look at the professor. This isn't the message she expected."

Professor Delight was crouched at the pedestal, examining the gem as if she were diagnosing a faulty machine.

The image of Invictus continued as if these were his last moments, "Magic not only requires a shield from madness, but checks and balances to ensure that no one can abuse it.   Friendship, teamwork, borrowed-family, these bind us together, make us stronger, and ensure the social fabric remains.   But once sides are taken, then our very civilization is at risk."

Invictus paused as if speaking had taken a toll on him. He gathered himself before continuing, this time without the weight that had burdened his previous speech.   Despite his appearance, that grandfatherly image came through his kind eyes.

"Today you second years will be placed into teams, and set at a task that will teach you the power of that which can only be found in trusting each other. This has been happening for exactly one hundred years. On this momentous anniversary, I want to sweeten the pot, and offer a special prize to the team that overcomes adversity and achieves victory in the Grand Contest. I cannot tell you what it is, but each and every one of you will wish you'd won, when you learn the truth."

Invictus bowed, and to Aurie, it seemed as if he looked directly at her, before disappearing. The bowl erupted into chaos. Professor Delight shouted for silence.

Aurie caught Zayn staring directly up at her. He winked, acknowledging her, and moved with the other fifth years to collect the memory gem. Her whole body warmed annoyingly. She didn't want to like him, since he was from a Cabal hall. Though it was doubtful she'd ever see him again.   The fifth years promptly removed the memory gem and marched back into the hole in the ground. Aurie watched him the whole way.

A crack of thunder brought the room to order.   Fury creased Professor Delight's forehead.

"Quiet! Despite the unexpected nature of the message"—

she paused, still shaken—"the team choosing will continue as planned. You will line up at the many doors around the bowl, it doesn't matter which one, just spread out. When you enter the room, you'll be given a test. Teams will be grouped by their score, but no more than one Hall member in each team. You may begin the challenge whenever you'd like, for as long as you'd like. Come back to this room when you want to work on it more. The doors will be attuned to your Hall pins. Good luck."

5

All anyone could talk about was the special prize for the competition while they waited to take their test so they could be sorted into teams.

"What do you think it is?" asked Deshawn.

"I'm not sure I care," said Aurie. "I just want to get a good grade."

"You can't tell me you're not even a little curious," he said.

"It's probably a trinket, or something minor from his personal collection," she said.

"See, I told you, you were curious," he said. "But it's not a single trinket. How would a team of six split it?"

"Fine, it's not a single trinket," she said, glancing at how slow the lines were moving. She wanted to get to the test. She was anxious to start on the project.

Deshawn went all starry-eyed. "Think about what could be in there. I mean, he was the most famous wizard ever. Practically created the modern magical structure with his patronage. The whole upper portion of the Spire is his domain, and nobody's seen it since his death. I'm sure he picked up some legendary artifacts along the way. Maybe those are the prizes."

Aurie thought about the Rod of Dominion. "I doubt he's going to give a dangerous artifact to a bunch of second years."

Pi leaned in. "What if it's a tour of his rooms? You know, Willy Wonka style?"

"I'm more curious about what kind of test we'll be given," said Aurie.

"You'll find out soon enough," said Deshawn. "It's not like you can do anything out here."

Aurie was anxious. She didn't know if it was the strange message from Invictus, learning Zayn was in assassins, or the test itself, but when she spoke, the words came out more harshly than she intended. "The test has to be something we all know how to do. Otherwise it wouldn't be fair to some Halls. So the magic will be simple. Probably requiring knowledge that's readily public, or generally cultural."

After their initial recoiling, understanding passed across their faces. Deshawn whistled in admiration. They hadn't been thinking about it, but Aurie had. She always thought three steps ahead—it was the only way she'd guided herself and Pi through their childhood.

A few minutes later, Pi touched her on the shoulder. She pushed her hair out of her face and didn't speak right away, as if something was weighing on her mind.

"What is it?" prompted Aurie.

"Do you think there are any records of our family anywhere?" she asked.

Aurie frowned. "You should be preparing for the test."

Pi rubbed the back of her neck. "Writing that background for my character made me realize I don't know anything about my history. Dad was an orphan and Mom wouldn't talk about growing up in Tehran."

"Pi, I can't really think about that right now. We should

focus on what we're about to do," she said, though the lack of history bothered her as well. She just hated talking about it.

"Do you think anyone's still alive in Tehran?" asked Pi.

"Doubtful," said Aurie, sighing. "I remember overhearing Mom and Dad talking about some news they'd gotten, and her mentioning she was the last of her family."

"I feel so blank," said Pi.

"We'll make our own history," said Aurie, even though she didn't quite believe it herself.

The test door opened, beckoning Aurie. She kissed her sister on the forehead and wished her luck. After a short hallway, she entered a nearly empty room. The only object besides an exit door and a timer on the wall that was currently set at 0:00.00 was a small black cube.

When the door closed behind her, a voice said, "Open the box."

The timer started counting right away. Aurie cracked her knuckles as she approached. She'd been watching how quickly the lines moved to get an idea how fast she had to solve the puzzle. Generally, it took about fifteen to twenty minutes, though a few times she saw the lines move at around five. If she wanted to get a good group, she needed to solve it quickly.

Aurie leaned forward to examine the cube. When her fingertips brushed it, an electric shock bit into them, making her recoil.

Her fingers were numbed. She shook them out and, undeterred, tried again. She was able to pick up the cube without further injury. The numbness wore off as she rotated the object. There was no obvious way to open it, no seams, no latches or handles.

Aurie cast a spell on her eyes that would allow her to see the presence of faez.

As she expected, the cube was magical. She peered at it

from up close, looking for clues. Nothing. The timer was at two minutes already.

"Maybe I'm over thinking this," she said, and tried a few spells on the cube. She cast various opening spells, but the cube absorbed them without change.

When the timer passed the three-minute mark, she said, "Open sesame!"

Nothing.

Frustrated from staring at an inanimate object, Aurie spun around so she could think more clearly, only to find a phrase written on the wall. It was visible because of the spell on her eyes.

ON YOUR UNLUCKY DAY DON'T FORGET THE WORDS TO SAY

"Unlucky day?" she asked no one in particular.

The phrase meant that she had to say something to open the box, so she hadn't been far off trying "Open sesame."

Unlucky day? What would an unlucky day mean? Thirteen was the traditional unlucky day. On a Friday?

Aurie spun around, tapping on her lips, until the answer came to her.

"Thirteen. Thirteenth birthday," she said.

The clock was nearly at five minutes. For kids with magical ability, the thirteenth birthday was a special occasion called Triskanatalis. The occasion was similar to the *bar mitzvah* coming-of-age ceremonies celebrated by Jewish kids. In fact, Jewish kids often combined the two, if they qualified.

The celebration involved a simple ceremony in which the child promised to use their magical abilities for good. A simple spell was cast, though it had no official binding and was only ceremonial. Her mom had taught her the spell the week before her thirteenth birthday. It was one of the last things they'd done together before she died.

Aurie stepped to the cube.

"*Mea promissum bonum operibus.*"

Nothing happened. The timer had passed five minutes. Aurie was sure that was the answer. What had she done wrong?

The spell had been cast after writing her name in a book of spells that was traditionally given on that day. She searched for something to write her signature with, but there was nothing else in the room. So she put her finger to the cube and wrote out her name with the tip like she did with those electronic credit card machines.

"*Mea promissum bonum operibus.*"

The cube opened, revealing a red button. Aurie jammed her hand down to press it. The click from the door opening was deeply satisfying.

She was about to go through the door when she noticed the timer was still going. It was counting past six minutes.

"Close enough," she said, going through the door.

The hallway led to a waiting area with the others who had taken the test. No scoreboards were present to give her an idea where she stood. She found the other Arcanium students who had finished the test and compared notes. So far she'd solved it the fastest of the group.

After about an hour, Pi came out of the room sobbing. Her eyes were puffy and red. Aurie gathered her younger sister in her arms.

"What's wrong?" she asked.

"I couldn't do the puzzle," she said, breaking away and then punching the wall. "Nothing worked. After an hour, the door opened up. I failed completely. Why am I even here if I can't do a simple puzzle!"

Aurie squeezed Pi tighter.

"What was that stupid thing, anyway?" asked Pi, once

she'd collected herself.

Aurie's breath caught in her throat. Pi didn't know because their parents had died when she was ten and on her thirteenth birthday, they'd been moving to a group home. Aurie had forgotten to wish Pi a happy birthday that day.

She felt like the worst sister in the world, twice over. On the ride, Aurie had been worried about making sure they stayed together. She'd heard too many horror stories about siblings being split up. It wasn't until a week later that she remembered that she'd missed Pi's birthday.

"Forget it," she said.

Pi's face wrinkled in anger. "Tell me. Don't treat me like a kid."

"It was the Triskanatalis spell," said Aurie.

The truth dried up Pi's tears as her jaw pulsed with anger. "I see."

"Don't stress about it. It's just a way to choose teams. The real competition happens after that," said Aurie.

Pi wasn't pleased. "What was your time?"

"Around six minutes," said Aurie, cringing.

"Yeah, doesn't matter says the girl with a top time," said Pi.

"I'll probably get stuck with a bunch of Coterie and Alchemists," said Aurie.

Pi moved away and collected herself in the corner. It'd been a while since she'd seen Pi this broken up. The reminder of her thirteenth birthday was probably about the worst thing, because it brought with it the memory of their mom and dad. They wouldn't have forgotten if they'd been alive, which made Aurie confused if she was supposed to be mad or sad. Eventually she settled on the knowledge that she was always letting her sister down.

The rest of the wait took another hour. When it came

time to find out the teams, they were sent through a portal. It would not only group them up, but give them access to their competition room. Each team could come and go as they pleased while solving the puzzle. It was expected to take the whole year. The earliest any team had solved it was by December.

Before they went into the portal, Aurie said to Pi, "Hope you get a good team."

"Doubtful," said Pi as she trudged forward.

After the portal flashed and Pi was whisked away to another location, Aurie took a deep breath. She was nervous about who her teammates would be. She reminded herself that she was likely to be grouped with some of the halls that formed the Cabal, though that didn't mean they were a part of those plots. These were just other students who were in the same position as she was, nervously hoping they could form a good team. She was glad she couldn't be grouped with Violet due to the one Hall restriction. Aurie hoped that she didn't get grouped with any of Violet's friends, the ones from the incident outside of Arcanium, but there was nothing she could do about it now.

Aurie crossed her fingers and stepped through the portal. Her skin tingled as if she'd crossed through an electric field. She blinked and arrived facing the last person she expected to see on the other side.

6

Five minutes. That's what she wanted her time to be. Even eight or ten would have been fine. She'd always been good at *everything*. When she was eight years old she'd broken her arm playing soccer, but finished the game because the score was tied. She'd scored the winning goal.

But her time? It wasn't even a number. DNF. Did not finish.

Pi wanted badly to be on a top team so people wouldn't think she'd gotten into Arcanium because of her sister. Starting over in Arcanium felt too much like the years of moving from school to school, making new friends, knowing she wouldn't keep them for long.

Pi was good at finding friends. She just didn't know how to keep them. They'd never spent enough time in any one place.

Friendships were insubstantial, surface things. She knew their favorite bands, favorite colors, maybe who they had a secret crush on, but nothing else. It was a lot like her family history. She knew her parents' names, facts about their lives and careers, but nothing about their hopes and dreams, the stories that create the fabric of history, of family.

The Triskanatalis ceremony was just another reminder of it. When she was younger, she thought the whole idea was stupid, but Pi remembered her thirteenth birthday, riding next to her sister on the Greyhound bus to Kentucky, waiting for Aurie to remember that it was her birthday. She didn't even really care about the ceremony. They could have joked about it, then Aurie would have taught her the spell. That would have been enough. It wasn't like Pi didn't understand that Aurie was under a lot of pressure being the oldest. She didn't expect anything special, she just wanted to be a part of something greater than herself. And for some reason, that stupid spell was a part of that idea.

Pi was the first one into the team room. Comfy couches formed a semi-circle around a table with a pair of custom laptops. A small kitchen was in the corner. The refrigerator and pantry were stocked with food and drinks. She was opening a Dragon's Blood alchemical booster drink when her first teammate appeared.

The girl had dark skin and thick glasses that made her eyes appear bigger than they were. She was small, mousy, and looked ready to break at the first sign of trouble.

Pi took a deep breath and introduced herself.

"I'm Pi, short for Pythia. Arcanium Hall. I'm excited to meet you," she said with her hand extended.

The girl glanced around the room as if she were in the wrong place, leaving Pi in an awkward position.

Without stepping forward, the girl said in a voice so quiet Pi could barely hear it, "I'm Raziyah Johnson. Stone Singers."

Pi tried to hide her disappointment. The Stone Singers were the civil engineers of the magical world. Very specialized, and good at their jobs, but not useful outside of road and building construction.

Raziyah seemed to sense Pi's discomfort and added, "I'm good at math."

"I'm sure we'll need it," said Pi hopefully.

"Are we the first ones here?" asked Raziyah as she looked around, disappointed.

A pithy response about being good at math and counting to two formed in Pi's head, but she left it unsaid. Being good at making friends meant not making comments like that. Not at first, anyway.

"Whoa, what a head rush," said a familiar voice from the doorway.

Her friend from Freeport Games, Hannah, stood in the doorway. Pi greeted her with a hug. She was simultaneously excited and disappointed. Excited because she knew Hannah, but disappointed because she knew she wasn't a great student. Not in the traditional sense anyway. Pi's expectations for team success started to fade.

"Sweet place we've got here," said Hannah after introductions. "We could totally have our gaming session here."

The fourth and fifth members of their team showed up right after each other. The fourth was Rigel Yamaguchi from the Theater hall and the fifth was Echo, whom she also knew from Freeport Games. She hadn't even realized he was in the Halls, though it explained why Hannah knew him then since they hadn't seen him in Freeport Games before.

Echo took a seat in the corner away from everyone else while Rigel in a Midwestern accent launched into a story about how he met Frank Orpheum, the patron of the Theater hall, in a rare book emporium while on vacation in Rome. The well-known mage had charmed his mother first by getting rid of her smoking habit with a little hypnotism, then by creating an illusionary pangolin that stayed with her the rest of the day.

Raziyah took an interest in Echo as if he were a younger brother. She got him some food and tried to talk to him without much success. He mostly stared at anything but another person. Pi gave Raziyah a shrug. At least she was trying to inspire teamwork, but overall, Pi was not feeling great about their chances. She was the only member of a major hall that taught general magic. The others were specialized practitioners.

"Where's our sixth?" asked Hannah after a few minutes.

"Maybe we don't get one," offered Raziyah. "If there aren't enough to fill out a team of six, the last place team probably gets shorted."

"Nobody solved the puzzle?" asked Rigel.

Raziyah said, "Thirteen was when my parents got divorced."

Hannah shrugged her broad shoulders. "My parents weren't talking to me. They'd sent me to special school to cure me of my queerness. Clearly it didn't take."

"That's terrible," said Rigel as he messed with his hair. It was shaved on one side and long on the other with dark blue accents.

"Don't sweat it. I enchanted phones at the school to change the word straight to gay. The place closed down a few months after I left," said Hannah with a wink. "What about you?"

"That was the year I was back in Nagoya. My parents wanted me to learn traditional Japanese theater. I think they felt guilty about moving to Chicago when I was a baby, but my heart's in the American stage. It was one of those things that just got missed flying back and forth all the time," explained Rigel.

Pi explained why she didn't know about the Triskanatalis spell, and nobody bothered asking Echo. They all just assumed he was too weird to have done normal kid-parent things.

"Hey, the portal's activating," said Hannah.

They all moved towards it, except Echo, who was doing something that looked like counting his fingers over and over.

"I think it's stuck," whispered Raziyah.

"I hope it's not malfunctioning," said Rigel.

Magic wasn't always reliable, but the portals around the school were top notch. Pi hoped their sixth member was someone from a top hall. She'd even take someone from Coterie, just to have a fighting chance.

When the sixth member stepped out of the portal, Pi choked on the name.

"Aurie?"

Her sister stumbled into the room, looking a little bleary-eyed.

Hannah, oblivious to the implications, launched herself forward and threw her arms around Aurie. "Aurie!"

"Wait," said Raziyah, at an almost normal volume, "you're both in Arcanium."

Aurie was confused. "What's going on? I can't be in this group. I solved the puzzle."

"The choosing algorithm must have failed," said Rigel. "Spells are fallible."

"Maybe it was confused because I was in Coterie last year," offered Pi, but she didn't think that was it.

"But that wouldn't explain how I got placed with you all," said Aurie. She opened her mouth to say something else, but then thought better of it. Based on the way her lips had been formed, Pi thought she was about to say Violet. It would make sense that Violet had sabotaged Aurie to get placed into the last group, but it backfired in the sense that Pi was already in it.

They went through another round of introductions and

were preparing to enter the puzzle room, which could be reached through a blue door, when Echo spoke up.

"Harpers."

Everyone froze as they tried to work out the meaning of the word.

"Harpers," he said again, emphatically, as if he expected them to understand.

"What's that?" asked Pi.

"Harpers. We're Harpers," he said forcefully. His eyes searched around for support, but when he found none, he looked back into his hands.

"Ernie," said Pi, "we want to understand, but you're going to have to explain. Give us context."

"Echo," he said without looking up. "My name is Echo."

"Echo, can you explain?" she asked.

"Hannah, Aurelia, Rigel, Pythia, Echo, Raziyah," he said.

Pi shared a dumbfounded look with her sister. She had no idea what to make of it.

Then Hannah clapped her hands. "Harpers! That's awesome!"

"It is?" asked Pi.

"Harpers," repeated Hannah. "Hannah, Aurelia, Rigel, Pythia, Echo, Raziyah. We spell out Harper. We're the Harpers. That's our team name."

Echo beamed up at Hannah. Pi didn't quite get it, besides that it was a nice succinct name, but the way his whole face was a light bulb was enough for her.

"Great job, Echo," she said, deciding at the last second not to pat him on the back. He didn't look like the type that enjoyed invasion of personal space. "Now let's get in there and start solving this puzzle."

The next room was a featureless white box with only one entrance, the one they'd come through, and an object floating in the center. One very large object.

"It's like the cube from the test," said Rigel.

"But much bigger," whispered Raziyah. "Much."

The cube in the test room had been small enough to pick up. About the size of a Rubik's cube. This cube was about ten feet to a side and floating in the air as if it were filled with helium.

They circled the cube, examining the six sides, glancing beneath it, touching it. It differed from the test cube in that it was made of obsidian, or at least that's what they thought it was.

They tried a few spells, including one on their eyes to check for magical auras. The only thing that glowed was the cube itself in a very homogenous way. There were no lines, or faez clumpings to indicate latent spells, no words written on the cube or walls like in the test. No one could really even explain how the cube was floating.

They spent a few hours examining it, trying to penetrate its secrets, but not a one of them was able to uncover a single clue. Eventually, they gave up, and made plans to rejoin at a later date. Everyone's next priority was the first day of classes at their respective halls.

Pi was anxious to actually start. The summer of direct tutelage from Professor Mali had been exhausting, especially the parts in the *Verum Locus*. She also wanted the additional access to the hall's libraries that second year students were afforded. She had a lot of research to do about the maetrie, especially the Ruby Court. She had no intention of becoming their slave for eternity.

7

The office of Semyon Gray was located in the underground waterfall, on the east side of Arcanium. Aurie had been sent to his office, rather than stay in the classroom with the other students for the second-year class on truth, which made her wonder if the incident with Violet was the reason. Before she'd left the classroom, Violet had given her a snotty parting glance as if she knew what was coming.

Aurie hadn't been in this part of the hall before, but a bobbing will-o'-wisp led her through the lower passages, so she had no problem finding her way. As the sound grew, she knew she approached the place where the water from the moat cascaded into the cave system beneath the school.

A deafening sheet of water burst past the stone stairs. The surface was slick, so Aurie had to hold onto the rock. The limestone cave shimmered with magical light, reflecting what appeared to be glass imbedded in the walls. The stairs curled around the waterfall like a corkscrew, until at last the path went into the pool at the bottom. Aurie had the impression of movement within the water, though she saw nothing more than darting shadows.

Aurie walked back and forth a few times, trying to figure out where she was supposed to actually go, when a female fourth-year student strolled out of the waterfall unaffected. The water diverted around the student, keeping her perfectly dry. A stone path was camouflaged by the roiling waters.

The girl stopped next to Aurie. "Don't worry. It's a little freaky at first, but you get used to it. Just don't step off the path, or the falling water will knock you into the pool."

The girl left, leaving Aurie wondering if this wasn't a prank. She was afraid she was going to take one step into the waterfall and get knocked off.

Summoning her courage, Aurie stepped forward. Once she realized the magic of the path protected her, she kept going. The water stream was a good five feet thick.

On the other side was a smaller cave with a series of partitions. A pair of voices, Semyon Gray's and Professor Mali's, carried to Aurie's location. The discussion sounded serious, and she wondered if she should announce her presence, rather than be seen eavesdropping, especially if she was in trouble.

"...the whole thing is disturbing," said Semyon. "How did we not know that other recording was in the gem?"

"Professor Delight has been performing that duty for years. She swears she didn't know it was there," explained Mali.

Semyon cleared his throat. "Can we trust her judgment?"

"Semyon..."

"Right. Sorry. I'd forgotten," he said. "How do we know that was him? That it wasn't the Cabal that put it there?"

"It doesn't seem like them, and why make him look so terrible? I've checked with a few of the others and they all think it's the real deal. The next question is what is the item? Invictus had some pretty powerful artifacts. What if it's one of those?"

"And give it to the students? Why would he do something

foolish like that?" he said.

"There are rumors of—"

"Yes, yes. But I don't believe them," replied Semyon. "It's just not possible."

"At the very least, we know the Cabal is looking for a powerful spell. What if it's—"

"Joanie. It's not possible. There's no way a single spell could do that. It's like asking a fish to do quantum mechanics," he said.

"Then what do we do?"

A heavy sigh. "Keep our eyes and ears open. You'd better get going. I have another appointment soon."

Before Professor Mali could roll out and catch her eavesdropping, Aurie backed into the waterfall. She was so focused on not getting caught that her foot went off the edge of the stone. The water pressure immediately pulled her to the left, launching her into the pool headfirst.

The thunderous waterfall pushed her deeper, knocking the breath from her lungs. She didn't know which way was up and flailed frantically.

She kicked hard towards what she thought was light, but only succeeded in slamming her head against a stone wall. Her mouth opened momentarily, letting in a bit of water, choking her.

Aurie started to panic. They were expecting her but didn't know she'd arrived yet. She was going to drown in the pool fifteen feet away from her patron.

Then something long and powerful wrapped around her in a coiling embrace. For a brief terrifying moment, Aurie thought she was getting pulled deeper, but then the thing stretched upward and deposited her gently on the stone. Aurie rolled onto her hands and knees and coughed out a mouthful of water, catching only the tip of something dark and snakelike slipping back into the pool.

Patron Semyon Gray stood above her with a look on his face that hovered between concern that she'd almost died and concern that she couldn't even walk through a simple waterfall.

He gestured, a series of movements with his right hand, like a maestro conducting a symphony, and the water squeezed from her clothes into a pool beneath her. The eloquence and efficiency of his spellcraft made her delirious with envy.

She opened her mouth to ask about it, but he'd already strolled back into the other area.

"Patron Gray," she began, but stumbled upon her words when she saw the miniature dragon curled on his desk snoring. The scaly silver creature raised a curious eyebrow, peeking momentarily at Aurie, before returning to glorious slumber. "I'm sorry about back there, falling in, my foot slipped, so I, uhm, thank you..."

He leaned against his desk, steepling his fingers. The gray in his tight black curls had spread. He looked weary.

"I watched a video the other day," he said in his upper-class English accent.

Aurie winced. "I should have been in more control. I'm sorry. It just happened."

"You *weren't* in control?" he asked.

The emphasis of his surprise worried her, making her wonder if she were in more trouble than she thought.

"Describe to me exactly how you created the spell that made their clothes fall off. Exactly. Leave no detail out," he said firmly.

Nothing came to her right away. That day had been a bit of a blur, mostly she'd been focused on how she felt, her anger in that moment, then later she was trying to comfort Echo, who had been traumatized by it.

"I don't know," she admitted sheepishly.

"How can you not know?" he asked, frowning. The creases around his mouth had deepened until they were valleys.

"I was angry at Violet for what they'd done to Echo," she explained. "It's hard to remember."

He slapped the palm of his hand against the front of the desk, startling the little silver dragon into lifting its tiny head and giving a snort of disapproval before curling back into a ball.

"So it wasn't an explicate spell. You weren't holding it back, releasing upon the trigger word," he said.

"No," said Aurie.

He loomed over the desk, flecks of anger making his expression twitch with disapproval. "How can you expect me to believe that you spontaneously made those girls' clothes fall off in front of Arcanium? How can you convince me that you didn't plan an ambush to embarrass and demoralize Violet and her friends from the Order of Honorable Alchemists?"

"I swear I didn't plan to do that," she said.

The way his shoulders sunk gave her the answer. His frown changed from disappointment to sympathy.

"For the sake of your continued schooling at the Hundred Halls, I need to understand how you performed that near-miracle," he said.

"I wish I could," she said.

"It appears on the video that you planned and executed a clever ambush," he said.

The sea of cameras recording the event came back to haunt her thoughts.

"Violet and her friends ruined Echo's things. I was just reacting to that," she said.

"The video appears otherwise. I'm not as familiar with these new terms, but I think the phrase is that video went viral."

"Could I be expelled?" she asked.

"No," said Gray. "But I'm worried about your control. If you didn't execute a cunning trick, then you have larger things to worry about."

"I didn't even know Violet was going to be there," she said.

"I believe you," he said. "But I need to understand what happened, what you were thinking, what you might have said, or did."

Aurie focused on remembering the incident.

"I remember wanting to get revenge on them for what they did to Echo's backpack. I was thinking about their purses, dresses, whatever, and wanting the threads to break, or loosen, so their clothes were helter-skelter. At the moment the faez converged, like a power grid had dumped its magic into me, I said the word ragged, and then, well, you saw the video," she explained.

"Could you do it again?" he asked, and handed her a piece of string.

She stared at it for a moment, trying to conjure the feeling she had with Violet. Summoning faez was easy, but it took a spell to convert it into something useful. Faez was like flour— you needed to mix it a certain way and bake it at the right temperature or it wouldn't be a cake.

"Ragged," she said to the string.

Patron Gray took it from her hands and pulled on it. She knew it wouldn't break, even before he tugged. He handed it back to her.

"Try again," he said. "This time, imagine you are speaking to it like an old friend. And focus your faez, that last effort was pathetic."

Aurie held the string across her hands as if her palms were a platform. She gathered her faez, let the word fill her mind, and spoke to the string, imagining the threads breaking.

"Ragged," she growled at it.

Nothing happened. She felt a little silly grimacing at the string in her hands.

He plucked it away, a thought perched on his lips. His gray eyes scoured his shelves.

"It might be that word is too emotionally charged for you right now," he said, pulling a cracked mug off the shelf. The coffee cup looked like it'd been dropped, and a large gap went through the middle.

"What are we even doing?" asked Aurie.

"Mendancy," he said.

"Mendancy?"

"The magic of lies."

Her mouth grew dry.

Patron Gray went on. "You understand, of course, the purpose of truth magic. Verumancy. That you take what's there and make it more of what it is. Truth magic is often thought of as enhancing magic. It's like a pep talk for the world."

"So lying magic is convincing something that it's not?" she asked.

"You've got the idea," he said.

"Oh my," she said, holding her hand to her mouth. The time with Violet wasn't the first. She'd been using it to fix her old clothes rather than buy new ones, or when she was working in the clinic. She just hadn't realized that it wasn't truth magic.

"Aurie," he said seriously, getting her attention. "You must understand that we do not normally teach this type of magic. It's quite dangerous."

"How?"

He pointed to the cup. "I dropped that the other day and haven't gotten around to repairing it. Convince it that it can hold water."

"Convince it?"

"Yes. Convince it."

She focused her mind on the glass mug, imagined it holding water, that it was whole, a complete thing. "You are whole."

The release of faez made her skin tingle. She nodded to Patron Gray.

He picked up a pitcher from his desk, being careful not to disturb the tiny dragon, and poured water into the glass mug. Nothing came out the crack. It held like it was whole.

Aurie whistled at her own work.

"That's cool. I still don't understand how it's dangerous."

"How long will that hold?" he asked.

Aurie shrugged.

"Imagine you convince a car engine that it's not really broken, and when you're flying down the highway, it fails, right when you need to swerve out of the way of a lorry. Or if you're walking across a broken bridge, convincing the planks that they can hold your weight. What if they fail then?" he asked.

Aurie started to see the problem. She held up the mug, admiring the way the water moved against the hole without coming out.

"This one looks—"

As the words left her lips, the spell failed, dropping the water onto her face, making her sputter and spit.

Once she'd wiped it off, she said, "Okay, I get it. It's dangerous."

"It's why we don't teach it. Too many wizards have died over the years. When you start lying, it becomes too easy, and you eventually forget what's real and what's not," he said.

"Then why are we talking about it?" she asked, guessing the reason, but wanting to hear it.

"Because you need to learn it. Clearly you have a knack for mendancy, and you're one of the strongest faez users I've ever seen. But if you use it incorrectly, you could get someone killed."

"I wouldn't do that," said Aurie.

"What happens when you're in a tight spot? The beauty of mendancy is that it's easy, and it works, except when it doesn't."

"I see," she said. "Which professor teaches lying magic?"

"We don't have one. As I said before, it's too dangerous."

Aurie squeezed her fists. "Then how am I supposed to learn?"

"I will teach you," he said.

"You? I'm honored," she said.

"Honor has nothing to do with it. I have a responsibility to my students, especially troublesome students with more power than sense," he said.

The rebuke stung. She lowered her head.

"Oh, don't feel remorse for your actions. While your methods were unorthodox, you were protecting your friend from harm. Trouble is not always a bad thing," he said, looking away, regret squeezing his lips together. "And you came to the Hundred Halls to learn control. If you already could, the Halls would be pointless."

"When do we start?" asked Aurie.

"Not today," he said. "I have other pressing matters. I will contact you in a few weeks, but in the meantime, keep practicing, on anything available. Just be careful and not pick anything that you need to truly rely on."

He looked distracted. She wanted to ask him about the gem, and Invictus, but didn't want him to know she'd been eavesdropping.

"Patron Gray," she said as she prepared to leave.

"Yes?"

"Thank you." She gave him her most earnest smile.

He straightened, tall and serious. "You might not say that once we begin lessons."

8

The air turned cool as autumn placed its arms around the city of sorcery, transmuting the sugar maples and yellow birch to fiery gold. Pi made her way to the Glass Cabaret, weaving around the heavy crowds that descended on the city near Halloween. She hated the way the tourists left their trash on the streets, overloading services, creating a heavy stink as she passed each alleyway.

Radoslav met her in the back room looking more dour than a corpse. A white rose poked from his pocket, accenting his pallid features.

"If I didn't know any better, I'd say you were concerned," she said.

He stared back at her blankly.

"Did I miss a funeral or something?" she asked.

"Let's hope this doesn't become one," he replied.

She knocked a loose strand of hair out of her face. "Confidence building. Let's see some confidence building."

"I'd prefer you nervous and paranoid. It will give you a higher chance of survival," he said.

She clapped her hands together, looking around the room

for clues. "Soooo...what now? What do I need to know?"

"Accept nothing from anyone. Do not eat or drink anything except that which you take with you. Expect that everyone is trying to kill you, or trick you, and above all, control your hubris. It will only get you killed in the Eternal City," he said.

"Don't sugarcoat it," she said.

He let a sigh out and plucked the white rose from his pocket. He pinned it to her shirt, right above her breast. He smelled like coffee and a rain-slicked street, washed clean. It was intoxicating, but she pushed it away. Now wasn't the time to get all moon-eyed.

"Good," he said, nodding with his eyes to show that he'd been testing her. "It will be even worse on the other side. This rose is both my sigil and a measure of protection. It won't protect you from stupidity, but it will keep you safe from the things you can't see."

She waited for him to continue. The explanation seemed extraordinarily short, considering the danger she knew she was under. She'd spent the last month researching the maetrie and their Eternal City at Arcanium, but even in the world's most extensive magical library, details were rather slim.

"Anything else?"

He adjusted his tie, a measure of sadness on his brow. "Know that I will not return to the Eternal City no matter what is at stake. This is the only message that matters. You can tell anyone who will listen. This is all I can do for you. Any other information might lead you astray. There will be things you will learn that might—no, will—be disturbing. You must decide for yourself how you will react. I will say no more."

He exhaled, smoke from his lips filling the room rapidly. The brick room faded as the obsidian cube came into view. Pi remembered the floating cube from the contest. She had an idea on what they might do next, but pushed it away. She didn't have time for distractions.

The brick room never quite faded completely. On the other side of the wall, Slyvan waited, looking like a cologne advertisement's version of a gangster.

Radoslav nodded. Pi stepped through the wall. The outlines of bricks looked like pencil drawings in midair. When she looked back, the Glass Cabaret was gone. She hadn't thought to ask how she'd make it back.

"Getting, how do you say, cold feet?" asked Slyvan.

"The only thing cold here is your heart," she said, then remembered Radoslav's warning about hubris.

But Slyvan didn't react as she expected. He hooked his finger at her. "Follow me."

Pi was glad she'd worn a light sweater and jeans. The air had a crispness to it that made her rub her arms.

The Eternal City lived in perpetual gloom. It wasn't day or night, rather that quasi-dusk that happened in the far north, where the sun never quite set or rose.

The books she'd read conflicted about the actual size of the maetrie's realm, as if the experience had been different for each traveler. Some said it went on infinitely—she didn't believe that—while others suggested that it was as large, or larger than the continental US. But most of these were speculations. The scholars also argued about what was past the edge of the city. Some thought it was nothing more than apocalyptic wasteland, or old sections of the city, forgotten and left like concrete graveyards.

Mage lights glowed from cast-iron lampposts, giving everything a distant quality, as if it wasn't actually there. Puddles from a recent rain glistened, though she saw no evidence of clouds. Or stars for that matter.

Looking up had her momentarily distracted. The buildings on the street they traversed looked like residences, five- to eight-story buildings, squat and solid. But above them, she saw skyscrapers, which reached beyond her sight.

"No dawdling," he said.

As they walked, she had the impression of movement from the buildings. Slight shifting up close, but more pronounced from the skyscrapers in the distance. Thinking she was going mad, Pi stopped and held her hand up for a reference point. It took a little while, but eventually the skyscraper shifted past her finger, indicating it was moving. Or maybe she was. She began to see the problem the previous visitors had had with describing the city.

In a short time, Slyvan had moved half a block up the street. Something in a dark alleyway spoke, and it sounded like knives being sharpened. Pi had the sudden impression she needed to get back to Slyvan immediately, but before she could take a step, a small compact object shot out of the alley, headed right at her. She had no time to do anything but throw her hands over her face. The white rose on her chest spiked with faez, sending out a wave of energy that deflected the missile.

Slyvan appeared by her side, eyes bloodshot with anger. He sunk to his knees and, in one fluid motion, scooped a hunk of asphalt from the street. The newly formed rock hissed with heat. Slyvan pulled a short knife from his inside sleeve, ran it across his tongue, then spit blood into the asphalt mixture as if he were mixing cookie dough, kneading and stretching, forming it into something small and humanoid.

Whatever was in the alleyway seemed to sense the danger, because it made a racket trying to get out.

Slyvan whispered to the material in his hands, then gently set it down. The vaguely humanoid construct, not half a foot tall, sprinted into the darkness, too fast for its tiny legs.

Inhuman screams reached them moments later. When

silence returned to the street, Slyvan gave her a bloody smile and wiped his lip. With a long black fingernail, he flicked the white rose on her chest.

"You're lucky Raddie was looking out for you. But make no mistake, that ain't stoppin' something with a serious hankering for mischief," he said, waggling his eyebrows. "No more dawdling, we've got a ways to go."

This time, Pi kept to Slyvan's heels, being careful not to get too far away. When she checked the rose, parts of it had black spots, as if the magic in it was finite. Not only did she regret showing weakness in front of Slyvan, she hated marring the beauty of Radoslav's sigil.

After an hour of heading in a forward direction, never once turning to the left or right, the air grew cold enough that puddles had ice crystals eating at the edges. Pi kept her complaints to herself until a light freezing rain fell, then an unending soliloquy of curses followed as if they could somehow create warmth, while Slyvan produced a midnight cloak that shed the water like an elegant duck. In minutes, her clothes were drenched and her teeth were chattering.

Slyvan gave her a sideways glance, followed by a malicious grin. He seemed to be enjoying her discomfort.

When she couldn't take it, she asked him to stop so she could do something about it. She pulled a piece of origami paper from her pocket. Nimble fingers folded it into a tiny umbrella. Then she tried to summon faez so she could enlarge the paper to protect herself from the rain, but it felt like her normal conduit was squeezed shut. Sparks shot from the sides of the paper umbrella, wisping into ozone.

"What a disappointing discovery," said Slyvan. "You're not as hot shit as you thought you were. Can't protect yourself, and can't even keep the rain off your head. What's a little mageling going to do?"

Pi crumpled the paper umbrella and shoved it into her pocket, growling to herself as she kept walking in the direction Slyvan had been headed. She glanced at the skyscrapers, noting they were on her right now.

Slyvan appeared by her side, bowing gallantly, his cloak folded over his arm.

"If you're not feeling up to the weather, you can borrow my cloak. It'll keep you warm and out of the rain," he said.

She stopped, blinked hard at him, and wrinkled her forehead. "You didn't actually think that was going to work, did you?"

"You'd be surprised," he said.

"I'd freeze to death before I took something from you," she said.

"That can be arranged—it's still a long way to the Ruby Court," he said. "Your lips are rather blue. A pleasing shade, I might add, but it's maybe another two hours, three tops."

Pi jabbed her finger at the skyscrapers. "Bullshit. You've been leading me in circles. I haven't noticed us turning, but that doesn't mean you're not doing it somehow. This city doesn't seem to obey normal rules."

Her response put a knife into his glee, turning it to vague disquiet. He looked as if he'd eaten something that had upset his stomach.

The pale, sharply dressed maetrie with dark hair closed his eyes. The street blurred around Pi, giving her vertigo. When the movement stopped, they stood at the top of a set of stairs heading into darkness. Statues of griffons crouched on pedestals to either side.

"After you," he said, extending his hand.

Pi started down, but not without wondering if he was going to put a dagger into her back. The air was warmer, which soothed her shivering. If she died warm, that would be something at least.

The wide stairs went down multiple levels. As she went, faint pings and gongs echoed upward, vibrating into her chest. It sounded like music was being played on sewer pipes, yet it wasn't unpleasing. Pi found herself hurrying downward to learn the origins of the strange symphony.

The stairs led into a massive grotto, at least a few hundred yards in diameter, a glittering cave of geometric stones. The inner surface looked like a giant geode had been sliced open, then a waterfall of pipes, great and small, had flowed through the middle.

Standing on a narrow platform halfway up the long run of pipes on the multiverse's biggest organ was a heavyset woman in padded leather armor with a two-handed striker in her hands. The platform went the width of the pipes. She ran nimbly from side to side, pounding the pipes. Each swing was the blow of a lumberjack splitting wood, the result of which created a haunting melody that hung in the air and had the whiff of sorcery.

They waited patiently at the edge of the steps while the woman, who Pi assumed was the Ruby Queen, played her song. The notes echoed through her, dissonant like the voice of the earth speaking in words so long they would take days to hear. The music brought forth visions of monuments waking and striding across the city like stone giants. The song made her melancholy, and it almost hurt to listen, not emotionally, but physically, as the pounding vibration shook her bones.

When the song was over, Pi was spent. She checked the rose to find no new spots, but wondered if it could protect from that kind of sonic assault. She started to understand why the Ruby Queen was wearing padded leather armor: otherwise playing music with the gargantuan instrument would drive her mad.

Pi wondered how the Ruby Queen would make her way over since there was no platform that connected the middle area to the steps, but like a mountain goat, she leapt onto the pipes, ran down the largest middle one, and leapt to the stairs when she reached the end.

Her physicality surprised Pi, especially given she was built like a shot-putter. She had short spiky blonde hair, and not a speck of color on her except for the rosiness of her cheeks.

"Pythia Silverthorne. I am Lady Amethyte," she said in a husky voice. "I owe you a debt of gratitude."

Pi didn't know whether to bow or speak, so she did what came naturally. "For what?"

"For putting my dear Slyvan in his place. He's been pouting since he visited Radoslav last, which has left me a measure of quiet, a rare gift in these lands," said Lady Amethyte.

Pi struggled to comprehend this energetic woman, compared to the others she'd met, finally chastising herself for assuming that the three maetrie she'd met somehow represented the whole of their race.

Not knowing what to say, her gaze fell upon the strange organ.

Lady Amethyte's broad lips stretched wide. "Do you like the *Ecacathodian*, the lungs of the city?"

"The melody was moving," replied Pi.

"What a prescient thing to say," said Lady Amethyte. "Don't you think, Slyvan?"

"Yes, Your Ladyship," he said, docilely.

"You may take your leave," said Lady Amethyte while she twirled the striker on her shoulder. "I want to speak to my new friend alone."

After Slyvan left, Lady Amethyte noticed Pi's blue lips.

"Why, we cannot have that," said Lady Amethyte, who promptly blew out a puff of smoke that, like a serpent, wrapped itself around Pi, tugging the cold water from her clothes. When it was finished, she no longer felt chilled.

"Thank you, Your Ladyship," said Pi.

"Just Amethyte is fine," she said.

Pi found herself liking the Ruby Queen. She wasn't at all what Pi had expected.

"Thank you, Amethyte."

"Radoslav must trust you keenly to have sent you in his place. What do you do for him?" she asked.

"Errands, things he can't trust his other employees with," said Pi, trying to keep it vague.

"Employees?" asked Lady Amethyte as they left the grotto, heading into a tunnel. "Why, that's rather impersonal. If you worked for me, I wouldn't keep you as an employee. You'd have a higher place of honor."

"One employer is enough for me at this time," said Pi.

Lady Amethyte looked down slyly, a husky laugh coming from her belly. "Deftly said. A refusal, while leaving open the possibilities of the future."

Lady Amethyte pushed through swinging double doors, releasing a wall of music, startling Pi in its intensity. They stood on a balcony inside a high-end juke joint. The dance floor was filled with constant motion as what could only be described as elvish swing music set to an up-tempo beat played.

The Lady herself had transformed her leather armor into a black suit with white pinstripes. A lit stub of a cigar stuck from the side of her mouth.

"May I offer you a drink?" asked Lady Amethyte.

"No thank you," replied Pi.

"It's safe, you know. I receive human visitors on a regular basis. It'd be bad for business if I trapped them here on a technicality, so I import food and drinks from your realm," she said, puffing on the cigar.

Thirst made her throat dry. The water sounded delicious, and she didn't want to be rude.

"Show me the bottle," said Pi.

"I'll do you one better. I'll let you open it yourself," said Lady Amethyte.

A server appeared from the private bar behind them with a tray, one single bottle of water perched in the center. The brand was Apenta. It was real glass. The thick kind that no one made anymore. The language looked like something Eastern European.

Pi popped the foil top and held the bottle to her lips. The water was a glorious rush of wetness. She downed the water in one go, and the server was back at her side with a second before Pi removed her lips from the first.

Sheepishly, she took the second, and turned her attention to Lady Amethyte, who was sipping from a martini glass and studying her.

"Why do you need Radoslav?" asked Pi, then she drank from the second bottle.

"Did he not tell you?" asked Lady Amethyte.

"I'd prefer to hear it from you myself," said Pi.

Lady Amethyte set the cigar on the edge of the balcony. "Such confidence for someone so young."

"I had to grow up early," said Pi.

"No wonder Radoslav likes you. He was the same way," said Lady Amethyte, a trace of sadness lingering at the corner of her lip. "Do you know why he left?"

"It didn't come up," said Pi.

"There was a war between the four courts, and after we won, he disappeared," she said.

"Four? I thought there were only three," said Pi.

"The war was the end of the Onyx Court. Prince Radoslav

slaughtered the last of them, and now they call him the Black Butcher, behind his back, of course," said Lady Amethyte.

A chill went through Pi as she set the bottle down. His enforced solitude became clearer. He was a mass murderer, or a war criminal, however you looked at it.

"Are you sure you still want to work for him?" asked Lady Amethyte.

"Yes," she said, leaving out that she was bound to him for two more years and had no choice.

Lady Amethyte winked. "I know you're loyal. I didn't think you'd say yes otherwise."

"My apologies, Lady Amethyte, but what do you want? I need to get back soon," she said.

"On one side of the War of the Four Courts was Ruby and Jade. On the other was Diamond and Onyx. After we destroyed Onyx, Diamond capitulated and signed a peace agreement. After all, it was they who started it. This peace has existed since, and I'd like to keep it that way, but Jade has been sneaking behind my back and talking with Diamond. I fear they're going to start a new war, except it'll be two against one," said Lady Amethyte.

"You want Radoslav in case it comes to fighting?" asked Pi.

Lady Amethyte straightened her jacket. "No. I want to renew my alliance with Jade and maintain the peace."

"Why is he so important? Can't you speak with the Jade Queen? Surely you don't need him," said Pi, bewildered.

Lady Amethyte set her martini glass down so hard some of the liquid splashed out. Her eyes were ringed with thought. "My darling Kikala won't speak to me, she won't even receive my messages. Even now, I fear it's too late."

"I'm sorry, Lady Amethyte. I can speak to him, but I don't think he'll listen," said Pi, moved by her anguish.

Lady Amethyte grabbed Pi's arm, a plea on her lips. "You must. He's the only one that can right this. If he doesn't then the city will fall into a terrible war. One that's never been seen before. Millions will die if he does not act."

"I'll do what I can, but you have to tell me. Why is he the only one? What's so special about Radoslav?"

"He's our son," said Lady Amethyte.

"Our?" asked Pi.

"Kikala and I," said Lady Amethyte, still holding Pi's arm.

"You're a man?" asked Pi.

Lady Amethyte quirked a smile. "Sometimes. I was for Kikala, when she asked."

Pi was stunned. The books she'd read had said nothing about the maetrie being able to change their sex, but then again, no one lived in the Eternal City, they only visited.

This was a family matter then, and Radoslav was the prodigal son. It explained why Lady Amethyte wanted him, but not why Radoslav refused. Wouldn't he want to repair the relationship between his mothers? Didn't he realize how important family was? Maybe those battles had taken too much out of him, or maybe he didn't know what was at stake. He'd said that he wouldn't come back no matter what, but it was possible he'd thought it a trivial affair.

"I understand your plight," said Pi. "I'll speak to him and try to get him to come back."

Lady Amethyte patted her hand, gratitude glistening in the corner of her eyes.

"It's all I can ask," said Lady Amethyte. "Would you like to leave now?"

"If possible," said Pi.

"A busy young woman," said Lady Amethyte with a wink. "I have another appointment waiting, so I'll have my server take you through that door and to my private portal. It'll bring you right to the back room in the Glass Cabaret."

Moved by the maetrie queen, Pi bowed. "Farewell. It was good meeting you, Lady Amethyte."

"You as well, Pythia Silverthorne."

The server led Pi through the swinging doors. Right as she left, Pi heard a familiar voice greet the Ruby Queen. Before the server noticed, Pi leaned back in, catching a glimpse of the fifth-year student Zayn from the assassin's guild.

The implications of why he was at the Ruby Court weighed on Pi's mind until she was back in the Glass Cabaret. She went right away to find Radoslav behind the bar, wiping down glasses.

He took one look at her and held up his hand. "I see that eager look in your eyes. You think you have something gravely important to tell me. But I don't care. So don't bother."

"But—"

He snapped his fingers, which made her lips clamp closed.

"I said, I don't care," he said, his black eyes smoldering. "You will not speak of what you learned with anyone, especially me."

"Then why did you send me?" she asked.

"I didn't," he said. "You wanted to go. Now you know. I hope your curiosity is sated."

Before she could speak, he walked through the back curtain into his private room, leaving Pi behind the bar alone. The heated exchange had drawn a few side-gazes from the clientele. With cheeks burning, Pi rushed out the front, angry at herself for ever getting mixed up with that murderous bastard.

9

Aurie was late for a meeting with the Harpers in the competition room. She'd been waiting for her sister, but Pi had never shown up, and no one had seen her in Arcanium. After she'd decided that Pi was on some errand for Radoslav, she headed to the Spire.

The sullen November sky was draped with shades of gray that Aurie could sense even when she passed beneath the over streets and various mezzanines that made up the center of the city. The lower areas of the Spire had been relegated for student use, while the mid-levels were either administrative or housed magical conferences. No one had gone into the upper section since Invictus had died. They used to hold fund-raising events or other important Hall meetings in his areas, but since those areas were blocked, everything had gotten shuffled downward.

Aurie was headed through a parking garage filled with administrative vehicles. She found herself constantly looking over her shoulder as she walked through the empty garage, her footsteps echoing. She kept telling herself that her unease was due to the unearthly drivers that haunted a few of the cars, but she'd come through the garage previous times without feeling this way.

A middle-aged male geist in the driver's seat of a bright blue Beetle watched her pass, and when its gaze flickered behind her, she knew someone was following. Aurie sped up her pace, hoping to either outrun whoever it was, or get them to reveal themselves.

The startling sound of squealing tires as a car entered the garage on another level gave Aurie the opportunity to slip behind a concrete pillar. Once the noise had abated, Aurie stilled her breath and listened.

After a dozen heartbeats, she heard quiet footfalls, confirming her suspicions. Rage filled her chest, turning her hands into fists until her fingernails cut into her palms. Why would someone follow her? They were going to pay the price for whatever mischief they were planning. As the footsteps approached, Aurie prepared an ambush.

At the right moment, Aurie jumped out, unleashing a spell upon her pursuer.

"Entangle!"

The laces on his shoes untied themselves and wrapped around his ankles, tripping him forward. The dark-skinned guy that'd been following her fell onto his face, barely getting his hands up in time to prevent busting his nose.

"Who are you and why are you following me?" yelled Aurie, nerves pulsing through her. "I'll turn your underwear into leeches if you try anything stupid."

The guy groaned and moved cautiously to his knees. About the time he spoke, Aurie noticed the web tattoos on his arms.

"Be a good trick, considering I'm not wearing any," said Zayn as he looked up at her.

Aurie's cheeks turned into a forest fire. "Oh shit. I'm so sorry, Zayn. I thought you were a stalker."

He rubbed the back of his neck. "Technically, I was. I'd seen you through the columns and was coming up to talk to you."

"Do you normally sneak up on people when you do?" she scolded.

"Probably?" he said, sort of laughing. "Habit I guess. Honestly, Priyanka would kill me if she knew that you surprised me like that. I was purposely not trying to be quiet."

"Priyanka?" she said, hearing jealousy in her own voice.

"She's the patron of my Hall," said Zayn. "She's why I was down here anyway. I'm her assistant."

Aurie didn't know that patrons took students as assistants, but then again, each Hall was quite different, as she'd learned from Pi's stories about Coterie.

He climbed awkwardly to his feet and indicated his entangled sneakers. "Could you?"

"Yikes. Sorry," she said, then released the spell. The shoelaces returned to their previous positions. "So what did you want?"

Suddenly, Zayn didn't know what to do with his hands. He glanced askance and bit his lower lip. Aurie wanted to rescue him from his nervousness, but decided against it, in case she was wrong about what he was about to ask.

"Do you..." he started as he crossed his arms and looked at his feet, "do you think you...could help me with a project?"

"Oh," she said, internally cringing at the disappointment in her tone. "Um, I don't know? I mean, why would you ask me? I'm a second year."

Zayn pulled his shoulders back as if he hadn't considered the question. His face went through a few contortions before he answered.

"My Hall has a narrow focus. The problem—project—I have requires a broader knowledge base. You're in Arcanium, and I saw you in action at Trials last year," he said.

Her fantasy of what he was going to say deflated as he spoke, but instead of being disappointed, she wanted to punch him.

"So?" he asked tentatively, his ice-blue eyes searching her for answers.

Zayn looked like he could free climb a building, probably knew deadly forms of hand-to-hand combat, and had learned the arts of killing from his Hall. He might have even practiced them. Hell, he was the assistant to his patron, a powerful woman who was probably the least moral of the Cabal. She didn't necessarily want to help him. She wanted something else entirely.

"No," she said.

He startled, clearly not expecting the answer. "No?"

"Not entirely no," she said. "We'll call it a maybe. Take me on a date. Nothing normal. We don't even have to eat, but it has to be something unique to you."

Zayn stammered over his words, and he didn't appear the kind of guy that was ever at a loss for them. "I'm, well, I mean, yes, of course." His brow furrowed. "Is this a date or a test?"

"I'll let you know afterwards," she said.

He chuckled lightly, as if he were amused that he'd found more than he'd expected. He quirked a grin.

"Well, alright. Something unique to me. I'll work on that," he said, looking forward to the challenge.

"Saturday," she said.

"I'm not sure..."

"Saturday," she repeated emphatically.

He held his hands up, laughing. "Okay, okay."

"I have to get going. We're practicing at sucking in the contest," she said.

His eyes went wide. "I could help you. I've heard a few

things."

"That'd be cheating," she said.

He gave her a look that said are-you-that-naive? "Do you really think the other teams are playing fair? Especially with that whole special prize thing from Invictus. Some teams have rich backers that are actively funding research into the contest."

"We don't need it," she said.

He raised an eyebrow. "Really? I've seen your score. You need help."

"You're keeping track?"

He gave her a funny look. "Everyone does. There's huge bets placed on the contest every year. This year is worse."

"Did you place a bet?"

"I'm not saying," he said, eyes sparkling with mirth.

"Goodbye, Zayn," she said, and started walking away.

"I'll see you Saturday, Aurie," he said.

Aurie purposely didn't look back, even when she knew that he was watching her. She made her way to the contest room. She knew he was probably the last person she should be getting involved with, but she didn't care. For years, everything she'd done was for her sister or to get into the Hundred Halls. She wanted to do something for herself for once.

Rigel was digging through the refrigerator for an energy potion when she stepped through the door.

"At least one of the Silverthorne sisters has decided to grace us with their presence," he said.

"Sorry. I was waiting for Pi. I think she had some class work or something," Aurie lied.

Rigel seemed to sense her deception, and he shook his head as he popped the top on his can and took a tentative sip.

Before she went through the portal, Aurie checked the scoreboard which had showed up on their wall after the first day. One hundred and fifty-two teams filled the space. The top team, the Indigo Sisters, had a score of 38,222. Another twenty teams had scores around that level, all of them heavily filled with members of the Cabal, as if they were sharing information. The next groupings were above the 10,000 mark, which was the score people got for solving the first room. At the bottom, Harpers didn't even have a score. There was just a dash line, not even a zero. They hadn't registered a single point in the Grand Contest.

Aurie stepped through the portal. Despite the score, the encounter with Zayn had left her flushed with excitement. She knew they'd get the first challenge down eventually.

The others weren't as positive as she was. The giant floating cube hadn't changed, but the tension had. It felt like she'd stepped into a pressure cooker.

Hannah was skating around the cube in her block skates, the wheels making a constant whirring noise, which clearly annoyed Raziyah, who seemed to be the only one actually studying the cube. Each time Hannah went past, Raziyah wrinkled her nose, which made her glasses shift. The drama between the two went unnoticed by Echo, who was seated on the cube picking at his fingernails.

Rigel walked in behind Aurie and made a sweeping motion with his hand to indicate the dysfunction of the group.

"Looks who's here," said Rigel. "Fifty percent of the Silverthorne sisters, not that one hundred percent has been doing us any good. And by the way, for those keeping score, which is hard not to do with that damn board in there, the Young and the Breastless team has officially climbed out of the bottom, leaving us as the one and only team not to have advanced past this stupid cube."

The whole team, minus Echo, groaned.

"Learn anything new?" asked Aurie.

Raziyah pushed her glasses up her nose with a single finger. "How can I think with that constant noise!"

Hannah slapped her hand against the corner of the cube. "I think better on these. At least I'm doing something, unlike Echo, who thinks he's a mountain goat up there, or Rigel, who spends his time sucking down free food and drinks and using the bathroom."

"I'll have you know, I have a delicate constitution. It upsets easily," he said, holding a hand to his stomach.

"Come on, Harpers," said Aurie. "We need to work together."

"Says the girl who showed up late and without her sister," snapped Rigel.

"Yes, I was late, but I'm here now," said Aurie, containing her anger. "Have you guys learned anything?"

"Hannah just skates in circles, doing nothing. At least Echo is examining the cube from a new angle," said Raziyah.

Rigel cleared his throat. "What Raz is so inelegantly trying to say is that we haven't learned one single thing this entire time."

"That's not true," said Aurie. "We've learned things that don't work."

Rigel huffed and put his hands under his armpits. "I guess we've learned it's not a box. There's nothing inside. Solid cube as far as we can tell."

"Good," said Aurie, "anything else?"

Hannah did a block skate pirouette. "It absorbs faez, though doesn't charge it."

"Probably not an artifact," said Raziyah. "Not that they'd have one hundred and fifty-two of them lying around for the contest."

"Good thinking," said Aurie. "We also haven't figured out why it floats, which could indicate some extra-dimensional magic. It might be held up from another realm."

"Heavy. It's very heavy," said Echo, from atop the cube.

His comment tugged at something. While the others clearly dismissed him, Aurie thought there was something to his insight. She didn't think he was saying it randomly.

"It's a portal," said Pi, who strolled into the room with a turkey sandwich in one hand and an energy potion in the other. Her mouth was half full, and her eyes were delirious with the enjoyment of eating.

"Sorry I'm late," she said through the food. "Prior engagement."

That was code for Radoslav. Aurie wondered what she'd been doing that she hadn't had time to eat.

"It can't be a portal," said Hannah. "There's nothing to go through."

Pi took another bite of her turkey sandwich. After she swallowed, she said, "I guess the technical term is a Dimensional Fusion Device. It shifts the alignment of two realms overtop each other so you can easily move from one to the other."

Aurie rubbed her forehead. "So it is trans-dimensional. That's why it's floating. Because in the other realm, it's on solid ground. They've shifted them in the z-axis so this one appears to float."

"How do we activate it?" asked Rigel. "I'm unfamiliar with these types of magics."

"These types of magics are the purview of Acoustic Architectural Institute of Design." When everyone rolled their eyes, Raziyah added, "Or Stone Singers. I haven't taken the class yet, but the theory is simple. You just need to..."

She placed her hands on the cube and closed her eyes. The white walls faded away immediately, giving Aurie vertigo. She barely had time to orient herself before movement from multiple directions had her backing against the cube.

Dozens of angular fast-moving insects, each the size of a bear, came chittering at them from every side. Aurie watched in horror as a giant bug rose above Hannah, then jammed a chitinous foot through her chest.

Rigel created a mechanical warrior, something out of Japanese anime, to protect him. Aurie saw right through the illusion, and to her and Rigel's disappointment, the bugs did too. They chopped him up like a frog in a blender.

To her right, Pi, turkey sandwich abandoned on the floor and lettuce sticking out of her mouth, lashed out with flame, but the insect came through the fire and tackled her onto the ground. Aurie had no time to watch, because two insects were bearing down on her. The first one had its leg snapped in half by Raziyah, who'd thrown a rock or something small from a squatting position, but the creatures kept coming. Aurie tried building a makeshift wall out of the earth beneath her feet, but the giant insects burst through it like rice paper. The last thing she remembered was a pair of glistening mandibles snapping towards her neck.

10

The first act of Professor Mali's bibliomancy class was to eat a book. They were meeting in the Tower of Letters, where ancient typeset blocks draped the walls. Each class, they met in a different location of the hall. For the first month, they'd learned the mundane practice of creating books using a printing press.

While Pi thought the exercise exquisitely boring, when they got to use the same press that Ben Franklin had made his pamphlets on, she started to come around.

The professor had ingested *Magical Wings of North America*, a book about butterflies. After the last corner was poked into her stern mouth, the professor swallowed, followed by an enormous belch.

"Excuse me," she said, pounding on her chest. "Now that I've had my fiber for the day, ask me any question you want from the text."

Everyone had their own copy of the book. They'd each printed and bound their own editions using special ink and paper.

Deshawn raised his hand first, and the professor called

on him. "What's the lifespan of a Brimstone butterfly, and what potions can you make with it?"

The professor closed her eyes for a moment, then opened them as if the answer had appeared in her mind like a light bulb. "Nine to ten months, and they can be used for fire breathing and, quite inexplicably, indigestion potions."

Other hands went up. Professor Mali answered each one with precision, though she'd never read the book. Pi wasn't a book lover as much as Aurie, but she recognized the power of being able to absorb a lot of knowledge in a short amount of time. The more research-oriented fifth-year students were said to consume two to three books a day, and could recite the most obscure facts about diverse subjects. Pi had no intention of doing that, but there were a few tomes of magical information she would like to absorb. Too bad they couldn't do this trick with spell books. Those had to be learned the hard way.

A groan went up around the room when Violet raised her hand. She gave the rest of the class a nasty look. Her clique had grown smaller after the incident with Aurie had gone viral.

"What are the Monarch butterfly's natural predators?" asked Violet.

Before the professor could answer, Aurie leaned over and whispered to Pi, "The blonde parasitic fly."

Pi clamped her hand over her mouth, but a little snort came out. The professor gave a darting glance in her direction, but answered the question without hesitation.

After the demonstration, Professor Mali moved to a different room so they could each eat their book and she would quiz them to the efficiency of their magical binding. The more facts you could recite, the higher the score. The room evolved into quiet chatter when the professor left.

Pi turned on her sister. "You're entirely in too good of a mood considering we got slaughtered by a room full of bugs two days ago."

"Moi?" said Aurie innocently. "Must I brood about everything? Anyway, I'm just glad we got past the first room and put some points on the board. We're still in last, but we're *tied* for last at least. I'm looking forward to getting back in there."

"Sucks we have to wait a week between tries now, though I suppose that's for the best. I've had nightmares about those stupid bugs killing us two nights running," said Pi.

"As far as I've heard, no one's gotten past the bug room yet, so we have time," said Aurie.

Pi eyed her sister suspiciously. "Are you taking mood-enhancing potions or something? What gives?"

"I'm not going to let that parasite over there ruin my time in the Halls," said Aurie, glaring in Violet's direction. "Besides, I have a date tomorrow."

"What? Who?" asked Pi, looking around the room.

A sly grin crept to Aurie's lips. "That fifth year from the Academy of the Subtle Arts."

"Assassins, you mean," said Pi, remembering that she'd seen him at the Ruby Court. "I'm not sure you should be messing with him."

"I'm not messing with him," said Aurie. "I'm going on a date. Anyway, I'm not blind. He wanted my help on something, but I'm not doing anything until I get to know him better. I'm aware this might be a trick, considering his Hall, but if it's not..."

Pi hesitated. She didn't want to bring up that she'd been in the Eternal City. Aurie would flip out. But she needed to warn her that he was mixed up in dangerous business.

"I saw him the other day," said Pi. "He was with some members of the Ruby Court."

"Stop it, Pi. I'm doing this," said Aurie.

"Couldn't you pick someone safer? Like Deshawn or Rigel?" asked Pi.

"Deshawn's a friend, and Rigel's got a cute girlfriend from Aura Healers. Come on, Pi," said Aurie.

"Fair enough. But please be careful. Zayn's cute, okay, strike that, he's drop-dead gorgeous, especially with those eyes, but think about the Hall he's in, and what he's going to be doing after he graduates this year. I can't see how you can trust him."

"Isn't it my job to be the big sister?" asked Aurie.

"And it's my job to be reckless and impulsive," said Pi.

"Aurelia," said Professor Mali, beckoning her into the side room for her quiz.

Aurie grabbed her book and nibbled on the side. "Bottoms up!"

Pi laughed, shaking her head, but really she was worried about her sister. It wasn't like her to be like this. Either she was cracking under the pressure, or this was the real Aurie beneath the crushing responsibility. Pi hoped it was the latter, though she vowed to keep an eye on her.

Suddenly, the wretched scent of musky plum invaded Pi's nose.

"Are you trying to attract flies with that?" Pi asked as Violet approached, holding her hands behind her back.

"You should be nicer to me," said Violet with a practiced flip of her hair.

"Actually no, that's not how it works. I despise you, your rich mother, and everything the pair of you stand for. Eventually karma will catch up to you, and the reaping will be glorious," said Pi.

"To think," said Violet, "I was coming over to offer an olive branch."

"Don't lie about that," said Pi.

"I'm not," said Violet. "I don't want to war with you two for our whole time in Arcanium. We don't have to be friends, but at least we cannot be enemies."

Pi eyed Violet carefully. She seemed strangely apologetic.

"I'll bite," said Pi. "What are you offering?"

"I'll back off with your sister," said Violet, "and keep my Alchemist friends from seeking revenge."

"And why would you do this?" asked Pi.

Violet's shoulders slumped, a measure of fear flickering across her gaze. She brought her hands around. In her grip was a stack of papers loosely shoved between bindings. The whole pile looked ready to fall onto the floor at any moment.

"Is that your book?" asked Pi.

Water welled up in Violet's eyes. "I'm terrible at this. I never did crafts as a kid. That was never my mom's thing."

"Doesn't she own a newspaper?" asked Pi.

"Yeah, but she runs the business side of it, she doesn't make them. I'm awful at all things books. If I don't get a better grade in this class, I'm going to flunk out this year, after I'm twenty, which means I can't reapply," said Violet.

"So you want my help with your book in exchange for backing off?" asked Pi. "Even if I wanted to help you, there's no time. Whatever that pile of papers is, it's not a book, no matter how much I might try to help you."

Violet's gaze lowered until it rested on the book on Pi's table.

"Oh, I see," said Pi, a pit forming in her gut.

"No one will mess with her. I promise," said Violet.

This project was a big part of their grade. Pi hated the idea of trading with Violet, but that gaggle of Alchemist girls could cause a lot of trouble.

Pi gritted her teeth. "You promise?"

"I promise," said Violet earnestly.

Pi handed her copy of *Magical Wings of North America* to Violet. When she accepted Violet's copy, a few pages fell on the floor.

"Sorry," said Violet. "I told you I was bad at this."

Violet was the next name called. When Aurie came back out, Pi hid the pile of junk that was called a book under her book bag and made small talk with her sister until it was her turn.

After scooping up the pages, and holding them together by cradling her arms, Pi hurried towards the side room. Violet came out with an aura of smugness on her lips so thick it made Pi choke.

Eyes glittering, Violet touched Pi's arm affectionately and whispered, "Thanks, Hick Pi. The professor was so impressed with my book that she awarded me extra points. You really know your bibliomancy."

"You promised," said Pi, intoning the words as a threat.

"I did," said Violet, holding her hand over her heart. "After all, I promised. But it won't matter." She winked. "Because my friends are terrified of you and Aurie. They're not going to come within a hundred feet of you ever, if they can help it."

She wanted to punch Violet in her perfect face, but then the book would have fallen to the floor. Violet gave her a patronizing pat on the arm before strolling victoriously back into the other room.

"Miss Pythia, it's your turn," called the professor from the other room.

Pi blew a breath out and marched forward. She was beginning to understand her sister's intense hatred for Violet Cardwell.

11

Aurie had been less nervous when she'd faced down the strange winged creature in the Enochian District than she was as she waited for Zayn. Her mouth was a little dry, and she kept having fears about tripping over her own feet, or the boot she'd been continuously repairing with mendancy failing at an awkward time. She fixed it twice again while waiting for him.

Cars flashed by, heading round the traffic circle. On the other side, a bronze statue of Invictus forty feet tall drew crowds. Hundreds of teenagers on winter holiday were taking selfies. The warm weather had been a boon for city tourism.

"We can go over and take one if you want," said Zayn, coming up from behind her.

He wore jeans and a simple black V-neck shirt, which was a relief. She didn't have any "date" clothes, and had worn her jeans with an aqua sleeveless light hoodie.

"Next you'll want to take a horseless carriage ride," she said, nodding towards a couple in the back of a white carriage. The girl had a rose in her hand and a bored look on her face. "I hope you can do better."

Zayn held a grin full of secret knowledge. He glanced at

her boots.

"Good choice," he said.

Aurie didn't bother asking about why she would need boots, because she knew he wouldn't tell her. She just hoped they held up during their journey.

They headed away from the statue toward a mixed residential area with cafes and three-story brick houses. The streets reminded her of a more urban version of her old neighborhood.

"Where are you from?" she asked as they walked shoulder to shoulder, occasionally bumping lightly as they passed around lampposts or other pedestrians.

"Alabama. A little town you've never heard of," he said.

"Really? I never heard a hint of it in your speech," she said.

"The first thing we learn in the hall is to remove our accents, especially southern ones. Priyanka says they make us sound stupid," he said, eyes crinkling with thought.

Aurie left her agreement unsaid. She didn't want to insult him.

They neared an outdoor restaurant called Olympias filled with smiling couples and families. Roast lamb and Greek spices permeated the air, making Aurie's stomach grumble. She thought they might go in, but instead, they went around towards the back. At the end of an alleyway, an archway led to a secret garden. Zayn touched bricks seemingly at random, and whispered a spell before they passed through. Aurie's skin tingled, and she guessed there was an invisible barrier.

At the center of the garden, hidden from the entrance by flowering lavender bushes, was an obsidian arch.

"It's a portal," said Aurie.

"You've used the Garden Network?" he asked, turning on her.

"No, I've just seen one before," she said, and when his brow bunched up, she added, "In a book."

It looked more permanent than the one her parents had constructed in the Undercity.

"Right," he said, not sounding completely like he believed her.

"Who made this?" she asked.

"Invictus," he added. "He wanted an easy way to move around the city. Only the patrons and a few other people have access."

"Like Priyanka's assistant," she said.

He gave a prideful shrug. "It has its perks. Now come here and hold my hand. We have to go through together."

His hand was warm and strong. He had calluses on his fingertips and along the ridge of his palm.

Before they passed through, he said, "Jaune-rouge."

The vertigo wasn't as severe as last year when she'd gone to Egypt, but she didn't want Zayn to know she'd traveled by portal, so she bent over on the other side, shaking her head.

"That's awful," she said.

"You get used to it."

They stood in near darkness. A faint glow from the portal illuminated a rock garden. Somewhere in the distance she heard water dripping.

"Undercity?" she asked.

"Let me guess," he said, "read it in a book."

She had to be careful with her knowledge. "My sister and I explored a little of the upper regions. Nothing too dangerous."

"I suppose everyone does it eventually," he said. "But it *is* dangerous. A kid in my class disappeared my second year when he went exploring alone."

"Never found him?"

"They didn't bother. He wasn't supposed to be there,

and the place is too big for an effective search. I've heard the Undercity is bigger than the city itself. If he's lucky, he's dead," he said in a way that told Aurie he'd experienced those sorts of things himself.

Aurie reached for her earrings to make light, but remembered that she'd used them to escape in the Enochian District. While she was preparing a wisp, Zayn put a spell on her eyes by lightly touching her forehead with his fingertips.

Suddenly, the world bloomed into existence, a plethora of blacks, whites, and grays with distinct lines like a charcoal drawing. The cave was much larger than she first thought. They stood in a pristine rock garden on a little plateau.

Zayn led her away, taking her on a path. The way was rocky, with frequent changes in elevation. A family of large rodents, two parents with a dozen smaller children following, crossed at one point. After they were gone, Zayn explained they were common to the upper areas of the Undercity. Not dangerous, and frequently the prey of other denizens.

At one point, Zayn had them climb into a crevasse that went down twenty feet. Aurie put a spell on her hands so she wouldn't slip, a practical spell that got a nod from him.

There was no path at the bottom, which made travel slow. The air was thick and slightly warm, bringing beads of sweat to her forehead, some breaking and running down her chest. After about what seemed like miles, but was probably only three hundred feet, they came out upon a ledge.

They scooted to the edge. It wasn't a complete drop-off, but a steep slope. Zayn reached into a cooler along the wall to produce a chilled bottle. She didn't think he'd prepared this for her, but it was a place he came to often. The water was cool on her tongue.

"What is—" she started to ask, but he put his finger on her lips and shook his head.

He said in a whisper, "We can speak, but quietly. We don't want to disturb the nest."

At the words—*the nest*—a shiver of fear went through her. Zayn pointed into the cave, which was about a hundred feet in diameter. The ledge was around forty feet up. Covering the far wall was a glistening white sheet, gently moving in an unseen wind. She didn't realize what it was until she identified the black specks moving across its surface.

"That's a web," she said.

He grinned with the kind of glee reserved for boys and their toys.

"There must be hundreds of spiders," she said, hiding her revulsion.

"Thousands, maybe more," he said as he searched her face for a reaction.

She reminded herself that she was the one that had demanded a date unique to him. She just hadn't expected hiding out in a cave full of spiders.

"Are they dangerous?" she asked.

"Only in swarms, though I suppose if you're a cave cricket, even one is dangerous," he said.

Zayn looked upon them like a kid watching a litter of puppies fall over each other. "Achaeranea magicaencia. One of the few colonies left in the world. They live near heavy faez usage, which is why they're in the Undercity. Which reminds me, don't use any magic. They're drawn to faez and can absorb it, making them deadly to mages."

"Wonderful," she said, remembering the thralls in the Enochian District. That night had been a disaster.

He looked back at her, touched her leg. "Don't worry. We're safe up here. I come here all the time."

"I thought you didn't like spiders?" she asked.

It took him a moment to remember. He seemed to prepare

his answer carefully. "Back in Freeport Games? I was afraid it might be poisonous."

She touched his elbow, running a finger along a line of web tattoo. "I don't think you were being completely honest with me that day."

"You caught me half naked in the closet. What was I supposed to say?" His voice echoed in the cave.

"Why do you come here?" she asked.

He looked at her with his ice-blue eyes. She tried not to imagine chewing on his lower lip.

"This is going to sound weird, but it reminds me of family. I have a lot of aunts and uncles and cousins back home. Everyone lives in the same town, so it's kinda like that spider colony, with everyone pitching in to help, swarming over problems no matter how difficult," he said.

"You miss them," she said.

"Yeah," he said wistfully. "I'd never been outside of my town until I came to the Halls. It's lonely."

"What about your other classmates?" she asked.

He snorted softly. "My hall isn't like most of the others. It's best to keep to yourself."

Sitting a few inches from each other, they stared at their feet. Aurie had a million things to ask him, but they all sounded forced and awkward in her head, so she stuck to a safe question.

"What was that project you needed help with?" she asked.

She regretted the question instantly. It was like the words had branded him. He leaned back, away.

"We don't have to talk about that now if you don't want," he said.

"It's okay," she said, curious. "I don't mind. After all, you showed me a unique part of yourself."

He searched for the words. "I feel like an ass asking.

There's a book in Arcanium's library that I was hoping to get a look at. I have this thing, and it might be able to help me."

"What's it called?" she asked, curious.

"*Impossible Magics*," he said, looking straight into her eyes.

A rock formed in her gut. Suddenly she was feeling manipulated. The duplicitous nature of his Hall came front and center in her mind. He was probably acting on orders for Priyanka.

"You okay?" he asked.

She realized she couldn't let him know her mistrust. If it was subterfuge, and it felt like it, she had to play the game better than him. But she wasn't a practiced liar, despite her gift for mendancy.

Before he could ask another question, she jammed her lips against his. He made a little noise, as if she'd spanked him on the ass lightly, and then they melted together.

She'd never considered that subterfuge could be so rewarding. His soft lips nibbled and teased, a playfulness that exposed a different side of him, tongue brushing hers but never demanding.

He tasted like sweet, glorious mint, and she didn't know how long the kissing went on. She was cradled against him, fingers rushing over his short hair, tracing down his back.

She put the sharp edge of her fingernails along his neck and clawed softly like a cat claiming its spot. He relinquished a moan which echoed her desire.

She was glad for the uncomfortable rocky surface, or she would have given her yearning its due, climbing on top and straddling him. She wasn't a virgin, but preferred to take her time.

Then he pulled away, turning his head to listen, while she quietly panted.

A soft squeaking from below put a dagger into her desire. Peeking over the edge revealed a young rodent who had fallen into the cave and appeared injured. Already, spiders mobilized in the youngster's direction.

"We don't have to watch if you don't want," he said.

"It's okay. I'm not squeamish," she said, catching his nearly imperceptible nod of approval.

"Once they get enough venom in the rodent, it won't feel anything. It's a powerful paralytic. Then like ants, they'll drag it back to the nest for feeding," he said.

The swarm of spiders came on rapidly. They were quicker than Aurie anticipated, and slightly larger, maybe the size of her palm, covered in fine black hair. The young rodent was only moments from death when its mother darted in from above, grabbed its baby by the scruff, and bounded away from the incoming spiders.

"Yay!" Aurie exclaimed, her cry of victory lasting until she realized the mother rodent was bounding up the slope towards them. With no more concern than if they were a pair of rocks, the rodent mother carrying her injured baby sprinted between them and out of the cave through the ravine.

Like a carpet of living earth, the spider swarm moved after the rodent, directly at them.

"Oh, shit," said Zayn.

Aurie was up instantly.

"Run," he said, pushing her towards the crevice.

The way in had been slow due to the torturous nature of the path, but with the spider swarm in pursuit, Aurie slipped frantically through the tight spaces, smashing her hips and legs on the rocky outcroppings.

The silent pursuit seemed almost worse than any chittering horde. Every time she looked back, Zayn urged her onward. She felt their presence almost directly behind them.

Aurie thought they might be breaking away, when her boot ripped at the seam, the magic of her lies failing at the worst time. Her unprotected foot slammed into rock, forcing her to cry out.

"Keep moving," he pushed at her.

The boot was ruined, and there was no way she could run over the sharp rock at the bottom of the crevice.

When she summoned faez to repair the boot, he said, "No magic!"

But she had no choice. She told the boot how it was almost brand new, that the threads hadn't broken, just stretched a little, and that everything was going to be fine. Mendancy felt warm and syrupy when she used it. With the covering back over her foot, Aurie continued down the crevasse.

She looked back and almost wished she hadn't as the swarm had nearly overtaken Zayn.

As the crevasse curved, part of the swarm broke off, heading over the edge to cut them off.

"Let's stop and fight," yelled Aurie over her shoulder. "We can burn them."

"No," he said. "It won't work. They eat magic."

Aurie growled in frustration.

"I have one thing left to do," he said through hurried breaths. "Keep going, don't look back. There's a white line painted on the rock in the place you have to climb up."

"Don't be an idiot. You can't face them alone," she said.

"I'll meet you at the portal," he said. "Just promise me you won't look back."

Her hands were raw from scraping along the rock. She couldn't imagine how many bruises she had on her legs.

"Don't be a hero," she said.

"Don't worry, I never am," he said, and the unrelenting anguish almost made her stop until he added, "No looking, and keep running! I'll meet you at the portal!"

Despite every urge to look, Aurie kept scrambling through the crevasse for what seemed like forever. Eventually she came to the white line and looked back. No spiders were following. She wasn't ready to chance their eventual return, so she climbed as if they were hot on her trail.

Thankfully, she'd been paying attention on the journey out, and found the rock garden, though she couldn't pass the archway. Standing in the darkness wondering if a horde of magic-eating spiders was going to appear at any moment wasn't the greatest of feelings, but Aurie survived it as well as she could.

An hour passed, and she was wondering if Zayn hadn't survived and if she would have to find her way out of the Undercity on her own, a prospect she didn't relish, when he came stumbling up the path.

Except Aurie didn't recognize him at first. He looked like he'd been hit with a heavy stick multiple times. He had lumps all over his body. Even his face was misshapen, which she assumed was from the poison.

"Zayn!" she said, holding him up before he fell.

Through one eye, he gazed wearily at her. He didn't look strong enough to stand let alone use magic to get them back.

Aurie used mendancy to convince him he was doing better than he thought. He perked up after the spell was over, and got them through the protective wall.

"Marron-gris," he said, bringing them through the portal.

Aurie half carried him out of the secret garden. He had foam on his lips and a pallor to his skin.

Once she was outside, she knew instantly where she was, only a few blocks from Golden Willow. Aurie spelled her tired limbs and carried Zayn the final distance like a firefighter, heading straight to the emergency doors.

When she stumbled through, Dr. Fairlight greeted her with a smile until she saw Zayn on her shoulder. Together they got him on a gurney.

"Spider poison," she said. "Achaeranea magicaencia."

Dr. Fairlight gave her a funny look, but marshaled her team. In moments, they whisked Zayn away, and she was left to collapse from exhaustion.

Curled up on a couch, Aurie slept until Dr. Fairlight woke her with a gentle shake.

"Is he okay?" asked Aurie, heart tearing as she remembered the horrible flight from the cave of spiders.

"He's fine," she said, nose wrinkling. "Or he'll be fine because you got him here in time."

"Can I see him?" asked Aurie.

Dr. Fairlight looked like she didn't know what to say. "He's in a private room now. He has other visitors."

"Oh," said Aurie, guessing someone from his Hall had come for him. "Priyanka?"

Dr. Fairlight raised an eyebrow, but nodded, releasing a bloom of jealousy. She wanted to be at his side when he awoke. But then she thought about her patron, Semyon. She imagined that if she were injured, he'd be at the hospital to check on her.

The subject changed to small talk. Dr. Fairlight checked up on how school was going, before she got called to another emergency.

When Aurie finally left, she was awash with mixed emotions, mostly because she liked him, despite the dangerous implications of his hall. It wasn't that good girl likes bad boys thing, or at least she hoped not, but that he'd seemed to be trying to tell her something through their conversation, something even he didn't necessarily want to admit.

She knew it because that's what she'd been doing for the

last year, until she'd finally been able to put her parents' death behind her.

One thing she did know for sure, she was going to get a look at this book *Impossible Magics*. Either it would tell her something about Zayn that he didn't want to admit or it was a clue to what he—or really, the Cabal—really wanted.

12

While the other Harpers were in the portal room, Pi confronted her sister.

"Are you going to tell me what happened on your date? You wouldn't shut up about it before when you left, but came back covered in bruises and haven't said a peep."

Aurie was wearing a shirt of light chain, which she kept shifting and adjusting. They'd borrowed the gear from Hannah's friends at Freeport Games who did live action role-playing.

"Because I already know what you would say," said Aurie. "You don't like him."

"What's not to like?" said Pi. "But I don't trust him, and neither should you."

"He seems to be genuine," said Aurie.

For an older sister, Aurie could be so naive. "Isn't that the whole point of his hall? To practice deception? Academy of the Subtle Arts is a nice way to say that they're practiced liars."

"There's nothing wrong with lying for the right reasons," said Aurie.

Pi put a hand to her forehead. "He's already gotten to

you."

"He hasn't, I swear," said Aurie, but Pi knew her sister. She could see that look in her eyes. She always believed the best in the guys she met, and was typically devastated when they turned out to be the jerks that Pi told her they were.

"I was the one to ask for the date," said Aurie. "He wanted something."

"Of course he did. Don't they all?"

"Not that. Well, probably, but that's not what he asked for. He wanted to see a book from the Arcanium library called *Impossible Magics*," she said.

"He's on orders from the Cabal, I bet," said Pi.

"The problem is that book isn't in the library. I checked with the Biblioscribe. Never had a copy. Nothing on the internet either. If it exists, it predates Hall records," said Aurie.

When neither sister had an explanation, they joined the others, who were milling around the obsidian portal cube nervously. Only Echo seemed impervious to the task. He was sitting in his traditional spot on top, wearing bulky padded armor. Everyone looked uncomfortable in their gear except for Hannah, who had a set of Army-issued body armor she'd acquired for cosplay.

"Are we ready to do this!" said Pi, trying to get her team pumped up.

Rigel gave his answer with a series of dry heaves along the wall, while Raziyah paced back and forth, mumbling and constantly pushing her glasses back up her nose. She had a bulletproof vest on that was two sizes too big.

"Time to take off the roller skates," said Pi.

"No way," said Hannah. "I'm better on these."

"But that courtyard is rocky and grass covered. You'll just get tangled up," said Pi.

"I'm *wearing* the skates," said Hannah.

Pi sighed. "Well, then. Positions everyone. Remember your jobs."

"I don't want to die again, I really don't," said Rigel, his color resembling old porridge.

"Don't worry," said Pi. "You'll respawn back here."

"It's not the respawn I'm worried about. It's the actual death. I've had nightmares since last time," he said.

"We all have," said Pi, "but we have to do this."

"Chin up, Rigel. We've got this," said Aurie as she placed her hand on the obsidian cube.

Rigel audibly groaned.

Everyone was in position, even Echo, who looked as uninterested as possible, but at least he was standing.

"Three. Two. One. Go."

This time, Pi had a moment to orient herself before the bugs attacked. They stood in an old stone fort, walls mostly intact, except for two areas that had collapsed. The greenish-blue bugs had six legs, were tall and angular, and had powerful mandibles. Once they identified their targets, they moved without hesitation, chitinous cow-sized insects intent on dealing quick death.

A bug came straight at Pi. She twisted fire and earth into a spear, the heat radiating off her face, and threw it. The bug was knocked back, one leg dangling at an obscene angle, but it kept coming.

Pi threw a second and third fire spear, collapsing the bug a few feet before it ripped her face off. On the other side of the cube, Rigel screamed. The bug had a leg through his midsection. She blasted it with another fire spear at the same time as Echo from atop the cube, killing the bug.

When the initial ambush had been turned back, the Harpers convened near the dead bug that had killed Rigel. Thankfully, his body disappeared. Seeing him die was bad enough.

"Not bad. We only lost one," said Hannah.

Raziyah squeaked. "We can't lose any if we're going to progress."

"Come on, Harpers. We've got to stay together," said Pi, then noticed Echo wandering away to look at some purple flowers along the walls. "Echo, come back. We need to stick together."

"I'll get him," said Hannah, half skating, half stepping across the uneven ground.

She was almost to Echo when a bug burst from the earth, showering everyone in dirt. Hannah went to turn, but her skates got tangled, and she fell to the ground.

Pi was going to throw a fire spear, but Echo was standing in the way. Everyone was shouting. The bug was on Hannah before she could do anything. It struck her neck, ignoring the body armor completely.

Everyone converged on the bug, killing it before it could move after anyone else.

"There might be more hiding in the courtyard," said Pi. "Let's sweep together and clear them out."

They killed three more, one at each corner, before considering the interior safe.

"It takes too many fire spears to kill one bug," said Raziyah. "We've got to find a better way if we're going to progress."

Though no one was sharing details about this phase of the contest, they'd learned that more bugs would attack the fort. They would have to withstand multiple waves, nobody knew how many, to get past the fort phase.

"Let's see how far we can get today." Pi pointed towards the gaps in the walls. "Can you fix those, Raz?"

Raziyah blinked hard. She frowned. "I can try. Echo, can you come with me to keep look out?"

Echo nodded and trudged off behind Raziyah. She seemed to have a soft spot for Echo. Whenever they had downtime, she was usually chatting quietly with him, trying to get him to open up about himself.

While Raziyah stood in front of the gap, singing softly and making gestures, Echo crouched down, pulled weeds from the earth, and looked at the roots as if they contained deep mysteries.

Pi climbed up a set of stairs to the top of the wall. Aurie followed. A forest surrounded the old fort. The whole scene didn't seem strange—they could be in the hills of West Virginia, or somewhere like that for all she knew.

"Any ideas?" she asked.

Aurie lifted one shoulder and had opened her mouth to speak when Raziyah screamed. A squad of bugs sprinted from the forest towards the gap in the wall. Raziyah had managed to raise a lump of earth in the space, but it would barely slow the bugs down.

Pi ran along the top to the gap. She didn't bother with the fire spear, there were too many for that to work. Instead, after using verumancy on her arms to give them more strength, she grabbed hunks of stone that had broken away from the wall and threw them at the incoming bugs.

The first one bounced harmlessly off the lead bug, then surprisingly, exploded into shards, knocking them back like bowling pins.

Pi hadn't made it explode. Only when Raziyah shrugged and yelled, "Throw another," did she understand. It seemed she was better at demolition than construction.

Pi threw a fastball at the bugs, who had closed the distance. Raziyah made a gesture like snapping an invisible stick between her hands, and the hunk of stone exploded, killing one bug and slowing the others.

Aurie moved past the mound of earth and knelt in the grass with her hands on the ground. The bugs were coming fast.

"Watch out," screamed Pi, but her sister didn't move.

Pi kept throwing rocks for Raziyah to explode, being careful not to throw short and get Aurie caught in the shrapnel. Echo was still on the ground, pulling weeds and inspecting the roots.

"Echo, do something," she said between throws.

The first bug was almost to Aurie when its legs sunk into the earth as if it were quicksand. The others toppled over the first, and the whole knot of them became tangled in legs and mandibles.

Then Aurie stood and pulled her hands back, as if she were withdrawing her faez. The bugs were trapped in the earth.

"Now!"

Pi lifted a rock larger than her head and launched it at the bugs. Her shoulders would pay for it later. When it hit the center, Raziyah exploded it, ripping the bugs into discarded legs and heads, orangish ooze leaking from the limbs.

The three of them gave a victory holler. The excitement didn't last but for a few seconds before movement from the other three sides of the fort brought them around.

Bugs flowed over the walls. Three more groups came from the undefended sides. Pi and Aurie shared a glance before they were overrun.

13

Broken glass covered the floor of the clinic, trampled to fine powder. Dust and other junk, blown in through the open window, gave the room a musty smell. It would take days to clean it up, even if Aurie had help.

"What the hell did this?" asked Pi, turning in a slow circle to survey the damage. The air had grown cold, but Pi still wore a white tank top and jeans as if it were still the middle of summer, which meant she'd enchanted herself to withstand the November weather.

"I don't think they were undead, or at least not the typical kind, like zombies or vampires, but you know, I'm not an expert," said Aurie. "They were attracted to light and magic. Undead faez eaters, or something."

"Whoa, cool," said Pi.

"You wouldn't have thought they were cool bursting through the windows hot after my blood," said Aurie, the echoes of her terror as the horde broke through the doorway making her heart rate double.

The strange thing was that the glass and debris on the outside had been swept up. Only inside her building did the destruction reign. Maybe the district had a janitorial elemental keeping it clean, since it was so deserted she doubted someone would have gathered up the glass on their own.

Pi wandered to the front and stuck her head out the door. "High noon. My kind of daylight in a district full of undead."

"I don't know if they're undead, though they don't come out during the day. I've been back a few times to check, and to see if I could find Nezumi. Haven't seen any of them, nor the winged thing that tried to kill me," said Aurie.

Aurie checked the back room. The mannequins had been torn apart, and mouth-shaped gouges decorated the hunks of plastic. That would have been her fate if they'd gotten hold of her.

"What gives?" asked Pi. "Are you doing this because of Mom and Dad?"

The question made Aurie pause. It wasn't hard to imagine that her parents had an influence on her, but something about the idea went deeper than that.

"Do you know why I picked Arcanium?" asked Aurie.

"No, actually. For the longest time, I thought you were going to Aura Healers, to follow in Dad's footsteps. Especially when you started working at Golden Willow," said Pi.

"I thought I would be in Aura Healers too, but Golden Willow changed that," said Aurie, holding up her hand, "but not for the reasons you'd think. I love working there. But on the other hand, it seems so futile. What's done is done. We can fix it, but it's just going to happen again to someone else. Some of those kids ended up in the hospital because their parents were mixed up in dangerous things. That's what had happened to Emily."

"So...the clinic is different from Golden Willow, how?" asked Pi, knocking glass from the front counter with her hand.

"Golden Willow is so removed from the world, so

bureaucratic. We brought them the Rod of Dominion last year, one of the most powerful artifacts on the planet, and I'm not able to assist them using it because of their rules."

Pi raised an amused eyebrow and placed a hand over her heart. "Aurelia Silverthorne can't take following the rules? What has the world come to?"

"I want to fix the world, *in* the world," she said, jabbing her finger on the counter. "Which means working where the problems are."

"You sound like Mom and Dad," said Pi, forlornly.

"What's that supposed to mean?" said Aurie, hands on her hips.

"Doesn't it bother you that we know nothing about our family? Were they ashamed?" asked Pi, throwing her hands in the air.

"They didn't talk much about it," said Aurie. "But why does it matter? We make our own history."

"You're not curious? Just a little bit?" asked Pi, nose scrunched. "What if we're the descendants of mass murderers? Or some weird supernatural creatures? Or royalty?"

"Secret princesses? Really? What does it matter? It doesn't change who you are," said Aurie.

"But it does! What if my true motives for doing things are hidden from me? My first and only instinct is to go for power. That bothers me. I'm always thinking about how to collect and acquire more. I almost stayed in Coterie, even when I knew they were bad people, because I knew they would be the best hall for my development."

"It doesn't work like that," said Aurie.

"Says the sister who got Mom and Dad's good side." Pi turned in a huff, crossed her arms, and faced the side wall.

"Pythia! Don't you think that what happened to them is the reason why you search for power? To protect yourself? To protect me?" asked Aurie.

"But what if that's not the only reason?" said Pi, over her shoulder.

Aurie was about to continue the argument, but she sensed the presence of someone standing outside the broken front window. Someone short of stature.

"Nezumi!" she said.

Then she saw his expression, and his clothes, and realized something was very wrong. Before, he'd been modestly dressed. A little bohemian, on the poor side, but generally well kept. Now it looked like he'd been rolling in mud and garbage. Smelled like it too.

"What is that stench?" asked Pi from behind her. "I think I'm going to retch."

Nezumi's eyes were ringed with sadness.

"Are you okay? How's your family?" asked Aurie.

"Annabelle coughs all time now. Undercity not good for little tail," he said meekly.

"If you bring her here, I could try and heal her," Aurie offered.

"No!" he said, recoiling. "Magic done bad enough. No more home. Now live in hole fighting for scraps."

"But you came back?" she asked hopefully. "You need help?"

"Came back to find Annabelle's wub-wub," he said, then added when they both looked at him strangely, "It's a crochet troll doll. She left it, you know, before."

"I'm sorry, Nezumi," she said. "I had no idea what would happen."

"Mages never do!" he snapped, baring his teeth. "Always power now, little people hurt later. Always pushing, never listening. I tell you about wakers, but you just arrogant mage."

The way he quivered with fear made her realize how brave

he was standing up to her. She was, to him, everything that was wrong in the world. He wasn't afraid of the wakers, but of people like her.

"What are the wakers?" asked Pi.

Nezumi gave her sister a sideways glance.

"Who she?"

"Pythia," said Aurie. "My sister."

"Mage?"

Aurie nodded.

Nezumi gave Pi a snarl before taking a quick step back. Pi laughed, which Aurie hoped wouldn't hurt his feelings.

"Bad mages," he muttered.

Pi took a step forward. "Would you rather have mages on your side or against you?"

"No mages," said Nezumi, emphatically.

"We can't help you there," said Pi.

Aurie opened her mouth to say something, but Pi cut her off.

"Look," said Pi. "I know my sister caused you major problems, but trust me, she didn't do it on purpose. She's the most good-hearted person I know. Tell her what those creatures are so that we can help."

"Mages only make worse," said Nezumi.

"There are good mages and bad mages. Bad things too, like demons or undead. But we can't deal with them unless we know what they are," said Pi.

Aurie wasn't sure this tactic was working, but nothing she'd said had helped, so she let it go.

"No," he said, shaking his head sadly. "You just make worse for someone else."

Pi moved in front of him so he couldn't leave. "I didn't give you permission to leave."

"Pi—" Aurie began, but Pi shook her off.

Behind Nezumi's back, Aurie pleaded with Pi not to do it this way.

"I get it," said Pi. "You're scared. People with magic are scary. But not everyone's bad. She's one of the good ones."

"What about you?" asked Nezumi.

Pi gave a halfhearted shrug. "You'd probably rather not know. But it doesn't matter. What matters is that she wants to help. We want to help. But we can't unless we know what we're facing."

Nezumi tried to step around Pi, but she wouldn't let him. It hurt Aurie to see him herded in that way, but she knew it was for the best.

"The winged creature," said Aurie, remembering the leathery beat of its wings in the darkness. "What is it?"

Nezumi was quiet a long time before squeaking out an answer. "I heard whispers from others it called Grat. A demon that some stupid mage let escape. It brought the wakers."

"How long ago?"

"I not know," said Nezumi.

"Do you know where it lives?" asked Pi.

Nezumi looked too afraid to speak. "I not say, or demon know and punish me."

"Nezumi, if you tell us, we can get rid of him so you can return to your home. Make the demon and the wakers go away," said Aurie.

He looked near to tears. His nose twitched furiously. Aurie hated doing this to him. He was worried about his family. She almost put an arm around him until she saw the gunk stuck to his sweater.

"Nezumi," said Pi as if she were speaking to a troublesome student.

He squeezed his eyes shut and, keeping his hand covertly by his side, pointed in an easterly direction.

"We need more than that," said Aurie.

Nezumi whimpered. "587 Merlin Avenue."

"Thank you, Nezumi," said Aurie. "You've been a big help. I swear to you I'm going to fix this."

"Can I go?" he asked as if any more time with them might cause him to spontaneously combust.

Pi stepped out of the way, and he scurried across the street to his old residence.

"You're not giving up, are you?" asked Pi.

"No," said Aurie. "If I can't handle this, how can I change anything?"

"That demon sounds particularly nasty. You can't go after it like this," said Pi.

"Not today," said Aurie. "But soon. I have to prepare. I want to get this clinic off the ground after the holidays, give people like Nezumi and his family a chance."

"I'd better be with you when you deal with this demon," said Pi, tutting her finger in Aurie's direction.

Aurie smiled back.

"*Dooset daram*, little sister. I wouldn't have it any other way."

14

The waterfall blocking Patron Gray's office gave her a bit of heartburn before she charged through, trying not to imagine suckered tentacles tripping her into the roiling pool. Aurie had asked around about the nature of the guardian, but no one in Arcanium had ever heard of a creature in the water.

Patron Gray was shouting into a cell phone about some ill-carried-out task when Aurie arrived. The little dragon was curled around his neck, its scaled eye ridges glowering with an intensity matching its master's.

After a flickering glance, her patron snapped his fingers and pointed to the seat opposite his desk while he continued pacing. Then he seemed to realize the nature of his conversation, quietly excused himself, and disappeared into a hallway behind his office. His angry responses turned muffled, then quickly disappeared, indicating the size of the area behind his office was much larger than Aurie first thought.

Aurie swore Patron Gray had bigger bags under his eyes than last time. She'd only caught a snippet of his conversation, but it sounded like hall politics. She guessed he was talking to a patron from another hall, but besides the Cabal, she didn't know much else about interwoven loyalties.

He'd summoned her on short notice for a lesson on mendancy. Her regular practice of the craft left her with a growing irritation.

Knees bouncing, Aurie scanned the room to keep her mind off what was to come. A glass globe the size of a softball swirled with pink mist on the desk. Aurie reached out to touch it, but upon seeing the mist react to the approach of her finger, she thought better and put her hand back in her lap.

Twin shelves dominated the left wall, filled with leather-bound books. She saw a few books she recognized, classic spell books of magical history, except these appeared old, edges nicked, indicating an earlier edition, well-read. Aurie was happily scanning the titles when her gaze fell upon *Impossible Magics*.

Seeing it was such a surprise that she jumped slightly in her seat. Aurie had thought the existence of the book had been a mistake on Zayn's part, since no records existed in the main libraries of Arcanium. She hadn't realized that Patron Gray had a private collection that didn't show up on the lists.

After checking for the sound of his voice, Aurie moved to the shelf and let her fingers linger on the binding of the book before pulling it out. The book was fragile, the binding loose, pages threatening to spill onto the floor, and one edge was blackened from fire.

Aurie leaned the book against the middle shelf for support and carefully opened it, using her chest to keep the pages from escaping. A spark of discovery traveled through her when she realized the author of the tome was Invictus himself.

A brief review of the table of contents revealed that *Impossible Magics* was a catalog of magics deemed uncastable due to the difficult natures of the potential spells. The list included things like raising the dead, stopping or manipulating time, traveling to distant galaxies, and summoning cities out of horsehair (no background was given about the need for this spell), to name a few. Each entry was a meandering thought-scape from Invictus about how such a thing might be accomplished, sometimes with fragments of spell ideas or lists of ways that he might narrow down the possibilities, almost as if he were free writing.

By scanning the tome, Aurie learned that raising the dead was possible, but only within a short time frame after death, much like an emergency room might save someone, and only if the specific issues that led to death could be dealt with. There was no grand unifying spell that could accomplish the task without discrete knowledge. A busted heart had to be repaired before the victim was brought back, cancer had to be removed or the subject would just die again, and a head blown off with a shotgun was beyond the repair of medical or magical science.

Not only was Aurie enamored with the study of the spells, but with the intense curiosity of the head patron. She could sense his childlike glee upon discovery, but also the deep wisdom as he analyzed the repercussions if the spells were possible, and how one might go about regulating their use. Invictus had been the one to bring magic out of the shadows with his patronage system, and she could sense his thought processes from his musing, much as one might of a Founding Father about America.

Aurie could have spent days reading the tome, but remembering that Zayn, and by proxy probably the Cabal, had interest in *Impossible Magics*, Aurie scanned the list for the most promising spells. The last one on the list made her skin tingle: wish.

She turned to the spell when a door closed from somewhere in back. Aurie quickly scanned the text, absorbing the highlights. Of all the spells Invictus had studied, he thought this one was the most impossible, because the spell would have to be capable of anything. Modern magical theory stated that spells were like computer algorithms, programmed to specific tasks. The complexity of a wish spell would require a spell infinitely difficult, which meant impossible. It was saner to consider each problem separately and design a spell for it rather than to try to make a catchall.

Yet when she read the last line of the section, it indicated Invictus still thought such a spell possible, though he didn't illuminate how.

Before she could close the tome, a group of pages slipped out, flipping through the air, right as the sound of footsteps approached. Aurie fell to her knees, scooping them up as fast as she could, jamming them back in, cringing as precious corners folded. She shoved the book into its home and threw herself onto the seat moments before Patron Gray strolled into the room.

"Apologies, Aurelia," he said, his gaze flickering to the shelves as if he noticed something was wrong, "it was a call I had to take."

"Was it about the Cabal?" she asked.

The lines on his forehead deepened. "I told you not to worry about them and focus on your studies."

The miniature silver dragon nibbled on Semyon's ear, bringing a forlorn smile to his lips. "I'm sorry, Menolly. I know I promised you food earlier if you were patient. But as you can see, I don't have time, so you can hunt minnows in the pool. No more than ten."

The dragonling uncoiled her tail and leapt from his shoulder like a cat on the prowl, quickly disappearing into the waterfall room.

"Where were we? Oh, yes. Mendancy. Time to see how well your studies are progressing," he said.

Aurie followed him through the hallways to a small garden with an obsidian arch.

The words "The garden network" tumbled out of her lips before she could stuff them back in.

Patron Gray, still in thought about his earlier conversation, merely raised an eyebrow and said, "Each patron has a private access to it. A necessity for moving around the city without creating distractions."

They portaled to a massive room with windows showing the surrounding city. The room was empty except for four posts thirty feet tall and a huge mat at the center.

"We're in the Spire," said Aurie, recognizing the view. It looked higher than she expected. "Are we in Invictus' quarters?"

"No one has access to those anymore," he said. "But this is directly below them. This is the room Invictus used for testing potential patrons."

"Why can't anyone get into his quarters?" she asked.

"That's a good question," he said, brow furrowed. "When he died, he took his secrets with him. Including how to replace him. The city of sorcery is slowly unraveling without a head patron."

"Is that what the Cabal wants?" she asked.

He tilted his head. "I told you no more questions about them."

Aurie opened her mouth, but his face warned her away from it. Whatever other secrets this place held, he was not going to reveal them to her.

"Put these on and climb that," he said, handing her two bracelets and indicating a wooden ladder on the nearest post.

The bracelets looked similar to the ones she wore during the final trial her first year that allowed limited flight. The rungs were rough, and scratched her hands on the way up.

On top of the pole, she looked down. "Now what?"

Semyon spoke a command word, and the wooden mat lifted into the air, forming a bridge across the room thirty feet high. The middle sagged due to the weight.

"Each of those slats have cracks in them. Some are broken in half and only held in place due to the nature of the magic contained in this room. On the whole, it's quite dodgy. Once you whisper the first wisps of mendancy, the room will cease to hold this bridge in midair. Your spell must bear the weight until you have crossed its length," he explained.

"Shit," she muttered at the daunting task.

"Did you say something, Aurelia?" he asked, though she was fully aware that he'd heard her.

"Can't wait to get started," she said, putting on a forced toothy grin.

"Very well," he said.

Aurie surveyed the woven mat. The nature of her challenge became clear. In one go, she had to convince the mat that it was solid enough to not only hold its weight, but hers as well.

"You won't have this kind of time in a pinch," he reminded, spurring her into action. "You should be able to do it without thought."

Aurie took a deep breath and summoned faez. Crouched on one knee, she whispered to the mat how rigid, how formed and solid it was, and before the first sentence was finished, the mat fell to the floor.

"Again," said Patron Gray, speaking the command word that brought the mat back into position.

She tried again, this time saying the words faster, to put the spell in place before the mat could fall, but she wasn't quick enough.

"Again."

Aurie tried again, flying through the words like an agile-tongued rapper, only to have it fall.

"Again."

This time with more faez.

"Again."

And fewer words.

"Again."

Aurie tried different versions of the spell, tried speaking them faster and slower, used other languages, and all manners of emphasis. After forty or fifty attempts, she'd lost count, she was feeling wobbly on the post.

"Again."

"I need a little break," she said.

He stroked his chin thoughtfully. "Why? You haven't accomplished anything yet. You're just trying the same bloody things that didn't work already. Give it some real effort, Aurelia. Your career as a wizard depends on it."

Aurie growled and went back to it. Her attempts didn't get any better; in fact, they started to get worse as she was drained of faez. She complained a few times, but he reminded her that her access to the raw stuff of magic was unprecedented and the exhaustion was only in the mind.

She kept going. One hundred, two hundred, she didn't know anymore.

Her legs were shaking from standing on the pole for hours.

She wasn't sure why, but when he said the word, "Again," she just screamed, pointed to the mat, and yelled, "Fucking bridge, you worthless pile of sticks."

When the mat held, Aurie looked down at her patron, surprised.

"Brilliant. Now walk across," he said.

The moment her shoe touched the mat, it collapsed, pulling off the pole. She plummeted face-first towards the ground, a scream trailing from her lips.

She jerked to a stop as the bracelets halted her fall, then

fell the remaining distance, landing heavily on her hands and knees with her hair hanging into her face.

Patron Gray's stoic expression did not give her much encouragement.

"Again."

The climb up the pole was excruciating. Whatever stores of energy she'd had left, they were spent in the terror of the fall.

She tried to recreate the brief success another forty times, but the bridge never held again. By the time her quivering legs could barely hold her up, her head swam with vertigo.

When Patron Gray spoke, and it wasn't the word, "again," she stared at him, confused for a moment.

"We're finished for now," he said. "But clearly you haven't been diligently practicing as I asked, or you would have made more progress."

Aurie was too exhausted to counter his claim.

"You may use this room as much as you'd like, though you'll have to come in through the administration offices. I've left instructions. Make sure you leave the safety links here. They won't work anywhere else."

"Patron Gray," she said.

"Yes?"

"Thank you," she said.

"Verbal thanks are unnecessary. This is my duty. What I expect is more focus next time. I don't think you're taking this properly serious," he said. "Now I must excuse myself. I have another appointment. Good day, Aurelia."

Too exhausted to stand, Aurie remained on the floor for a half hour before removing the bracelets and climbing to her feet. She felt rice paper thin. She wasn't sure what was worse, dying to the bugs in the contest, or learning mendancy.

15

Pi was in her room reviewing a lesson on somniancy, waiting to be tired enough to practice the spells, when Deshawn stuck his head through the open door.

He had a stupid grin plastered to his lips. "Some cute girl in glasses is here to see you."

"Me?"

He nodded enthusiastically. "She's waiting on the other side of the drawbridge."

"Thanks," said Pi, then added when he lingered in her doorway, "and let me guess, you want me to get her number for you."

"If it's not too much trouble to ask," he said.

Pi closed her book and grabbed a hoodie from the bed. "You owe me."

"Now and forever," he said.

The end of January had brought a cold front down the east coast. There wasn't much snow on the streets, but the lakes were frozen and the brisk winds made being outside long perilously cold. Pi cast a warming spell on her hoodie before venturing outside of Arcanium.

A single figure in a parka with the fur-lined hood pulled up waited for Pi. She had a premonition of danger, and almost went right back inside. Pi looked around to make sure no one else was around. The normal tourist crowd that lingered outside Arcanium had disappeared during the cold spell.

Once she crossed the drawbridge, Raziyah revealed herself, bringing a sense of relief.

"Hey, Raz, what's going on?" asked Pi. "I didn't think I'd see you till our next attempt after finals."

Raziyah laughed nervously. "I actually asked for your sister, but you can help just the same. If you're willing."

"Everything okay?" asked Pi.

"I'm fine," she said, pushing her glasses back up her nose. "But I'm worried about Echo. I try to keep in touch with him, make sure he's okay and all, but I haven't been able to get a hold of him the past few days. He lives in a pretty dangerous area, and I didn't want to go alone."

"Where?"

"Southside of the thirteenth ward," said Raziyah.

Pi chuckled. "Yeah, no problem. That's where Aurie and I used to live. You came to the right person."

Raziyah blushed, and pulled her coat tighter. She was squarely middle class. Exactly what Pi would have been had her parents lived.

They took the Blue Line to the Red Line, chatting about the contest along the way. They'd been stuck on the third wave of bugs for the last three attempts.

"I don't think we're good enough," said Raziyah. "I'm last in my Stone Singer class, Echo would rather spend his time smelling flowers in the fort, Hannah keeps getting killed because of her roller skates, and Rigel doesn't have much to offer with theater magic since the bugs see through any illusions, nor will they succumb to any hypnotism magic.

We're lucky you and your sister are in our group."

"That's not true. We just haven't found a way to leverage everyone's abilities yet," said Pi.

"The top teams are on wave seven. I hear there are flamer bugs and jumper bugs from five on. I have nightmares just thinking about getting burned alive," said Raziyah, squeezing her coat against her chest.

"The good thing is that no one is past the bug section, which means we have time to catch up," said Pi.

"I don't know," said Raziyah, "those top teams have a lot of outside help working on strategies. Plus, they've got the top people from their halls. It's like some of them spread out into different halls just so they could compete together. Of course, you'd know that."

The train lurched to a stop as Pi said, "What?"

"The Indigo Sisters," said Raziyah, as if Pi should already know what she meant. "That girl, the one whose mom owns the *Herald of the Halls*."

"Violet Cardwell?"

"Yeah. We think she's in Arcanium so they would win the contest. Why else would she not be in Alchemists?"

The realization was like a smack to her forehead. It made sense. Violet had been planted in Arcanium, which meant the Cabal had known about the special prize long before this year. Or she could be a spy, since Patron Gray opposed them.

"Something wrong?" asked Raziyah, looking at Pi's hands.

Pi unclenched her fists. "No." She looked up. "Let's go, our stop."

No one else got off at the station, and a few people gave them are-you-crazy looks. It wasn't the stop she'd used to get to her apartment, but the one deeper into the thirteenth ward. There was a good side and a bad side, if that could be believed, and they'd lived in the area that despite being poor, people looked out for each other.

While they were second-year mages at the Hundred Halls, with more power at their fingertips than a normal person, a gun could still kill them from a distance before they could do anything. And people who lived in the City of Sorcery were well acquainted with what a mage could do given the chance. It was better to shoot first and deal with the consequences later if there was any question of magic.

Pi led them on a roundabout way to get to the address that Raziyah had for Echo. She'd lent him a cheap phone to keep in touch, since he couldn't afford one himself.

When they arrived at the address, they learned it was a group home for autistic adults. A lot of his behavior became clear upon seeing that sign.

"Is this why he doesn't live in his Hall?" asked Raziyah.

"What hall does he even belong to?"

Raziyah blinked. "I don't know. I've never gotten that out of him. Maybe it's one of the smaller ones that doesn't have a building to live in. They use rooms in the Spire for lessons."

A knock on the door brought an older woman with heavy bags under her eyes.

"We're friends of Echo's from the Halls," said Raziyah.

The older woman didn't seem to understand.

"Ernie," said Pi.

"Oh, Ernie," she said, her face drooping with sadness. "Have you seen him? He hasn't come home the last three nights. I thought he might be, you know."

The woman didn't look like she'd come to terms with him being able to wield magic, which Pi decided would be a concern in a home like this.

"That's why we're looking for him," said Raziyah. "He hasn't responded to my texts or anything."

The woman touched Raziyah's arm. "Bless you both for

befriending him. He's a good kid, but I don't know what to do with his abilities. Sometimes strange things happen in the house that I can't explain. The others have begun to fear him, and blame anything that happens to them on him. I'm afraid he might have run off."

"How did he come here?" Pi asked.

The old woman sighed. "He's a ward of the state. That's all I know."

"If he comes back, could you contact me?" asked Raziyah, then she gave the woman her number. "I'll let you know if we find him."

"Bless you both," said the woman before she slipped back inside.

Pi and Raziyah shared worried glances.

"This is not good," said Pi. "How do we find him?"

"I have an idea," said Raziyah, "if you promise not to freak out."

"Try me," said Pi, suddenly curious.

Raziyah pulled out her phone and started typing away on it. "Before I knew I was strong enough to get into the Hundred Halls, I was working on being a programmer. Like I said, I'm good at math, but I'm even better at hacking."

"I'm shocked," said Pi.

"I've only ever done, you know, white-hat hacking, but I know how to get into his phone and check his GPS," she said.

"Whatever gets us there," said Pi, wondering what Raziyah would think if she knew about the demon she'd summoned to get into Coterie, or that she was bound to the Black Butcher, a city fae of ill repute.

After a few minutes, Raziyah said, "Got it. Not far from here. Three blocks."

The place was an old abandoned apartment building with the windows boarded up. A couple of gang members with guns sticking out of their pants were hanging around front.

They stayed way back and discussed what to do about it.

"You know, it's possible that they stole his phone and he's not in there," said Pi.

Raziyah looked shaken. "But what if he's in there?"

"We're going either way, don't mistake me. But I want you to be prepared if he's not and we've done some not so very nice things," said Pi.

"Maybe we should get the rest of the Harpers," said Raziyah.

Pi shook her head. Aurie was in the Spire practicing mendancy, and she didn't keep her phone on her. Hannah had taken the train south to visit family, and Rigel was auditioning for the lead role in a play in the theater district.

"I think it's just us two," said Pi. "If you're not up for it, I can do this alone."

Raziyah blew out a steadying breath. "No. I'm good. I just hope you have a good idea on how to get in there."

"Well, they're not going to let us walk in. Honestly, I don't think we can get near without risk of getting shot. Can you make us a bridge from one roof to another? We could go over?" asked Pi.

Raziyah sunk lower. "Even if I could, they'd hear my singing."

"Good point," said Pi. "I don't think we want to go in anyway. Probably a drug operation inside. If Echo's in there, they're probably using him to make drugs. A good mage can speed up the process, make it more potent, and so on."

"How do you know so much?" asked Raziyah.

"The dealers near our apartment made us many offers before we joined the Halls. Thankfully, they were the less persistent ones. I've heard of underage mages getting pressed into service before they had a patron, going mad from faez making drugs."

"No one tried with you or Aurie?" asked Raziyah.

"We made it clear that if anyone tried anything, we'd burn the motherfucker down rather than work for them. Being known as a crazy bitch in these parts has its advantages," said Pi with a wink. "Which gives me an idea. Maybe we don't have to go in. Maybe we can get them to come out."

The pair crept around to a back alley. Standing back from the apartment, Pi lobbed a ball of flame into a dumpster. Flames sprung from the beaten blue box immediately.

They waited for a minute as the fire simmered, but no one came to investigate, and the fire was only burning inside the dumpster.

Raziyah pulled back her sleeves. A hint of ozone filled the air. Then a brick at the corner of the wall exploded. Then another, and another, eventually collapsing a section of the wall. The guards from the front came running around and started yelling into handsets.

The pair hid in the shadows. When the guards weren't looking, Aurie lobbed a ball of flame against the hole, catching the wood inside the building on fire.

Within minutes, gang members were fighting the fire with extinguishers, and when that grew to be too much, they evacuated the building. It looked like an ant farm upended. Guys in hazard suits and face masks came stumbling out of the front door. When Echo walked out, handcuffed to a gang member, Pi and Raziyah quietly cheered that he was still alive.

The pair waited down the street. The gang was making headway on the fire as more of them brought extinguishers, so Raziyah called 911.

There were a lot of guns in the street, which made the pair nervous while they watched. They kept expecting the sirens to make them scatter, but no one came. Pi began to suspect that the emergency services either thought it was a prank or didn't care enough about the area to bother. The gang was getting the fire under control, which meant they would be going back in soon. Echo looked bruised and beat up, his head down like a whipped dog. Pi couldn't let them take him back in.

"Shit," said Pi. "Stay here, and tell my sister I was an idiot, if she asks."

Raziyah tried to pull her back in, but Pi was away in an instant. The gang didn't notice Pi until she was halfway to them. She stopped when they trained a half-dozen guns on her.

"Whoever you are, girl, you need to get the fuck out of here," said one gang member wearing a skull shirt. He had an AR-15 tucked under his shoulder.

"I can't," said Pi, holding her hands up and nodding towards Echo. "You have my friend."

"He ain't your friend if you dead," said Skull Shirt.

"I promise you that gun is useless, and even if you did manage to kill me, I summoned a demon the next block over. If I die, then he's been instructed to kill you all. A task I'm sure he'll relish, and it won't be a quick death either," said Pi.

The gang members shared glances.

"You ain't a mage," said Skull Shirt, taking a step forward, jabbing his AR-15 in Pi's direction.

Pi made a fire spear in her right hand. She was used to creating them at the bug fort.

A wave of expletives traveled through the gang members.

"Maybe I think you lyin' about the demon and kill you anyway," said Skull Shirt.

"I didn't come alone," said Pi.

And as if on cue, a rock near Skull Shirt's foot exploded. Half the gang threw themselves on the ground.

Once they picked themselves up, they whispered amongst

themselves while keeping an eye on Pi. At each glance, she was sure they were going to shoot. After a full minute, Skull Shirt motioned towards the gang member who was chained to Echo.

"Fine. You can have him. We done anyway," said Skull Skirt.

Pi sensed a trick, but didn't want to try any spells and spook them.

They uncuffed Echo and pushed him in her direction. The whole time, Pi expected them to shoot. When he neared, she whispered, "Keep going. Raz is back there."

As she turned her head, she caught movement from Skull Shirt. He lifted his AR-15. Pi was too slow with her spell.

As the first shot popped, an explosion ripped through the building, and a bullet sung past Pi's head. The gang was knocked to the ground.

"Run!" yelled Pi, grabbing Echo's hand and sprinting down the street.

She expected a hail of bullets to rip into her back. When she reached the corner, Raziyah came running up from the alleyway. They ran the whole way back to the train station. Once the doors had closed, they checked on Echo. He had bruises up and down his arms and a burn mark on his neck, from what looked like a cigarette.

"I'm so sorry, Echo," said Raziyah with tears in her eyes. "I wish we would have figured this out sooner."

His eyes were glazed, and he mumbled something below hearing, repeating it over and over. Eventually, he leaned against Raziyah, fidgeting with his hands the whole way.

Once they got away from the thirteenth ward, Raziyah had him put up in a hotel near Stone Singers so he didn't get picked up by the gang again. She said she'd work with the home to find him a safer apartment, maybe even the university would help. Pi offered to help, if she needed it, but by the time she left for Arcanium, she was sure that Raziyah had it all taken care of. Pi just hoped that the experience hadn't irrevocably injured Echo, and if it had, she'd go back and make that gang pay for what they'd done.

16

A light snow covered the Enochian District, giving the squalid streets a fresh coat of fluffy paint and washing clean the normal smell of garbage collecting in the alleyways. Icicles ringed the dragon fountain like teeth. Aurie broke one off, the ice snapping like a muted gunshot.

"It's like the rest of the city forgot this little idyllic corner," said Aurie, hugging her arms to her chest. The air didn't feel as cold as it had near Arcanium.

"Just like you seem to be forgetting the murderous horde of faez-eating thralls and the winged demon that controls them," said Pi.

"Minus that," said Aurie. "It'd be neat to see this place filled again like it used to be when Mom and Dad used to come here."

"I thought this wasn't about them," said Pi, frowning.

"It's not, but it'd still be cool," said Aurie, kicking the snow playfully.

Pi scooped up a handful of snow and threw it at Aurie. "We need to work on what you think is cool, big sis."

"I will take your disapproval as a compliment," said Aurie.

"Enough dillydallying. We've got a demon to banish."

"Nobody says dillydallying anymore," said Pi, accessing the GPS on her smartphone. "The address you gave me is over there, down that street. Are you sure it's living there?"

"Technically the mage that summoned it bought that place. It could be living anywhere, but I suspect it didn't bother finding a new home," said Aurie with a shrug.

"Don't you think it's strange that the demon doesn't come out during the day?" asked Pi as they wiped away snow on the porch numbers to find the correct house.

"I'm not an aficionado of demonology, but it's possible. Living in a faez-thick realm creates some pretty weird things," said Aurie.

"I still think it's odd," said Pi.

The modest shotgun-style brick three story looked normal enough from the outside. Aurie was expecting the door to be ripped off and fissures venting black smoke to cover the sidewalk outside.

"He must go out a different way. The snow in front of that door has piled up, and it hasn't snowed in days," said Aurie.

"A big demon has ornamental wings," said Pi.

"He was human-sized," said Aurie. "Let's go around back and check the other door."

They had to go up the street to find access to the alley behind the row. Each house led to a small backyard. Despite the vine-choked fences and old junk abandoned between the houses, the neighborhood seemed rather well preserved.

"It's amazing what fear will do to you," said Aurie, slightly disgusted. "This whole district is filled with great houses that were left by people who couldn't stand living next to people a little different than themselves."

Pi coughed. "Faez-eating thralls?"

"I did some research using the city records. The recent

exodus happened about three years ago, but many other non-humans have lived here for longer," said Aurie. "The demon must be the alpha predator, or something like that."

The backyard was as pristine as the front, except for tiny cat prints that went in and out of the open gate. Aurie slipped through and crept towards the back of the house. A storm door went into the basement.

Aurie pulled out a worn key and whispered to it, explaining how it would fit like two lovers embracing, which only made her think about Zayn. Now wasn't the time to entertain such thoughts, she reminded herself, and started the spell over. The trick to mendancy was to tell the lie so convincingly that the object was temporarily transformed by the magic. Not a lot was known about how the magic worked. Some magical researchers thought the objects had memory and could revert to a previous state, but Aurie knew that was bullshit, since this key had never been used in this lock. It was something else, something she thought had to do with perception, or that the universe was really a hologram. Real science-y stuff.

Sometimes it bothered her that she was so good at mendancy, at liar magic. Knowing it felt like a crutch, like she was taking a shortcut, or that she was flawed and that when the wrong thing happened, she'd cleave into two.

When she was in a good mood, the mendancy wasn't really lying magic, but believing the best about something, even when it was a little broken, much like people. She'd done that throughout her whole teenage years after her parents had died, convincing herself that she could keep going, even when it felt pointless. Mostly for Pi. When she was depressed, the magic was a mirage that would collapse at the wrong turn, and she felt that she never deserved happiness or any of the things that she'd ever accomplished, that magic like that was reserved for other people, privileged people. Not her.

But today she had a positive outlook. She'd had lunch with Zayn—*stop those thoughts, Aurie*—at a falafel restaurant in the fifth ward. They'd talked about nothing, really, but that had been the best part.

So when Aurie told the key that it would fit perfectly, she knew that it'd worked even before she put the key into the lock. The nubless shaft of metal slipped into the hole, and the lock clicked satisfyingly. Aurie kissed the blank and stuck it into her pocket, receiving an eye roll from her sister for the display.

The steps went into the darkness. She wished for the spell that Zayn had cast on her eyes, but without that, let a conjured wisp drift downward, illuminating the way while she followed, Pi right behind.

The bones of the house were old, stacked stone with sloppy mortar jammed between. While the façade of the building had been renovated, the cellar had been hastily repaired, evidenced by the musty smell and water puddles in the corners.

The demon's presence hadn't scared away the arachnids, as webs clung to the beams above their heads.

Crawling on her knees, Aurie created a circle with a bag of salt, leaving one side open to capture the demon. Neither of them were prepared to lure the infernal creature into the center themselves, so they'd created a tiny simulacrum to provide as bait.

Pi pulled the plastic doll out of a bag: its normally blonde hair had been colored black with a magic marker and chopped short to match Pi's, and runes had been etched into the pink plastic skin. The simulacrum worked like a voodoo doll in reverse. It was a representation of Pythia, not physically, but in spirit. Once they'd gotten the demon's attention, it would draw the creature into the circle like a bloodhound after a scent. That was the theory anyway. They figured they could bug out if something went wrong, retreating to the snowy daylight.

Aurie hated that her sister was the one acting as bait—she'd planned on doing that herself, as it was her clinic that they were trying to rescue—but when Pi had that determined look in her eye, she'd learned to let her sister take the lead. If something went wrong, then she could be the one to "rescue" her sister, which would only annoy her later.

The doll had been placed at the center of the circle, bent into a stiff-legged seated position as if it were waiting for a black metal tea party. They each found a spot to hide along the wall behind dusty old shelves. A single forgotten can of Spam was Aurie's lone companion on her side of the cellar.

From her spot, Pi funneled faez into the doll. It worked like a power conduit, the trinkets that mages used if they wanted to maintain their power in other realms. Each mage had a specific access to faez, but it worked best in their own realm. If you went into another, the mage's power was weakened.

In this case, the simulacrum collected and broadcasted Pi's location. Demons had notoriously finicky senses of smell, so it should detect the doll quickly.

After waiting for about ten minutes, Aurie moved towards the basement stairs. If the demon hadn't been alerted to Pi's faez, it probably wasn't in the house.

Aurie made it to the fifth step from the top before something heavy landed on the floor above her head. A host of wood groaning in response followed, eliciting visions of the bat-winged demon dropping down from the ceiling, where it'd been previously hanging.

"Shit," she mouthed, turning to creep back down, every step screaming as her weight shifted.

Heavy ponderous steps moved towards the basement door while Aurie rushed to get back to her hiding space. Pi waved frantically for Aurie to hurry up, but she didn't want to go too fast or the demon would hear.

She moved off the last step and slipped into the cubby as the door opened, almost forgetting about the light wisp, sending it away a moment too late.

Aurie held as still as she could manage behind the dusty shelf. The demon had to have seen the light. She listened for footsteps on the steps, but the quiet was unbearable. The only thing she could hear was her own breathing, which sounded like she'd run a marathon.

A long, painfully slow squeak announced the creature had moved onto the first step, followed by grumbling exhales right at the edge of hearing, like a bear moving through underbrush. Aurie cursed herself for not remembering that they wouldn't be able to see in the dark once the demon entered the cellar.

It was too late now. She'd have to wait for the creature to enter the circle before using light, and hope to close the salt before the demon escaped. The timing would be tricky, but with her sister's help, she knew it could be done.

She was a little confused about the scraping sound she heard following each step, until she remembered the demon's wings, which probably didn't fit in the compact stairwell.

Before the demon reached the bottom, Aurie realized she could see slightly. It appeared the demon was luminous, because the faint outlines that she could see had reddish shadows opposite the stairs.

It stopped at the bottom. Aurie heard its wings brush against the ceiling. It made no move toward the doll, and since she was around the corner, she couldn't tell what it was doing.

The delay worried Aurie. She had the suspicion that it sensed the deception and was investigating its surroundings before moving. They'd kept the salt circle as thin as possible so the demon wouldn't notice, and since it wasn't closed, it would not be seen as a magical barrier.

The only thing the demon should notice was the

overwhelming amounts of faez emanating from the doll and the aura of ozone.

The demon moved around the broken salt circle as if it sensed its presence, while Aurie tried to convince herself not to run. It walked around the arc and then back around like a dog testing an invisible fence. Aurie wished she could communicate with her sister. Clearly it knew they were there. If they hit it with heavy magic at the same time, maybe they could get away before it could retaliate, but without coordinating the attack, she didn't want to chance it.

The demon looked less formal than it had the last time, wearing nothing but a pair of dark jeans, the muscles on its bulky back flexing as the wings shifted, flickering like the tail of a horse shooing flies.

To her surprise, the demon stepped into the circle and reached down to pick up the runed doll. Aurie hadn't been expecting that, so she wasn't in position to close the salt circle.

The demon had its back to her, examining the doll, sniffing it like a beast. Aurie crept forward, one careful step at a time, her muscles quivering with the effort of staying silent. One foot scuff and it would rip her throat out.

When she pulled the bag of salt out of her pocket, a handful spilled onto the ground. In the quiet of the cellar, where even a heartbeat was a drum, the falling grains sounded like thunder. The demon snapped its head around as Aurie fell to her knees, dumping the salt into the opening and pouring faez into the circle, springing the trap.

From the darkness behind the demon, Pi's voice rose as she began the banishment spell, the perfect enunciation bringing hope to Aurie. Her excitement at their success lasted until the demon faced her and, with the toe of its boot, kicked away the salt, breaking the circle.

That was not good.

She didn't have time to analyze how they'd failed. She shot a burst of sparks from her hands, not to injure, but distract, and sprinted towards the steps.   Cold, pitiless laughter followed.

Aurie burst onto the main floor, orienting herself towards the front door.   The reddish-skinned, bare-chested demon marched after her. Its body shimmered as if it were gathering power or something. She didn't bother with the locks on the front door—there wasn't enough time. Instead she went up the stairs to the second floor.

Something black and spectral, like a tendril of darkness, whipped past her head. Its glowering animosity was like a brand on her back, driving her forward.

She paused at the second floor; something was different about it. There were no rooms, but one large area. She caught a whiff of familiarity and moved to peek around the corner when the demon raged, and more tendrils came slithering up the staircase. Aurie ran to the third floor, found a room, threw herself in, and locked the door.

Aurie wasn't prepared to make her last stand against a powerful demon. Even with Pi at her side, such a battle would be ill-advised.

She only had one option, and she cheered when the window opened easily, letting in the freezing air. Aurie climbed out, whispering to her hands that they were as sticky as a spider's web.

Grabbing on wasn't the issue as she shivered in the cruel wind. At that height, the wind through the neighborhood, unhindered by taller buildings. Within the first few holds, her hands were stiffening.

"Hurry, Aurie!" yelled her sister from the backyard.

Aurie looked up in time to see the demon lean out the window. Whatever mischief it had planned for her was cut short when Pi sent a battering blast that exploded the window in its ferocity. This gave Aurie an opportunity to shimmy further down the wall, risking a jump into the snow when she was a story up.

The snow puffed around her as she landed, sending the white stuff into her eyes and mouth. She ran to Pi, and together they escaped through the alleyway, constantly glancing back for pursuit.

When they reached the main square with the dragon fountain, they paused.

"That didn't go so well," said Pi, knocking the hair out of her face.

"Better than having my heart ripped out through my neck," said Aurie. "For a failed demon banishing, that wasn't terrible."

"How the hell did it break our circle? If we can hold a demon lord, we can certainly hold this fella. He looked more like a model trying out for some infernal cosplay show than a real demon," said Pi, clearly exasperated.

Aurie nodded along. Something about the demon bothered her as well. "I'm not sure it was a demon. As I ran through the house, I was surprised by how well it was kept."

"Is Grat a hipster demon?" asked Pi, one eyebrow raised. Despite the quip, she didn't sound as irreverent as she normally did.

"Maybe it's not a demon at all, since the circle didn't work," said Aurie.

Pi frowned deeply. Something was bothering her, but Aurie let it go and knocked the snow from her jacket. The tumble had stuffed her pockets with the cold stuff. "Back to Arcanium. For now. I think we have some more research before we try him again. Though I don't want to wait too long. Poor Nezumi and his family are stuck in the Undercity until we can cleanse the district."

"Nezumi," said Pi with a cold distance. "Yeah, I think there's a problem."

"What? Did you see him or something?" she asked, looking around.

"When you escaped up the stairs, I followed at first, in case we had to do battle. I didn't want you to fight alone. Once I heard the door slam, I figured what you were going to do and went out the front, but before I left, I saw something."

"Spit it out, Pi."

"I saw the doll. The wub-wub. Annabelle's crochet troll doll," said Pi. "You know, the one Nezumi was looking for last time."

Aurie put a hand to her mouth. "That's not good. That is *not* good."

A personal item like that, especially a well-loved one, could be used in various unsavory ways. The least of which would be a way to find Nezumi and his family. The worst, well, Aurie didn't even want to think about that.

"We can't leave it," said Aurie.

"We don't have to," said Pi, pulling the dirty green crochet troll doll from her jacket. A leg had been cut off and it was covered in candle residue. "But it's too late. He's already been using it. Looks like he might have been scrying them. Probably heard Nezumi give us the house directions last time and is going to be pissed now."

"We made it worse," said Aurie, sinking her face into her hands. "We have to go back. Kill that thing right now."

Pi put her hand on Aurie's arm as she moved back towards the house. "No way. We'd get slaughtered. He wasn't fooled by our simulacrum, which means he knew what we were. And we don't know what he is."

"We can't leave Nezumi to him," she said.

"We don't need to. We can get a message to him with this," said Pi, shaking the doll. "Then we can get them somewhere safe."

Aurie thought about it for a while. They could find a place for them to stay, put protections on it. It wasn't a great option, but it was better than leaving them vulnerable or charging in and dying today, which still wouldn't help Nezumi and his family.

"I hate to tell them they're still at risk," said Aurie. "We've put them through so much already."

"Leave that to me," said Pi.

"I don't want to know," said Aurie.

Pi grinned. "Nope, you don't. You work on figuring out what that thing is while I make sure Nezumi and his family have a good place to stay until we've gotten rid of the demon."

"Or whatever it is," said Aurie, moving in the direction of the train station. "You know what we need now, right?"

Pi looked over inquisitively, then realized what Aurie was about to say. "No. No you don't!"

Aurie began, "When the going gets tough—"

Pi stuck her fingers in her ears and started making random noises.

"—the tough study more."

As much as her sister hated the saying, Aurie knew it was true. Good magic required preparation and study. They hadn't beaten Grat because they hadn't understood what it was. Maybe it hadn't known they, in particular, had been coming, but clearly it'd prepared enough so that it wasn't affected by the salt circle. Or it was something similar to but not a demon.

Pi stopped making noises and tentatively pulled a finger out. "Are you done yet?"

"Never," said Aurie, winking, leaving Pi to groan.

17

A few years ago, the Wild Sorcery was Pi's favorite place to get away when she was fighting with her sister. She'd seen the mages that frequented the bar, with their trinkets and spell tattoos, sipping frothy cocktails that looked like miniature cauldrons, and thought that was what she wanted when she joined the Hundred Halls.

The place hadn't changed much since she'd moved on from the idea. She sat at a corner booth with a view of the front door. The setup was a little on the nose, but it was still good practice.

Cheap mood lights cast a bluish glow across the tables, turning every face into a mask. Mages with little skill made glowing letters float in the air. Pi didn't know if they had patrons or were guaranteeing they would eventually succumb to faez madness.

Pi saw him right away when he entered. The crappy lighting revealed something about him that she hadn't realized before.

"Slyvan," she said, motioning toward the opposite side of the booth.

The maetrie's nose didn't so much wrinkle in disgust as sneer at everything around him. When he spoke, it was as if he were about to cough up a hairball.

"If this is what you think passes for a clandestine meeting, then I mistook you for a smart girl," he said, turning to leave.

"Wait," she growled, hoping to convince him to stop through sheer intensity. "Sit. Please. Give me a minute to explain."

His impeccable suit was practically a second skin on his lithe body. His revulsion to his surroundings made it shift constantly as if he expected to contract a disease.

Slyvan pulled a handkerchief out of an inner pocket and wiped the leather booth covering. When he was finished, he wadded the cloth up and tossed it into the corner.

"One minute," he said.

"When I first came to the city of sorcery, I thought a place like this was where real mages came to hang out. But once I got in, I realized that people with real power wouldn't need to display it with gaudy tattoos that sparkle or drinks with silly names like Gelatinous Shots, or Kobold Juice. It became clear pretty quickly that half the clientele were posers, pretending to be mages, or low-level wizards with self-esteem issues."

Slyvan's contempt was barely disguised as disinterest. He looked ready to escape at any moment, so Pi hurried to her point.

"Which makes this the best place to hide. No self-respecting mage or maetrie would be caught dead in here. Think of how much you detest this place. Could you imagine Radoslav coming in here?" she asked.

In the pause afterwards, he went through the stages of realization that she was right, while she worried if she was doing the right thing. She hated going behind Radoslav's back, but he hadn't talked to her much since she met the Ruby

Queen.

"I might acknowledge the cleverness if it weren't like hiding in a dumpster fire," he said.

"Fair enough," she said.

"What do you want?"

Straight to the point. She should have expected it. It wasn't like they'd had friendly exchanges in the past, which made her regret the bracelet trick.

"I want to help," she said.

His sigh was like a work of art, an exquisite gesture of reluctance and disappointment.

"You want nothing of the sort," he replied. "Or you wouldn't be working for Raddie."

"I didn't say for free," said Pi.

"Good. I detest do-gooders. I cannot trust someone who doesn't want something," he said, idly examining his fingernails.

"Tell me something," said Pi, girding herself for the expected reaction. "Why did your brother leave?"

Slyvan's gaze flickered with fury.

"Half-brother," he said, then added after a thought, "Because he's a coward."

"I'd hardly call someone who acquires the nickname the Black Butcher to be a coward," said Pi.

"He left our realm to hide amongst you humans. He could have had anything he wanted, but he left, and for what, to own a shitty bar in a place that's a pale imitation of the Eternal City?" asked Slyvan rhetorically, as if to even consider it was pure madness.

Slyvan perched his chin on his hand in a thoughtful pose. Pi decided to push her luck with his verbose mood.

"Did he really deserve that name? The Black Butcher?" she asked.

His gaze had a faraway quality, remembering times past. There was a hint of admiration, twinned with disgust.

"The Raddie you know isn't even a shade of the real one. He's the son to two maetrie queens. Even without his full powers here, he's still a formidable bastard," said Slyvan.

The maetrie looked back at her as if he'd realized he was talking too much. He'd underestimated her once again, one of the few advantages of being a young human girl. She now knew what the figurine was that Slyvan had taunted Radoslav with. It was a power conduit. He must have hidden it somewhere in the Eternal City, but Slyvan found it. Knowing that her boss's abilities had been reduced explained some of his reactions, but not why he didn't charge back into the Eternal City and take his power conduit back. It also made this little game even more dangerous. Clearly the Ruby Queen had been planning this for a while if she'd waited until they had found his figurine before acting. She wanted to believe that Lady Amethyte was trying to repair the peace, but knew there were probably other considerations.

"How can I help with the Jade Queen?" she asked, deciding that waiting any longer would work against her.

"You can't," he said. "We need Raddie."

"As you said before, I'm his mageling. Surely that counts for something," she said.

He looked bored. Pi hoped that was a facade. She'd decided before he'd come that everything he said or did would be a lie. It was the only way to be safe.

"What do you want? You're not doing this out of the kindness of your little human heart," he said.

"Information," she said.

He motioned with his hand. "Out with it."

"No," she said. "I'm not asking until I know if we've got a deal."

"How do I know I can help you if you don't ask?"

Pi made sure she was sitting up straight and looking him dead in the eyes. It was hard because she wanted to fawn over him. To counteract his aura, she tried to picture him as a snake with a human suit over top.

"You have the information I want," she said. "That much I am sure of. And I know you have an idea how I can help you, or you wouldn't have come here in the first place. The fact that you showed up at all told me everything I needed to know, including that he was your brother, or half-brother, my apologies."

He made that sigh again and studied his fingernails as if they were more interesting. She kept quiet and still, worried that she'd pushed too hard. When he brought his gaze up, she knew she'd struck true.

"I suppose you could help," he said, reaching into his inner coat and pulling out an envelope and a jewelry box. "Soon we will celebrate the anniversary of our peace at the Reaping Celebration. Her Ladyship would like you to be Raddie's representative. Lady Kikala will be disappointed that he could not make it, but she will, I think, take a liking to you. As a token of faith from Lady Amethyte, you will deliver this necklace. It's an old disagreement between them. Her Ladyship hopes to smooth away the past problems by returning something that the Jade Queen has long desired. The invitation, of course, will get you into the celebration. We'll send an escort when the time comes."

Pi eyed the items suspiciously, keeping her hands well away from them.

The corner of Slyvan's lip tugged downward. "These are safe for you to accept, since they are not, by the rules of the realm, for you at all."

"I'm not going to agree to anything until you tell me what

I want to know," she said.

"Which I cannot do, since you have not told me," he said, his anger not well veiled.

"I need to know what Priyanka Sai wanted from the Ruby Queen," said Pi.

His surprise was such that she knew any surprise he'd shown before had been false. For a moment, she thought he might reach across the table and throttle her, but he contained his emotions, smoothing his coat as if it were made of feathers and had become ruffled.

"I suppose you earned that," he said. "I'm not sure how you learned about this arrangement, but it's fortuitous for Her Ladyship, because it is something that she can offer in return for your service."

Despite her success, this was the part she dreaded. What if the information she'd asked for was useless, or trivial? She'd put herself into a dangerous position by going against Radoslav's wishes and involving herself further in the political machinations of the maetrie courts.

"Then we have a deal," said Pi, pulling the items closer. "I will act as Radoslav's representative at the Reaping Celebration."

After a pause he began, "Priyanka came to Lady Amethyte because she is in search of something important. A spell specifically. Something so powerful that it could be used in any number of ways. I see by your eyes that this is what you're looking for."

Pi cursed internally for giving away that information, but he was right. She'd practically floated above the table when she heard it.

"That's not enough. I already knew that," said Pi. "What's the spell? And did Lady Amethyte tell Priyanka where it was located?"

Slyvan chuckled, half-lidded eyes relaying supreme amusement.

"It's Invictus' greatest achievement, the wish spell," he said. "And they're not looking for it—they know where it is, and they're trying to figure out how to use it when they get it."

Pi sat in stunned silence. The wish spell, they knew where it was. That could only mean one thing. It was the prize at the end of the contest, the contest they were sucking at. It explained why so many halls were pouring resources into winning.

Slyvan pushed the envelope and case across the table as he got up.

"Tell Raddie we miss him," he mocked. "And be ready when we send for you. Her Ladyship takes a hard line on those that go back on their promises."

"I'll be there," said Pi, hoping she hadn't gotten in over her head.

"I'm sure you will."

Slyvan strolled out of the club like a victor that had gotten everything he wanted. Pi stared at the envelope and case for a long time before finally shoving them into her carryall. She'd gotten what she'd wanted, but maybe she'd gotten more than expected.

18

Aurie shivered, curled up on the couch in the waiting room, nibbling on a piece of chocolate, contemplating her last death. The others had left right away; everyone had their rituals for dealing with the aftermath of being killed in the game.

They'd gotten past wave three during the last two attempts, but hadn't come up with a solution for the burrowing bugs in wave four. But Aurie wasn't thinking about strategy. She was trying to shake the feeling she was really dead.

Pi hopped over the couch, startling Aurie into dropping her chocolate into the crack between couch cushions.

"Dammit, Pi. I thought I was the only one here," said Aurie.

Her sister's hair was a disheveled halo around her head. Mud splatters covered her face, except for a line where the helmet had covered her forehead. They both stunk of sweat and bug guts, which smelled like rotten cabbage.

"The floor behind the bar is cool," said Pi. "I hate the few hours after we lose. I feel like I've been split in two, and another version of me is wandering the world as a ghost."

"I thought they were being generous with the energy

drinks and chocolate bars that first day. I wonder no longer," said Aurie.

"Barely above last," said Pi.

Aurie's gaze gravitated to the top of the leaderboard. Violet's team, the Indigo Sisters, had maintained their domination of the contest since day one.

"We're never going to catch up at this pace," said Aurie. "February is nearly finished. I've heard they think the queen bug is at the tenth wave."

Pi crossed her legs and faced Aurie with a serious demeanor.

"We have to win the Grand Contest," said Pi.

"Haven't we been trying?"

Pi looked into her lap. "I mean because of the reward. I think I know what it is."

Aurie had been thinking about it as well, but the way her sister said it made her think she had learned something. Aurie had a sinking feeling in her gut that Pi had done something dangerous again.

"You remember that book, *Impossible Magics*," said Pi, receiving a nod from Aurie. "They're looking for a wish spell."

"That's—"

"Impossible, yeah, we both know it," said Pi. "But you said that Invictus thought it could be done."

"He left the possibility open, but like I said, I skimmed the text quickly before Semyon returned," said Aurie, growing suspicious. "What gives? We've talked about this before."

Pi chewed on her lower lip, which was a sure sign she was hiding something.

"Why would Zayn bring it up, if he wasn't trying to manipulate you?"

"Stop with the Zayn stuff," said Aurie, her face bursting with heat. "I told you I'm in control of my feelings. He's not going to get me to betray Arcanium for the Cabal because he's a good kisser."

Pi's eyes opened wide. "So you've kissed him?"

"Only a couple of times since the cave," said Aurie, but even thinking about it made her blush. She liked him more than she cared to admit to her sister.

When Pi stared at her, she added, "But I make sure to stay in public places, and he hasn't asked me about the book since."

Not that she hadn't thought about taking him somewhere outside the city so they could spend a weekend in private. She ached with desire, but didn't trust herself with the relationship if they had sex. If she trusted sharing that kind of intimacy with him, then she wanted to be able to share her deepest thoughts and fears. To do it the other way would feel backwards, so she'd kept it light.

Pi rubbed her forehead in faux pain. "Why, why, why? I mean first, tell me he's a good kisser, but you know he's got to be working for them! He's his patron's assistant!"

"He kisses like you'd imagine that David Beckham would," said Aurie.

"Wow," said Pi, then shook her head as if she were trying to wake up. "But not good."

"Why are you so against him? What if he's good? What if he needs our help?" asked Aurie, knowing full well that her sister disagreed.

"What if he's not good? I think the evidence is stacked against him," said Pi.

"Out with it. You're holding something back," said Aurie.

Pi squeezed her eyes shut and said the words quickly. "I saw him asking the Ruby Queen for information about the wish spell, and confirmed that the Cabal knows where it is. They're trying to figure out how it works once they get it."

Aurie practically came off the couch.   "Ruby Court? Are you crazy? What are you doing there? You know how dangerous that is."

"We've got to take chances, sis," said Pi.

"Not stupid ones," said Aurie. "At least talk it over with me first."

"You'd never agree, so why bother? And I can do what I want, I don't need your permission," said Pi, jaw pulsing with intensity.

The rebuke was a slap to Aurie's face. She held a hand to her mouth. It hurt down to her bones to argue with her sister, but it'd hurt even worse to lose her.

Pi spoke quietly as if she were trying to bridge the pain between them. "The wish spell *has* to be the reward for the contest. That's why they're putting so many resources into winning it. I hear some of the Cabal halls have suspended classes to focus on practice fighting bugs. Thankfully they can't bring magical artifacts into the contest or they'd load up their teams with every useful device on the planet."

"Maybe that's why Violet was placed in Arcanium," said Aurie, musing over the subject. It was easier to focus on their task than battle with her sister.

"That's true," said Pi. "I heard that from Raz."

"She's a nice girl, but she is a terrible Stone Singer," said Aurie, thinking back to their most recent battle against the bugs. Raziyah's failure to reinforce the earth against them had doomed them to failure.

"They mean well, but damn, sometimes I wish for better teammates," said Pi. "Echo makes a better gardener than a mage. I'm not sure he's killed more than five bugs this whole time."

"Even if I don't understand how it could be possible, I bet I know why they want the wish spell," said Aurie, the words frothing to her lips so fast she could barely get them out. "They want to get into Invictus' place at the top of the Spire so they can claim the role of head patron."

"If they had that they could do anything they wanted," mused Pi. "As the saying goes, *he who controls the Halls controls the world.*"

"We've got to stop them," said Aurie.

"Even if it means giving up on Zayn?" asked Pi, looking her directly in the eyes.

"That was a low blow," said Aurie.

"Am I right?" asked Pi.

Aurie pulled her arms to her chest and squeezed herself tight. "I promise I'll be careful with him."

Pi raised a single eyebrow.

"Maybe we can use him for information?" offered Aurie.

"I suppose," said Pi.

"You be careful with the maetrie," said Aurie. "They're more dangerous than the Cabal."

"Always."

"Dooset daram."

"Love you, too."

19

The bug exploded, guts splattering across the wall in a disgusting pattern. No matter how many times Pi smelled them, she couldn't help but gag. She climbed onto the wall and surveyed the carnage. They'd survived the third wave—again.

"South corridor clear!" she shouted to the rest of the team.

Aurie motioned from the north wall. "Clear here."

Hannah was still struggling up the east wall slope in her block skates and armor. Even after countless deaths, they couldn't get her to change to sensible hiking boots.

"Clear!" yelled Raziyah from the west wall.

Pi gave the dark-skinned girl a salute. Her spell work was suspect, but she made a good teammate, unlike Echo, who was digging in the dirt again. Pi'd given up trying to use him, which meant they were a person down for the battle.

Hannah finally made the top, and yelled, "Bug sign, coming in hot."

In the fourth wave, the bugs came from random directions each time, so they had to watch for the motion in the trees. There would be two groups of burrowers and three groups of darters. While the poisoned spikes the darters shot were a pain, it was the burrowers killing them every time, because they didn't know where they were going to come up.

Every time, a few escaped the defenses they set up and killed someone before the rest of the team could react. The only person they hadn't killed was Echo, who was usually sitting by the flowery bushes at the center of the fort, as if they knew he was useless to its defense.

They had a few minutes before the bugs arrived. Pi took a moment to survey the countryside. The idyllic hills rolled into the distance with no sign of civilization in any direction, though it was hard to completely tell since the fort was nestled in a valley. Though the trees looked similar to the foliage on the coast, there were no chem trails, or other signs of Earth life, which meant they were in a different realm, or a pocket universe created solely for the contest. This seemed important to Pi, but she couldn't figure out why.

Echo had wandered back to the garden and settled cross-legged near a scraggly bush sprouting purple flowers. She would have yelled at him to get back into position, but he seemed so peaceful, which only made her feel guilty, because it was an effort to get him into the contest each week. More than anyone else, he took the deaths keenly. His eyes were puffy with tears by the time they got him into the contest room. The only thing that made it worth it was that he seemed to do better once they got inside.

Pi wondered what kind of life he had before the Halls. Neither she nor Raz could get him to talk about anything, and attempts at finding where he'd come from had come up empty. His history was a blank sheet of paper, much like hers, which made her even more reticent to push him.

Aurie didn't seem to care as much about not knowing anything about their family. Having an unbelievably hot boyfriend was a good distraction, but even before that she hadn't cared.

Pi flicked the bug guts off her shoulder armor and checked on the bug sign. The foliage on the trees shook, indicating the attack was imminent.

It wouldn't be long. Twenty seconds, maybe less.

She glanced back at the rest of the fort: four broken walls creating a slight depression in the earth filled with purple flowers. If it wasn't the location of her weekly death, it might be a great place for a picnic.

"Why is this place even here?" she asked Raziyah, who was busy channeling her faez into the ground to create an anti-flanking barrier.

"The contest?" asked Raziyah, though she wasn't really paying attention.

Pi felt like she had something. Rather than face the direction of the bugs, she looked behind them, tried to see the fort with different eyes.

It was...

An explosion ripped across the yard as a bug emerged into one of Hannah's tinker bombs.

Pi had no time to regather her thoughts as a hailstorm of projectiles flew from the darter bugs as they exited the trees. She took a piece of circular steel she'd brought, tossed it high, and yelled, "Expand!"

The steel stretched until it was paper thin, catching the majority of the spikes before they could injure anyone. The rest went wide of the team. She'd spent the morning working the metal with faez so it could easily change size.

Aurie was in front, doing her trick with the sticky-earth. Last week, the burrowers had slipped between that area and Raz's wall, killing half the team before they'd begun. This time, it seemed to work, and the earth around her dimpled as the bugs thrashed in the trap.

Rigel stood to the left side, sending sparks into the trees where the darters were hiding. A few flames caught, but not enough to hurt the bugs.

"More faez!" she yelled to him, then over her shoulder, "Echo, we need you!"

Even one bug could make the difference between losing and surviving the wave.

Echo hadn't moved, and he had a crown of flowers on his head. Pi sighed. Even without him, they could still pass. This was their best start yet.

Pi was preparing the next steel shield—the darters would launch a second volley soon—when Hannah looked down at the ground with a perplexed look on her face.

"I think—"

The ground exploded as two bugs burst upward, mandibles snapping. Pi dove away, warned only by Hannah's expression.

The screams were silenced as a rock bomb, set off by Hannah, destroyed her and the attackers. She was out of the game.

Pi staggered to her feet, ears ringing, her combat helmet thrown towards the field of battle, and was preparing to regroup when chaos fell upon the rest of the team. Within seconds Rigel was down, and her sister and Raz were almost overrun.

She was going to make a last stand with Aurie, but decided that no matter how many times it'd happened, getting killed by giant bugs was never fun. Pi leapt from the wall and ran the other direction. She made a grab at Echo as she passed.

"Come on! Come on!"

She tugged on his arm, but he wouldn't come. The look of overwhelming sadness nearly made her stop to embrace him, but the bugs scrambling over themselves after her nixed that idea. Before she could go, he took off his crown and placed it on her head.

The head start wouldn't last, so she used verumancy to give her legs more speed. She passed the edge of the fort and made the trees, branches pawing at her arms, whipping her legs. She hurried, fear of the bugs, fear of death, driving her forward.

While the speed verumancy made her legs go faster, they did nothing for her endurance. By the time she reached the top of the nearest hill, she was tanked.

Bent at the knees, heaving, Pi tried to keep an eye out while trying not to barf up the two chocolate bars and the energy drinks she'd eaten before the attempt. The flowery crown dipped into her vision, making Pi think that for a moment, some critter had fallen onto her. She yelped and yanked it off, mashing the pretty purple flowers in the process, and releasing an awful stench.

"Wretched," she said, before she remembered she was being hunted by killer bugs, and slapped her hand over her mouth.

In the valley below her, the trees moved with the swaying certainty of insects. Pi knew bug sign when she saw it.

She was going to die, there was no doubt about that. The bugs were coming from three directions, but if she could learn something for the next attempt, it'd be worth it.

Looking up, Pi knew what she needed to do. She jammed the flowery crown back on her head and pulled herself into a wide oak-like tree that had long droopy leaves like stunted willows. The bark was rough, which hurt her hands, but made good gripping material. Her legs still shook from the mad dash, but her arms were fresh enough to haul her up the trunk.

She was halfway up when the first bug arrived. Using its long limber legs, all six of them, the bug ambled up to the tree, armored head searching the ground while its mandibles dripped yellow foam. Pi held still, waiting to see if the insect could detect her presence. It seemed to know she was nearby, but not exactly where.

As it moved around the base of the tree, other bugs arrived, and she found herself fascinated by the details she hadn't noticed before. During combat, the only thing she saw was the knifelike legs and the powerful slavering mandibles ready to pinch her head off. Without that immediate fear, she studied the bugs, hoping to glean information that might help them. They were angular and tall, legs like jagged-edged protractors in their stiff-legged marching, moving in two speeds: slow fascist march and hyper-skittering annihilation. Chitinous armor had overlapping plates, protecting the soft joints, colors to blend into the forest with natural swirls and designs. Darker coloring and thicker armor seemed to indicate older bugs.

The only other bugs she'd gotten to study at leisure were the bugs first killed in the fort. The ones initially guarding the portal had thicker armor like these, while the bugs hiding in the ground were softer, adolescents.

Pi was so busy staring at the bugs, the flowery crown slipped off her head to float through the branches until it landed right next to a curious bug. At first, she thought the movement of the flowers would give her away, but the bugs seemed not to be interested in where the flowers had come from. But over the next minute, their attention slowly climbed upward, as if they were starting to realize she was in the tree. She had a good suspicion of why they hadn't noticed her. Something to do with the awful smell of the flowers hiding her human scent. When the first bug put its leg onto the trunk, Pi fled upward.

This seemed to incite them to a frenzy, and a sea of clacking drove her upward. She pushed through the canopy to come out much higher than she expected. To her disappointment, the rolling hills continued in all directions. No sign of anything that might indicate where the bugs were coming from.

Pi looked down to see a bug a few feet below her.

"It's never easy, is it?" she told the bug as it paused and shook its mandibles at her. A moment later, she summoned a fire spear to each hand and leapt downward, a war cry on her lips.

20

It was preview night in the Magelings Theater. Aurie and the rest of the Harpers, minus Raziyah, who had gone home for spring break, had come to support Rigel, who had the leading role in the play *The Last Mage*. The theater wasn't a large one, mostly run by the initiates from the Guild of Magical Dramatics. The theater reeked of spent faez and cigarette smoke, the latter a lingering ghost from pre-smoking-ban times.

The show wasn't going to start for a half-hour, but they'd wanted to get good seats and wish him luck before the show.

Rigel came out from the back and met them at their seats.

"Thank you all for coming," said Rigel, a grin on his face, but eyes wavering with nervousness. He kept squeezing his hands together and taking cleansing breaths.

"We wouldn't miss it even if you banished us to another plane," said Aurie.

Laughing, the others added their agreement.

"Hopefully I'll do better here than I do against the bugs," he said. "Otherwise y'all will think I'm useless."

"You're not terrible," said Aurie, putting a reassuring hand on his arm. "Your illusions are amazing. It just sucks that the bugs see right through them. The fault is mine that I haven't found a way to use your unique talents."

Rigel raised an eyebrow in exquisite mockery. "That's a euphemism if I've ever heard one."

"Not fair. I mean it," said Aurie.

Pi leaned in. "Are these unique talents I'm hearing about getting murdered by giant bugs in new and interesting ways? I think one chopped your head off last week and it rolled between Hannah's legs. I was going to award it two points, but I caught a dart in the leg."

"I still have nightmares about that," said Hannah from the end of the row. "Thank you very little for bringing it up."

This was the part about the Harpers that Aurie loved. They hadn't had much success in the contest compared to the other teams, but no one had started blaming anyone else, and everyone kept trying. They'd even made it to the fifth wave last week, which felt good, despite getting promptly slaughtered. The only one she was disappointed in was her sister, who kept disappearing during the first two waves on scouting missions.

"How's your mom doing?" she asked Rigel.

"Mom's still a bit wobbly, being the first anniversary and all," said Rigel, eyes heavy with sadness.

His father had died last year in a boating accident on the lake. Rigel seemed to have come to terms with it, but he was worried about his mom.

Aurie gave him a squeeze on the arm. "Sorry, I shouldn't bring that up now."

"Actually, it helps keep my mind off what's to come... oh no, he's here," said Rigel, staring across the theater and looking ready to pass out.

The group of them turned their heads to see the legendary Frank Orpheum, patron of the Dramatics Hall, entering the theater with a beautiful woman on his arm. After Invictus, he was probably the most well-known individual from the university, and one of the most liked in the world due to his extensive charity work, and of course, his beaming star power.

He'd sung for every pope and president, once did improv with the Dalai Lama in a Tibetan temple, performed a magic trick that made the moon disappear for everyone in the northern hemisphere, slept with every actress or actor who ever made the World's Sexiest lists, once hypnotized a stadium full of people into believing they were statues, and not one of them blinked for over two hours, created the iconic Magelings series about a fictional Hundred Halls, and done a billion other things. Before he'd stopped performing, people jokingly called Hollywood Frankie-wood due to his utter domination of every aspect of entertainment.

"Great balls of fire," said Hannah. "That's Priyanka Sai on his arm. I didn't know they were dating. I can't believe that hasn't hit the *Herald of the Halls* yet."

Pi poked Hannah in the arm. "You read that piece of trash?"

"Sorry, Aurie," said Hannah, with a not-so-sorry grin.

While Frank Orpheum welcomed the fawning attention from those in attendance, the Indian patron was studying the crowd as if she were about to teach a class on advanced mathematics.

The difference between what Aurie had in her head and reality was rather surprising. As the leader of the Academy of Subtle Arts, Aurie had expected more cockiness, like a female James Bond. Priyanka projected quiet confidence instead, more professorial, reminding Aurie that her hall did more than teach the tools of dealing death. They were the world's best diplomats and spies. Aurie gathered that she inclined more to the other aspects of her hall than the former, which was a relief.

"It's okay, Rigel. Don't hyperventilate," said Aurie.

Rigel put his hand on his forehead. "You don't understand. It's not just a show. I'm trying out for the summer production circuit. All the biggest stars got their start there. If I impress him, then I get to travel the world, if not, then I'm destined for a life of doing Sunday theater for blue-haired old ladies who cough through the entire show."

"Don't focus on that," said Aurie. "Have a good time. If you have to look anywhere, look at us. We'll be cheering you on. Remember, you're doing what you love."

This brought a measure of relief to his eyes. "You're right. Thank you. I'm so glad you guys are here. I think I'd hide in my dressing room otherwise."

The theater was filling up, so Rigel went backstage. While they waited, Pi kept Echo entertained playing Five Elements, and Hannah chatted with her girlfriend, a short girl with hair that kept changing colors.

Aurie was a little jealous. She'd asked Zayn, but he gave her a vague reason for not joining her. They were seeing each other more often, but she never felt like they were actually dating.

When the curtain went up and lights went down, everyone settled in. Rigel came onto the stage in orphan rags and with bruises on his jaw.

His first couple of lines were delivered in a shaky voice, but when he looked at the Harpers, he visibly relaxed and started to shine. The play was about a boy who became a great mage in Guangzhou China, eventually going on to serve the emperor and win famous battles, mostly through his cleverness. Aurie had seen the movie version of the story on a bootleg copy back when she and Pi lived in the thirteenth ward. She was excited to see how Rigel and the other actors would pull off the illusions to create the battles.

During a lull in the action, Aurie snuck out to use the bathroom, since she knew there were no parts with Rigel coming up, so she didn't think he'd mind. Alone in the corner stall, Aurie mentally griped about all the homework that Professor Mali had given on Friday.

Before she finished, someone came into the bathroom, stiletto heels smacking the white tile with precision. The woman was talking into a cell phone.

"I don't care what his problem is," said Priyanka Sai. "Tell him who made the request. That might loosen his schedule a little."

Aurie pulled her feet up and held her breath while Priyanka paced. The voice on the other side of the call was distant and squeaky. Aurie thought she heard something about a team.

"We don't have that kind of time. I need this now," said Priyanka.

Aurie wanted to hear what was being said by the other party, but it was too quiet. As carefully as she could, Aurie touched her ears and performed verumancy. Almost as soon as the spell was finished, Priyanka's heels stopped short.

"Hold a moment," said Priyanka.

With her enhanced hearing, Aurie sensed that she'd been detected. She should have realized that the patron of assassins would be paranoid. Detecting faez would be the first sign of an attack.

Priyanka marched down the sinks and stopped in front of Aurie's stall. The slider on her door started opening on its own. Aurie searched for something with which to counter the spell, but she'd left her purse at the seat and the toilet paper was no use.

The voice on the cell phone was asking, "Hello? Priyanka? Are we doing this or what?"

Using mendancy, Aurie reached out and told the phone

to lose its signal. The subsequent click startled Priyanka, and the handle on the door stopped opening.

"Son of a...," said Priyanka.

Dialing beeps echoed through the room. She'd delayed the inevitable, but still needed a way out.

Then the door opened and a trio of women came in chattering. The stiletto heels marched out of the room, leaving Aurie in her stall.

After Priyanka was gone, Aurie flushed, washed her hands, and found the window. The lock was easy to circumvent. She climbed out the window to a ledge three stories up, closed it behind her, and found a rickety drainpipe to climb down. The bolts had rusted out, and the first time she put weight on it, the whole thing groaned.

Another dose of mendancy convinced the pipe to hold her weight and she started climbing down. Occasional shifts and clicks gave Aurie momentary heart attacks, but she was able to make it down to the street level without incident.

There was no way she was going to go back in now. Priyanka would be waiting to see who came out of the bathroom. Eventually, she'd figure out what had happened and check the entrance to the theater. Aurie hated to disappoint Rigel, who would surely notice her absence, but she didn't want the patron of assassins to know she'd been eavesdropping, especially when it sounded like she was requesting something that would impact the contest.

Aurie had no doubt that the wish spell was the prize at the end. Otherwise, why would Priyanka Sai be worrying about it? Her position within the Cabal made the involvement perilous.

After the play was over, Aurie snuck back in amid the chaos, finding a crowd at the side of the stage with Rigel. As Aurie walked up, Frank Orpheum was leaving. Rigel looked like he was about to bump against the ceiling.

When she stopped next to Pi, her sister gave her a funny look. "I'll tell you later."

"Did you get it?" asked Aurie.

Rigel was looking at his hands as if they didn't exist. "Not only did I get it, but he said that performance was better than the latest version on Broadway, and that he might put a few scenes of The Last Mage into the traveling show to showcase my performance. I think I'm numb from shock, actually numb."

He shook his hands a few times and laughed gleefully. "Where'd you go the second half? I looked for you."

Aurie poked herself in the gut and made a grimace.

"Gotcha," he said. "You'll just have to see me again this summer."

"You can count on it," she said.

Afterwards, they went to a nearby diner that named sandwiches after famous Dramatics alumni like Frank-O-Furter for Frank Orpheum and Garbanzo Bean Salad Sandwich for Jillian Garbanzo. Rigel spent the time giving moment by moment recollections of his interactions with Frank Orpheum and contemplating his future culinary namesake at the diner, while the rest of them cheered him on. Aurie laughed in all the right places, but she couldn't help but be distracted by what she'd overheard from Priyanka Sai. The Cabal were going after the wish spell, and the wish spell had to be the prize at the end of the contest, which meant the Harpers had to win the contest. If only she knew how.

21

A haunting saxophone played over the speakers in the kitchen of the Glass Cabaret. Pi was placing enchantments on the dishes and silverware to keep them clean, even after use. The tricky part was making it so the utensils would work during the meal, but not let the food slide off the tines. Radoslav hadn't told her how to perform the spell, so she'd had to deconstruct it from the spell residue.

The work was tedious, but she didn't mind. It helped soothe her simmering rage. After Rigel's play a few weeks ago, Pi noticed that Aurie was pushing the team harder in the contest. The last attempt had been disastrous. No one stuck to the plan, trying to compensate for Aurie's intensity. The bugs had overrun them at wave three two weeks ago, and wave one last week. No one had even scheduled the next attempt, despite the spring semester winding down towards finals.

In the meantime, she was taking on more and more duties for Radoslav since the encounter with Slyvan earlier in the school year. She wondered if the Ruby Court had diminished his powers through their control of the power conduit.

Pi was hunched over the stainless steel table, sprinkling

dried clouds on the row of spoons as a faez binder. The seed of a headache was germinating at her temples from the focused work, so she didn't hear the door whisk open until it was too late.

Radoslav's anger had twisted his lips into bent razors. A column of hard smoke shot from his outthrust hand, launching Pi into the subzero refrigerator. The impact sent stars through her vision. She had no time to defend herself before chains of vapor grabbed her arms and held them to the cold surface.

"You double-crossing piece of shit," he said.

A curl of smoke slipped from his lips like a snake and wrapped around her neck. It gave her throat a muscular squeeze, restricting her air.

If Pi had ever wondered how he could be called the Black Butcher, she wondered no longer. His eyes were jet black, his pale skin smoldered like ash.

"I'm trying to help," she choked out.

"Help?" he said with absolute condemnation. "You know nothing about what you're doing. You think for a moment that because you've survived a few minor skirmishes that you can suddenly maneuver your way through the courts of the maetrie and come away unscathed? You're putting countless lives at risk with your idiocy."

Pi fought against the smoke around her throat. "At least I'm trying to do something, instead of hiding out in this bar."

When he squeezed his hand, she thought he was going to kill her. The smoke crumpled the refrigerator as if it were an aluminum can. Pi recalibrated her understanding of his remaining power. Even with Slyvan tampering with his power, Radoslav was as scary as a Hall patron. Maybe scarier.

"I am not hiding here," said Radoslav. "What I am doing is keeping my people from destroying themselves."

"They might do that with or without you," she said.

"Wouldn't you rather help?"

He paced back and forth in front of her like an angry panther desperate to get out of his cage. Pi sensed that at any moment he could finish what he'd come to do, which was kill her. She had no doubt of that. He was convinced that she needed to be stopped.

After a few tense minutes, he paused in front of her and held his finger to her chest. The smoke bindings rippled and squeezed, reflecting his mercurial mood like tentacles.

"No more meddling. No matter how you think you might be helping. If I find out that you stepped even one foot into the Eternal City, I will kill you." His eyes narrowed. "I might be a fool for not killing you right now, but I'm trying to learn from my mistakes. Don't make me regret it."

Radoslav didn't wait for her to reply and charged out of the room. The smoke released her, and she collapsed on the floor. The kitchen was a shattered mess, broken dishes everywhere. Pi took a deep breath, recaptured her hair into a ponytail, and went back to work.

22

The lattice of broken slats fell to the floor with a resounding thump, an all-too-familiar result for Aurie. She turned around to face her sister, who had a bemused expression on her lips.

"That was terrible, sis," she said.

Aurie put her hands on her hips. "I thought I brought you here to help."

"If you want lies, I'll send for Rigel, and he can make some illusions for you," said Pi.

"Don't bother, I can see right through them," said Aurie.

"You can?" Pi scrunched her face up. "When he makes those illusionary spiders, I can practically feel the hair on their legs."

"Nope," said Aurie. "Might as well be poorly made plastic spiders for me."

"Weird," said Pi. "I wonder if that has to do with mendancy? Since illusions are a bit like lying. Maybe that's something that could help you here."

Aurie's jaw ached, which was weird because she hadn't been punched or anything. Probably been clenching it too much. As she massaged her jaw, she said, "I'm not sure how.

Being able to see through illusions isn't going help anywhere, especially in here. I'm not going to pass this class with Semyon if I can't pull off a feat of mass mendancy."

"You need to try harder," offered Pi.

"I am!"

She got so mad she almost fell off the post.

"Do it a few more times while I watch," said Pi. "I need more than one viewing to see if I can help."

Aurie did as asked, but wasn't able to make the slats hold enough to take even one step. After a dozen attempts, Pi called it off.

"Have you ever gotten them to hold?" asked Pi.

"A few times," said Aurie. "But not many. There's just too many things to fix. I can't do it all at once."

"But you made the clothes on Violet and her twit friends fall off with a single word," said Pi.

"Yeah," said Aurie, shaking her head. "I don't honestly know how I did that. Maybe it was a mistake. What if it was really Echo that caused it?"

Pi frowned. "I doubt it. Otherwise, we'd be doing better in the contest."

"What then? I'm out of ideas," said Aurie, frustrated.

"Anything special about that day? Anything you remember?" asked Pi.

"Other than Violet being a total jerk? No," said Aurie.

She'd been over this a thousand times in her head. Aurie had no earthly idea why that day she'd been able to perform a nearly impossible feat of mendancy, yet she couldn't do anything significant since.

"I'm getting down," said Aurie. "There's no use trying this if I don't have any new ideas."

To her surprise, Pi said, "Yeah, you should get down."

Her sister had a strange look on her face, one she didn't

trust.

"Why did you agree with me? That makes me nervous," said Aurie.

Once Aurie was on the floor, Pi started climbing up the pole.

"What are you doing?" asked Aurie.

When Pi reached the top, she stared down at Aurie and stuck out her tongue.

"Pi, get down. You'll break your neck if you fall. You don't have the levitation bracelets," she said.

"I'm not getting down," said Pi, and she hit the button, making the slats lift into place. They would fall again at the first whisper of magic.

Seeing her sister on the pole, thirty feet in the air, made Aurie jumpy inside.

"Pi. Seriously, you're scaring me," said Aurie.

Her sister made small steps as she turned around in a circle. "How do you stand up here for hours at a time? This is insane."

"What's going on? Why won't you get down?" asked Aurie, biting her lower lip. She'd climb up and get her down, but would probably only make Pi fall. It was like when they were eight and six respectively and Aurie had knocked Pi off the bed and broke her arm. This time it was quite a bit higher.

"What if it's an illusion? Maybe I need to have faith to walk across this area," said Pi, holding one foot out as if she were going to step onto the fragile slats.

"Stop! Get down, Pi. This isn't funny, and it's not an illusion. If you step forward, the slats will fall and so will you. You're going to break your neck," she said.

Pi held her arms out and looked straight down at her sister with a look of pure determination. "Then you'd better figure it out. I'm going to step forward on the count of three. One."

Aurie started to run forward, but realized she'd never have enough time to climb the pole.

"Two."

She stopped, bunched her hands into fists.

"Three."

At the final number, Pi lifted her leg and took a large step forward onto the slats.

A thousand things went through Aurie's mind in that instant. She imagined her sister lying on the floor like a discarded marionette, eyes blank and unfocused. Or her parents quietly scolding her for not taking care of her sister. The first time that Pi walked, when she was a chubby cheeked toddler. Halloween, dressed as two Jedi. Making sparklers turn different colors with faez, even though they knew it was dangerous. That fierce I-don't-care-what-you-think twinkle in her eye, smile like a thousand hugs that you never wanted to let go of, the sweet smell of her hair when they cuddled on the hammock watching fireflies, the thump-thump of her heart, blinding love that hurt so much when she thought too long about it, carefree, mischievous, best sister in the world.

The toe of her sister's sneaker touched the wooden slats. Aurie had no time to think, no time for anything. The faez came like a flood.

"Bridge!" she screamed, the faez bubbling up and through her like a geyser. The wealth of magic gave her vertigo, as if one person was not meant to hold so much.

Pi's weight fell upon slats, and held. Aurie wanted to cheer, but the danger wasn't over yet. She concentrated on the lie, that the connecting slats were really a bridge, a solid foundation built on deep rock. That Pi could drive a tank over it and it'd still hold.

At each step, the slats groaned and creaked. Pi walked forward calmly, eyes straight ahead.

Through sheer force of will, the bridge held. Aurie would not let it falter while her sister was upon it.

And then it was over, and Pi was on the other side.

The lattice of wooden poles collapsed with a clatter, followed by Aurie dipping to one knee.

She didn't even need to look up at Pi to know there was a smug smile on her face.

"I hate you," said Aurie.

"It worked," said Pi.

"Why didn't you tell me you were going to do that?" asked Aurie.

With unsteady legs, she stood.

"Then it wouldn't have worked," said Pi.

"Why did it work?" asked Aurie.

"Really? Sometimes, Aurie, I swear. It worked because you're too damn selfless. You'll do amazing, and stupid, things for other people, but you forget about yourself. The mendancy worked that day because you were protecting Echo," said Pi.

"But I wasn't protecting him. They'd already ruined his backpack. It was petty, and he wasn't in danger," said Aurie.

Pi shrugged and started climbing down. "It's not like you knew what you were going to do."

Aurie rubbed her temple. "I still don't see how this is going to help me."

"This is everything," said Pi. "It means you can do it."

Aurie wanted to feel better about the situation, but she wasn't as excited as her sister about the successful mendancy.

"Yeah, I did it once, when you were in danger," said Aurie. "But how am I going to prove it to Semyon?"

"One step at a time, sis. One step at a time," said Pi, clearly proud of herself.

Aurie wished she was as confident as her sister.

23

The Reaping Ceremony had come marching towards Pi with the subtlety of a steam train. Despite the threats from Radoslav, she'd known she was going to attend the ceremony on Lady Amethyte's behalf from the moment he'd left her.

Standing on 4th and Magenta, Pi waited for her ride to the Eternal City to arrive. The stylized runes on the invitation had suggested a formal affair, so Pi had borrowed a dress from Ashley. It was a bright red swanky number with a slit for her leg to stick out as if she were some Hollywood starlet. She didn't quite manage to fill out the top of the dress since she was rather flat chested, but a few spells had cinched it tight enough that the shoulders didn't slip free.

The enchantment on the dress wasn't the only one she'd cast, but it was the most mundane. Despite Slyvan's assurances that this would be a boring event, and the gift mostly a formality to spark new negotiations, Pi treated it like she was being sent into a warzone. The hardest part about the spell work had been making them unobtrusive. She knew that if she went in bristling with invasive enchantments, she could do more harm than good, so her work had to be subtle.

Pi hoped she'd been careful enough.

At least she hadn't had to worry about the weather, as the spring had brought temperance to the coast. Not that a few spells wouldn't have fixed that.

She held a clutch purse and the case containing the necklace to her stomach as cars flashed past. A bunch of young men in camo hats catcalled her from their oversized truck with a Confederate flag on the bumper, so Pi flipped them off and put a spell on the tires to have a slow leak they would never be able to find nor fix. One perk to being a mage was never having to take shit from guys like them.

She was beginning to wonder if she was waiting in the wrong spot when she heard squealing tires and honking horns. A half a block down, a grainy portal shimmered into existence like a mirage in the desert, and a horse-drawn carriage came bursting through, forcing normal traffic to veer away.

The horses were anything but ordinary. They were made of polished steel, glowing contour lines accented their muscles, and their eyes were bright and ominous. The carriage was black metal and polished silver, looking like something out of a theatrical heavy metal concert: the vehicle in which the lead singer would arrive to flame jets and ball-busting bass notes.

Pi expected smoke to billow out of the door when the carriage stopped next to her. The horses' steel hooves cracked the concrete at each blow as they stomped in place.

She was aware that every eye on the street was watching her, and she silently cursed this unsubtle arrival of her transportation. There was no way that Radoslav wouldn't find out about it, which had probably been Slyvan's intention, a payback for the bone bracelet trick. But it was too late now—she'd made promises that she had to deliver on.

Pi stepped into the carriage and seated herself on the red velvet bench. Almost as soon as she leaned back, the door slammed shut and the steel horses burst into motion, making a hard turn back toward the portal, throwing her into the side, forcing cars to go screaming out of the way. There was a crash, metal impacting. People were yelling, and cameras everywhere captured the moment.

While she'd planned for the possibility of being spotted while in public and placed the proper obscuring enchantments on her person, the meaning of the grotesque display wouldn't be lost on her benefactor. No one else in the city would know who had gotten in the carriage except one person: Radoslav.

But she pushed it out of her mind as the carriage entered the portal into the Eternal City. The difference from the city of sorcery was remarkable. Invictus was bright, noisy, people-filled, a bit garish in its American mercantilism. The Eternal City brooded like an old crone chain smoking, eyes clear with the threat that she would cut you open for getting even a speck of mud on her filthy carpet.

Streets and buildings flew by at a rapid pace. The carriage barreled through the city as if it were being hunted. Unlike her first visit, Pi saw people this time, though everyone looked like they were prepared for a fight, spells dripping off them like deadly ink.

The carriage headed deeper into the city where the skyscrapers walked. Her destination became apparent when she saw the massive structure at the center of the pack, though to her surprise, it wasn't moving. They looked like metal and concrete giants with their heads in the clouds. A faint green glow emanated from the windows of the middle building, a subtle nod to the Jade Queen.

"Oh, Pythia, what are we getting ourselves into?" she said, the window cold against her splayed fingers.

Before she had a chance to wonder how she would reach the upper levels of the superstructure, the carriage leapt into the air, sending her stomach into her throat. Pi stuck her head out the window to see the metal hooves creating sparks each time they struck the empty air. As she rose further, the city unfolded, stretching to a greater horizon, and though the gray clouds that hung beneath a tortured sky obscured the tops of the tallest buildings, she saw the city that went on forever.

The ride ended when the carriage trotted to a stop on a landing platform near the bottom of the sky. Other guests exited vehicles more outlandish than hers: a ball of pulsating goo that ejected its travelers with a sickening plop, a host of radioactive butterflies that carried their hosts then exploded into crackling fireworks once they had landed, and others too strange to comprehend.

In comparison, her heavy metal carriage seemed mundane, and she wondered if she'd mistaken Slyvan's intent. Maybe the carriage had been the least of what he could have sent.

At least the fashions weren't reflective of the vehicles. Pi had worried about her choice, but the going haute couture could have been a product of the Paris runways.

The door guardian was a mountain of a man with gray skin and black eyes like the rest of the maetrie, but pulsing greenish lines ran across the sides of his head and down his neck. They looked like radioactive electronics. Pi wasn't sure if they were functional or for show, and she hoped she wouldn't have to find out.

Pi handed him the invitation.

"You're quite the bouncer," she told him. "I know a guy who would love some tips from you like how do you get blood out of your shirt, or what do you do when someone summons a vomit demon."

The door guardian took the paper without comment. It looked miniscule in his granite hands. He pushed the door open, letting her pass.

"I guess all maetrie are as moody as Radoslav," she muttered to herself.

The inside was a grand ballroom. Lots of polished chrome with those glowing green lines that she'd seen on the guardian. It felt like she'd been miniaturized and placed on a circuit board.

Pi didn't know where to find the Jade Queen, so she milled around, clutching the gift for Kikala tightly against her stomach. It felt strangely warm. Or maybe she was cold and the case radiated heat from when she was standing on the street in Invictus.

Most of the guests were maetrie, their allegiance unclear, bunched together in groups. She spied a few humans and non-humans amongst the crowd. What looked to be a talking dog was chatting with a gold-skinned nearly naked woman.

A knot of human mages surrounded a woman in a black dress. Pi recognized Celesse D'Agastine, the patron of the Alchemists Hall, so she went the other direction. She doubted Celesse would remember her from the delivery last year, but she didn't want to chance it.

Other areas were blocked by silvery doors. Sometimes maetrie went in and out of them. Pi didn't know if they were fancy bathrooms, or other rooms for the celebration.

Cutting around a glowing green pillar, Pi saw Slyvan standing by himself. He wore the same black three-piece suit she'd seen him in the first time back at the Glass Cabaret, and that same dismissive expression. He looked like he'd been waiting for her.

"You are aware that emo is a stage that you're supposed to grow out of," she told him on approach.

"Says the girl who looks like she's on a prom date at Denny's," he said, looking down his nose at her.

"Wow, nice one," she said. "I didn't know you had it in

you."

Slyvan let a nearly imperceptible sigh out of his lips as if having to be in her presence was a special agony that only he had to suffer.

"So...where is the Jade Queen? I'd like to get this over with," she said.

Using only his eyes, Slyvan directed her towards the wall of black mist that few guests had been going through. As if on cue, a tortured scream echoed from the mist. A short, plump maetrie in a gray shirt ran out of the blackness and down the stairs, only to have a tentacle reach out and grab him around the midsection. The scream rose to a crescendo then ended abruptly as the maetrie was pulled back into the mist. The partygoers resumed their chatting as if nothing had happened.

"That was quite the shit show," said Pi, trying to calm her beating heart.

Slyvan smirked. "The Watcher knows if you have intentions of causing harm to the queen and eliminates the threat."

"Wonderful," said Pi, remembering her precautions, then blowing out a breath added, "Anything else I need to know?"

"Be polite," said Slyvan. "Lady Kikala isn't as informal as Lady Amethyte. She will take offense easily, so you might think about keeping that tongue of yours restrained."

Pi mimed zipping her mouth shut, then remembered one more thing and unzipped it. "What am I to say to her? Here's a gift from your ex-girlfriend? Can we be friends, and by the way, your son would like you to not to kill your dad, who's also kinda your mom?"

"You never seem to be at a lack of words, you'll think of something," he said.

"Great. Off to see the wonderful wizard of Oz," she said, moving towards the black mist. "Wish me luck."

Slyvan said nothing.

"Ungrateful bastard," she said, and glancing back, found he was gone. "Probably went to find a mirror to preen in front of, maybe take a few selfies, post them on Instagram like a proper teenage girl."

Before she went in, Pi liberated the explosive seeds she'd made from her pockets, dropping them on the steps. She didn't want the Watcher to confuse her intent. The rest of her enchantments, she hoped would be considered merely defensive, but she was going to miss the seeds. Since her faez was limited here, it'd been a way to circumvent the restriction. She only had to use enough faez to detonate them.

The black mist was cool upon approach, almost soothing, until she felt the presence probing her mind. The touch was so alien and forceful, Pi nearly panicked and unleashed faez to defend herself. Sparks formed in the darkness, a precursor to the tentacles. The Watcher filled her mind, violating her thoughts, laying them bare with the cold precision of a scalpel. It weighed her intentions, and to her horror, she sensed it deciding whether or not to destroy her. The enchantments she'd placed on herself as protection had drawn the ire of the Watcher. It plucked the strings of magic, and she felt tentacles stirring in the darkness. Pi thought of Radoslav, of her link to him, to prove to the Watcher that she posed no threat, and after a long fateful pause, she found herself stumbling through to the other side.

Pi stood in a throne room of mirrors and green glowing lines that made the space seem almost infinite in its reflections. The Jade Queen sat on a black throne in absolute stillness. Her straight black hair ended past her shoulder blades, the edges as sharp as a razor. She was clothed in silver thread, which left her nearly naked.

Pi'd expected to see others, and upon finding it empty

except for the two of them, she stepped nervously forward.

"Hi," she said, cringing at the informality. "I mean, greetings, or it's lovely to meet you, Your Highness."

She'd bumbled from one mistake to another and felt the fool by the end. If the Jade Queen smote her on the spot, she deserved it.

Lady Kikala's somber expression deepened. "How is he?"

"Radoslav? Yeah, of course," she muttered. "He's well?"

"Who are you to him?" she commanded.

Pi almost gave an obfuscation but decided against it. "I work for him. Made a deal with him last year in exchange for my service. I'm a student in the Hundred Halls."

The Jade Queen appeared offended. "Why did he send you?"

Pi felt like a mouse in a buffalo stampede. There was nowhere to run. "I was available?"

The look that crossed Lady Kikala's face betrayed the sense of loss she had without her son. Pi suspected she had thought the choice of representation an insult, which was dangerous for Pi if she wanted to make it out alive. In these circles, honesty was usually not the best practice, but in this case, a little more clarity might save her life.

"Actually, he didn't," said Pi. "I shouldn't have said that. He told me not to come, but I did anyway."

Lady Kikala sat up straighter, her hair swaying sharply at the movement. "You are a strange girl. Since you weren't sent by my son, tell me why I shouldn't have you killed."

The case in her hands moved, or at least she thought it did, but Pi was too distracted by the queen's growing wrath to bother investigating. "I came because Radoslav couldn't. Lady Amethyte found his power conduit, threatened him."

The air tightened around Pi as if it were a constrictor. Lady Kikala leaned forward.

"You're lying.   Something about you isn't right, Pythia Silverthorne.   Out with it now or I feed you to my Watcher," she said.

Pi opened her mouth to refute the accusation, until the case moved again as if something was waking inside it.   Both their gazes went to the gift.

As the case opened on its own, Pi threw it behind her.   The stench of faez made Pi's nose itch.   A massive hulking spider larger than the Jade Queen's throne expanded into the center of the room.   Pi recognized the type of spider because Aurie had told her about it from her date with Zayn.   *Achaeranea magicaencia.*

She dove out of the way as Lady Kikala blasted the critter with twin bolts of lightning, but the spider absorbed the magic without damage, and grew a few inches.

Pi knew now what Zayn had given the Ruby Queen in exchange for information: a way to assassinate her rival.

Lady Kikala was standing tall, fury clouding her brow. She was about to cast another spell.

Pi yelled, "Don't.   It'll only eat the magic and get stronger."

To make matters worse, the building lurched as if it'd been hit by an earthquake.

Lady Kikala cried out.   "They dare attack me, today?"

The massive spider advanced on Lady Kikala, who didn't look like she planned to move, oblivious to the danger the spider posed.   Pi scrambled behind the throne, looking for a suitable weapon.

The mountainous guardian from the outer door came running through the black mist and leapt onto the spider. Pi cheered the development until the spider flipped him over and sunk its fangs into his chest.   His limbs quivered as he screamed, foam filling his mouth as the poison claimed him.

The look on Lady Kikala's face was the realization that the

Ruby Queen had outmaneuvered her. She stared at the spider with consternation, but lifted her arms for magic no longer.

Pi hated that she'd been used, so she decided to help, even if doing so seemed ridiculously stupid. She ran around the edge of the room, staying away from the spider until she was near the black mist, but far enough away the tentacles couldn't reach her, she hoped. Unless Pi proved otherwise, the Jade Queen would probably think she was part of the assassination attempt.

Pi threw a fire spear at the spider, and as expected it absorbed into the furry body. But it didn't stop its march on the queen.

"Why are you doing that? You said not to," said Lady Kikala.

"Trying to distract it," yelled Pi.

The assassin spider had no reason to deviate from its goal, so she had to stop it another way. Pi reached into her clutch purse and pulled out a piece of ice. Like the metal shields she used in the contest against the bugs, it'd been magically reduced.

She threw it towards the spider, yelling, "Expand!"

The cube hit the ground, followed by a sheet of ice stretching beneath the spider's feet. Its legs went straight out as it scrambled to stay in the same place, trying and failing, again and again, to stand.

To her horror, once the spider had completely given up and rested its hairy body on the ground, the ice began to disappear, absorbed by the magic. The spider grew another few feet, making it even more dangerous.

"That didn't work so well," she muttered.

The spider started advancing on the queen again. She needed something that would hurt the creature without using magic, because otherwise the spider would grow stronger.

"I'm not going to like this," said Pi as she had an idea.

Moving a little closer to the black mist, Pi made another fiery spear, but rather than throw it at the spider, launched it towards the Jade Queen.

"Watch out!" she told her.

Lady Kikala knocked it out of the air easily, then screamed, "What is the meaning of this?"

The Watcher was stirring in the mist, but she didn't know how to get it to leave and attack the spider, or even if it could.

She shouted across the room, "Can't you get the Watcher to come out?"

Lady Kikala backed around the throne. She kept eyeing the mist as if she expected reinforcements. Pi guessed the Ruby Queen had attacked at this moment to distract her guards. It might be a slaughter in the other room for all she knew.

The spider leapt onto the throne, knocking Lady Kikala onto her back. It bent its eight legs, preparing to leap.

Pi sensed a presence in the mist, noises, shouting. A chunk of tentacle came sliding out of the darkness, smearing purple blood in its wake.

Then a maetrie came charging through with a massive runed two-handed sword made of obsidian. Pi almost didn't recognize Radoslav. His skin smoldered like ash, his eyes glowered. The single glance he spared for Pi was like realizing she was in a pool full of hungry crocodiles.

But Radoslav turned his attention to the massive spider. He blurred across the room, his obsidian blade screaming as it sung through the air.

The spider cleaved in two, pus and entrails spilling onto the floor. Noxious gases hissed from its split body, a mixture of spent faez and guts. It slowly reduced in size as they watched.

Lady Kikala sprung to her feet and upon reaching Radoslav,

slapped him with the impact of a two-ton sledgehammer. He barely reacted.

"You abandoned me," she said.

The reunion was cut short when cold laughter entered the room from the other side.

Slyvan strolled through the fading mist, softly clapping his hands. Pi backed against the mirrored wall, sensing her chances of survival had gone to nil.

"Brother of mine, you always had to be the hero. I knew you'd come," he said. "You're such a fool, Raddie."

"This ends now," said Radoslav. He flexed his muscles, and black armor formed across his body. He was an obsidian knight. The runes on his sword pulsed with a faint green light.

A figurine appeared in Slyvan's hand. "Forgetting something, Raddie?"

Radoslav lurched to a stop, his sword held at the ready.

Slyvan winked at Pi. "Thank you so much, little mageling, for helping this whole thing come to fruition. I can't tell you how long we've been trying to get to her so we could lure him back to the Eternal City."

"Why?" asked Pi.

Slyvan sneered. "Watch and learn."

He whispered to the figurine. Radoslav turned and advanced on Lady Kikala. She backed against the wall, then thrust her arms forward, covering Radoslav in electricity. It did nothing to stop him. He raised the blade to strike the blow.

"Hold," Slyvan whispered to the figurine.

"That's not a power conduit," said Pi. "That's like a controller. What is he?"

Slyvan peeled his lips away from his teeth. "Ol' Raddie wasn't born out of the love of two soul mates. He was created with the sole intent of wiping out the Onyx Court. Only everyone realized after he did it that he was a power unto himself and could kill every single maetrie if he wanted. Too much power in the hands of one person. So after the battle, the queens conspired and created this figurine to control him, only before they could do anything, he stole it and fled the realm. But now he's back, and we have him, and after we're done with Lady Kikala, we'll eliminate the Diamond Court, and Lady Amethyte can finally rule as she was meant to do. So on behalf of the Ruby Court, thank you, Pythia Silverthorne. For your part in this you've earned a quick death."

Things were not looking good. The only tricks she had left, the explosive seeds, she'd dropped outside the mist. She could make them detonate, but the impact wouldn't reach him from there. Unless she could use them another way.

Pi took a step forward, let a cocky smile rise to her lips. "But you know what you forgot, Ol' Slithering Slyvan? We knew about your deal with Priyanka Sai for the assassin spider"—the surprise on his face was instant—"and that you were going to move the Ruby Court into position to attack. I'm not an idiot, I know what the *Ecacathodian* was for. Lady Amethyte gave it away when she said I was prescient about it being a *moving* piece. And now it's our turn for a surprise."

The seeds exploded on the other side of the mist, which had faded enough that the greenish lines of the great hall could be seen. When Slyvan looked back expecting an attack, Pi fired a force bolt at his hands. The figurine went flying out, sliding across the floor to bump against the mirror.

Pi leapt into action as Slyvan did the same. She was quicker and had her hands on it before he could.

"Defend me!" she said, hoping that was all that was required.

Slyvan's eyes went wide, and he ran out of the room before anyone could stop him. Radoslav chased him until he reached Pi's location, and stood over her with sword at the ready.

"Holy shit," she said, realizing what kind of power she had with him at her command.

Lady Kikala approached, cautious steps betraying her concern.

"They will be pulling back now," she said. "If you send my son after them, he will slaughter them to the last."

"Is that what you wish?" asked Pi.

Lady Kikala's nostrils flared. "I would reward you in any way that you desired."

The obsidian helm kept Pi from guessing Radoslav's thoughts. She looked at the figurine in her hands. It looked like a black knight from a chess set, carved from obsidian.

What should she do? Radoslav had warned her that he would kill her if she came. If she let him go, he might decide that her interference deserved death. On the other hand, if she let Lady Kikala have her wishes, Pi would be responsible for the murder of untold numbers. She wanted power to protect herself, but not this.

Pi began to understand why Radoslav had retreated to her world. They'd made him to be a killing machine, the Black Butcher. If he stayed, his people would kill themselves over his services.

She handed him the figurine. "It's yours to decide."

The armor and sword disappeared at once. Radoslav grasped the figurine with both hands like a drug addict finally getting a fix.

Lady Kikala glowered at Pi. "You're a stupid, stupid girl. Unfit to wield power."

"Probably," she said.

Radoslav faced the Jade Queen. "Goodbye, Mother."

She said nothing.

A portal opened up, and Pi followed Radoslav into the back of the Glass Cabaret. Once the portal closed, Pi tensed up, waiting for the inevitable tongue-lashing and punishment, and she didn't blame him. She'd nearly caused the annihilation of his people through her foolishness.

"Thank you," he said softly.

"Wh-what?"

"Thank you," he said. "I may hate them for all they do, but they're still my family. Thank you for not sending me against them. I could not take it again."

"You're welcome. I thought you'd be mad about me going even though you said not to," she said.

"There's time enough to be mad later," he said, a distant pain haunting his gaze. "However, this means I will tack another year to your service for disobeying me so carelessly."

"I guess I deserve that," she said.

"You will, of course, say nothing of this to anyone, including your sister," he said.

"I promise," she said right away.

He eyed her suspiciously, then nodded.

"What are you going to do with that?" asked Pi.

"Find a new place to hide it," he said.

"Can you destroy it?" she asked.

"I would die," he said.

She winced. "I'm sorry."

He lifted his chin. "It's not your burden."

But she could see he didn't want that burden either. How would that feel to know you'd been made for the purpose of destroying your own kind? No wonder he'd fled the Eternal City. And what a bunch of shits his parents were. At least she and Aurie had gotten to spend a good ten years with their parents, good parents, before their deaths. It was a reminder that some people had it worse, much worse.

She left him with the obsidian figurine. The red dress she'd borrowed from Ashley was torn in two places and the slit practically exposed her panties, but she was too tired to care. Pi called a cab and rode back to Arcanium slumped against the cold glass, relieved that she hadn't sparked a genocide of the maetrie.

24

Around the time that Pi was heading into the Eternal City, Aurie entered the practice room. Beyond the glass, the city of Invictus glittered, a moving landscape on fire with life and magic. A giant illusionary dragon soared above the Frank Orpheum theater in the distance, but that's not what drew Aurie's gaze. The field of interwoven slats lay in the exact position that she'd left them just a few weeks ago. She hadn't attempted mendancy since.

Aurie pushed those thoughts from her mind. That wasn't why she'd come to the Spire. The possible events of later this evening brought a warm glow to her face.

As if on cue, she heard a foot scuff, a purposeful noise meant for her. She hadn't heard him enter, but here he was.

"Zayn," she said, his name slipping off her tongue.

His gaze bounced around the room, but eventually came back to her. "How did you get access to this place?"

"It doesn't matter," she said. "We're not staying."

"We're not?"

A few weeks ago he'd reminded her that he'd taken her on a thoroughly unique date in the Undercity—ignoring the fact that they'd both almost died from a horde of magic-eating spiders. It was her turn to reveal something of herself, so she chose the flip side of the city.

Aurie opened the window. A brisk wind billowed into the room, throwing her hair around her face. The latch had been magically held, but was no match for her craftwork.

After slipping off her sneakers and socks, she stepped onto the ledge, hanging on with one hand, swaying back and forth. She couldn't help the sly smile slithering to her lips. The night city was beautiful, but she didn't have time to enjoy it yet.

"You can climb in those, right?" she asked.

Zayn looked down at his dark jeans, black button-down shirt, and stylish boots. He cocked a smile, the boy in him coming through. "I can climb in anything."

"Meet me at the top," she said, pulling herself onto the ledge above the window. Before he'd arrived, she'd cast the necessary spells to make the climb. Her fingers had ridges like gecko fingers, while dime-sized suction cups covered her toes and the balls of her feet.

Zayn leaned out the window, looking up. "Are you sure about this?"

"Are you afraid?"

"Fear isn't a bad thing," he said. "Keeps you safe. Keeps you from doing stupid things."

"It's not stupid if you're prepared," she said. "I *know* you can climb, or you wouldn't be in your hall. But since you seem to lack the proper motivation, I'll wager you that the first person to the top gets to make the other do whatever they want."

The dare had the expected reaction. She could see the hungry look in his eyes.

"You wouldn't stand a chance," he said.

"I'll see you at the top," she said, and took another pull upward.

"I never said I agreed!" he shouted into the wind.

"Too bad!" she yelled over her shoulder, staying focused on moving upward at a good clip.

This wasn't the first time she'd made the climb. A few weeks ago, she'd gotten frustrated with mendancy and started poking around, hoping she could find a way into Invictus' apartments. She knew the likelihood was nil that she'd actually discover a way in, but it was better than doing something she knew she'd fail at.

She'd climbed the Spire in the hopes of getting a glimpse of his rooms, but the windows were made of black glass. Only after a couple of sessions of exploring did she realize the patrons, and especially the Cabal, would have already tried to get in this way.

The wind was brutal the further up she went. From the open window to the roof was seven hundred feet, give or take a few stories, since she hadn't exactly been measuring. It would only get worse as she went. Her fastest time was forty-seven minutes.

Aurie glanced down to see something dark moving perpendicular to the window. It moved out of sight before she could get a good look at it. She assumed it was Zayn, but it hadn't looked like him. Whatever spell he'd used had made him look hairy, and maybe with an extra leg or arm or something.

Gusts did their best to throw her off, but she'd gotten used to the rising whistle as the wind raced around the Spire and crouched against the glass when it got too bad. Halfway up, her arms grew tired, but there was nowhere to rest, except the roof.

She made the top an hour before midnight, rolling onto

her back to catch her breath and reverse the gecko finger and octopus toes. Forty-two minutes. A new record.

The top of the Spire was fifty feet in diameter. A metal tower at the center rose into the clouds with alternating red and white beacon lights warning away low-flying planes.

The clouds were restless like an upside-down sea in a storm. Aurie watched as the gondolas soared far beneath her, tiny lights moving across the sky on invisible wires.

Watching the city made her skin tingle with expectation. For as long as she'd known she could wield magic, she'd wanted to come to Invictus. Not just the Hundred Halls, but the city itself, revel in its shops and sights, breathe the air that always had a hint of ozone about it. When she was six, she'd drawn a map of the city on the wall of her bedroom in crayon. Her parents were mad at first, but when they saw the detail she'd put into the cartography, they let it stay.

"This view is amazing," said Zayn, coming up from behind her.

Once again, he let her hear him, but she knew he could be as silent as thoughts.

Zayn put his arms around her. She leaned into him, resting the back of her head on his shoulder. He was only a few inches taller than her, so he cradled her against him, breath softly exhaling against her neck, bringing gooseflesh to her arms. She wanted him, but was content to wait for the right moment.

"I didn't know this place was up here," he said after a time.

"Not many do. There are names carved into the concrete around the rim, some with years. Students have been coming up here for a long time," she replied.

He pointed to the left, into the fifth ward. The Stone Singer Hall was lit up like a colorful flower. The massive concrete petals were usually open during the day and closed at night, but it appeared there was some occasion happening. It could have been her imagination, but she swore she could hear music rising up through the air from that Hall, even though it was too far away to be possible.

"You can see every Hall from here," he said.

"If you know where to look. I found about thirty-one and then I gave up."

She pulled away and slipped the knapsack covered with buttons off her back. Zayn eyed her curiously, examining and flicking a button reading "I Heart Dusty Tomes" with his fingernail. Ignoring him, she opened the empty sack and after maneuvering her hand around, pulled out a couple of bottles of chilled water.

"Nice trick," he said, poking the canvas with a finger. "I thought that thing was empty."

"It is." She held it up. A mist swirled inside the canvas bag.

He grabbed her arm, jaw dropping. "You've got a portal in there."

"It's not as impressive as you think. Only goes back to a trunk in my room where I left a few things for tonight," she said.

He examined the construction of the miniature portal, forehead bunched, shaking his head as if he were looking at a talking pig.

"We embedded runic switches into a titanium wire frame with obsidian chips creating the scaffolding for the portal," she explained.

"Ignoring how you acquired runic switches, how did you come up with this? You're a second-year initiate. A damn good one, but this is mastery work," he said.

Aurie knew it was good, but she hadn't considered it was

that remarkable. The idea for the construction of the device had come from her parents' notes. She and Pi had been working on it in their spare time, knowing it might be useful later. It didn't have much range—the portal could only reach the length of the city—but it was handy.

"Are you done admiring? Or did you forget that you lost the bet?" she asked, lips parted slightly, tongue resting on her teeth.

"Um...I am ready to submit to your wishes," he said, responding with his own playful grin. At one corner, a little dimple formed.

"Good," she said, placing a single finger into his chest. "Jump off the tower."

He had a brief epileptic reaction. "What?"

"Jump off," she said, letting the corner of her grin grow wider. "Or are you afraid?"

He glanced around him, suddenly worried. "I don't understand."

"I won. So you have to do as I say. I want you to jump off the tower," she said, relishing his unease.

At that moment, a gust of wind battered them both, streamers from the clouds whipping past the tower. The smell of a storm brewing tickled her nose.

"Fine," she said, shoving the canvas knapsack into his gut. "If you won't jump off, I will."

Before he could say a word otherwise, she sprinted to the east side, and in one leap, cleared the safety wall. A rush of adrenaline turned her into one big laughing scream as she fell. She knew he had to be freaking out, and the moment she went over the edge, she was too, no matter how many times she'd done it.

After about thirty feet of falling, the safety enchantment kicked in, slowed her descent, then reversed her movement, sending her stomach into her throat, before launching her back onto the roof like a slingshot.

Zayn had reached the edge about the time she came flying back up. She hit the concrete and tumbled onto her knees and side, laughing as if the world was laughing with her.

"What the fuck," he said, face etched with worry. He looked near to tears. "You gave me a heart attack."

She let him help her up. Kissed him on the cheek as a reward before pulling away.

"Let me guess," he said, slowly recovering. "There's a reverse gravity field surrounding the tower."

She nodded enthusiastically. "Your turn."

He didn't seem eager, but he reluctantly handed over the bag. He took off in a northern direction. Aurie quickly grabbed his arm.

"No, not that way," she said.

"Now you're just messing with me," he said.

"No, really. The enchantment's weaker on that side. I'm not saying you'd fall, but let's not chance it," she said.

He backed up and jumped in the same location she had. A string of expletives followed him over, then like a Doppler effect when a car goes screaming past, the curses came back. He landed on his feet like a gymnast after a tumbling pass. Aurie was jealous, since she usually fell.

"I can't believe I just did that," he said, holding his hands out, fingers splayed, as if he were trying to keep the world in one place.

Then before she could approach him, he turned and ran the other way, leaping to the west side, a howl of victory disappearing and then reappearing. He went back and forth a few times before finally strolling up to her, eyes wide, tongue wagging, and generally wigged out from adrenaline.

"I'll never ride another rollercoaster again," he said. "That was sick. Sick, sick, sick. Jump with me."

He reached out to her, and she stepped inside his grasp, bunching the front of his shirt in her fists, latching onto his lower lip with her teeth gently, but firmly. He mewed with enjoyment and tucked his arm around her neck, cinching her closer.

They kissed: sweet, probing, hungry.

While he'd been jumping, she'd pulled a blanket from her room and laid it on the concrete. She pushed him down, straddling his leg, putting her fingernails against his neck.

The clothes came off faster than she'd planned, but she was a victim of her own success, rising to his need. She traced the dark webbing on his chest, nibbling, biting, digging.

She guided him towards her as he quivered with excitement.

"Did...you?" he asked, trying to form the word.

"I cast the proper spells," she said, enjoying the way he was enraptured of her touch.

Once they had joined, there was heat, a slow burn, rising and falling. She was worried he was too excited, but he seemed to catch himself, and they rocked together on the top of the Spire, winds proving a touch of cool air, lasting until the sky crackled with electricity.

They came together, screams lost amid the approaching thunder, collapsed, cradled together, and whispered soft words to each other. It was exactly as Aurie had wanted it.

Propped on an elbow facing him, she traced her fingers across his naked chest, while he kneaded her hip absently. Their feet were tangled, and all seemed right in the world. It was, as far as she could remember, one of the happiest moments of her life.

"What will you do after you graduate?" she asked, trying not to sound needy.

He closed his eyes tightly and shook off the question. "I'd rather not talk about it."

A twinge of jealousy hit her in the gut. Did he have a girlfriend back home when he returned? Was his relationship with Priyanka more than as an assistant? The thoughts were brief, and painful, but she shut them off before they could spiral out of control. Better not to borrow trouble.

His eyes brimmed with sadness, burdens carried with quiet stoicism.

"What is it?" she asked him. "You can talk to me."

"I want to. I really do. I've really been enjoying this," he said.

She kissed him. He didn't quite kiss back. An idea formed, born on the suspicions her sister had confided. She decided to test him.

"Are you worried about the wish spell?" she asked.

He was a better liar than she would have guessed. He acted like it was the first time he'd heard of it, even though she knew better.

"What are you talking about?" he asked.

She pushed herself into a sitting position. It seemed rather odd to be naked on the roof of a building having a serious conversation, but it seemed silly to put clothes on now.

"Back when we first met, you mentioned a project you needed help with. You asked about a book called *Impossible Magics*, but you never asked again about it," she said.

He sat up, crossed his legs, and looked her in the eyes. "I figured since you didn't mention it that Arcanium didn't have a copy."

"Are you sure you're not looking for a wish spell?" she asked, drilling her gaze into him.

The intense focus made him look away. "Of course not."

She decided to drop the hammer. "Then why did you ask

Lady Amethyte about it?"

His head snapped around. "No. I don't know how you know about that, but no. That's not what that was about. I told you. There's a project I'm working on. Lady Amethyte was answering some questions for me."

Aurie sighed. "Zayn. There's no reason to lie to me. I know you're looking for the wish spell. You work for Priyanka Sai. I know she put you up to this. I've wanted to believe in us all along, but if you're not going to be honest with me..."

He grew angry, squeezed his hands into fists beside his head. "I'm telling you. It's not what it looks like." He bit his lower lip and shook his head back and forth slowly as if it caused him great pain. "I can't explain why, or what it is that I'm doing, but trust me. This isn't for *them*."

The way he said it, the way he said them, she knew exactly what he meant. The Cabal.

"Zayn, you can tell me. I'm...well, I like you a lot. Whatever's going on, I can help," she said.

Zayn grabbed his clothes and started shoving his legs into his jeans, the muscles on his stomach rippling.

"No, you can't. I mean, you can, but you can't," he said. "Stop talking about this."

"See!" she said, latching onto his moment of indecision. "I can help. You said so."

He looked at his palms as if he were seeing something there. "No. I shouldn't have come. We shouldn't be doing this. I don't want...I don't want..." He paused, looking straight at her. "I don't really want you. I've been using you. It's a game at the hall. We have to pick a girl and seduce her. Make her believe that we like her."

His words were cold shards of glass against her throat. "You don't mean that."

He stood taller, face slowly hardening into a mask of a

person she didn't know.

"Are you really that naive? I told you I'm Priyanka's assistant. You're a second year. Don't you think she knows exactly what I'm doing all the time? I needed something from you and now I don't. It's over. You can go back to your pathetic hall."

It felt like ribbons of hot metal were constricting her chest so she couldn't breathe. It took every ounce of self-control not to lash out with magic. He sensed the faez bubbling up and tilted his head in a dare.

"Zayn. What is going on? I don't believe any of this," she said, desperate to return to the feelings she had only a short while ago.

"It doesn't matter if you believe it. It only matters that you leave. Go back to your hall. Forget about me. Worry about your silly contest, and figure out who your real enemy is," he said.

A bolt of lightning slipped past the Spire, blinding Aurie, the instant thunder making her duck. As she cleared her eyes, she realized he was gone.

A void opened in her chest, sucking all her emotions into it. For a moment, she'd thought the old Zayn had been speaking to her, but realized that was only her wishful thinking. She'd been a fool to think they had a relationship.

Aurie stood naked on the top of the Spire, watching the storm cross the city, the tiny hairs across her body attuned to the energy, contemplating where she'd gone wrong. No cathartic rains fell, leaving her agitated, thoughts swirling like the clouds in the sky. Eventually, Aurie realized if she didn't get moving soon, she'd be spotted climbing down when the sun came up.

Clothed and enchanted, she took one last look at the spot where she and Zayn had been together, memories already turning bitter in the hazy light of reality. Life was like that, sweetest before the fall, marbled with fears and laughter. No guarantees that even the brightest moments wouldn't fade away as quickly as looking away from the sun. She began her climb downward, heavy, sad, alert. She wouldn't make the same mistake again.

25

A headache as big as a dragon was sitting behind Pi's forehead, exhaling flame against the back of her eyes. She lay on the couch outside the contest room with a bag of ice on her forehead moaning softly.

From the kitchen she heard Aurie pop the top of an energy potion and chug it. Pi wanted the sweet release of sleep, not to be awake enduring the post-mortem echoes that haunted her.

"I swear it's getting worse each death," said Aurie, holding the can to her forehead.

Pi sat up, and instantly regretted it. "I think the death residue is building up. Violet's little posse of cheaters is going to win soon anyway. If the Cabal gets the wish spell, we're all screwed."

Aurie didn't speak and stared at the blank wall as if it held dark secrets.

"Sorry, sis. I shouldn't have brought her up," said Pi. "We've been stumbling from one disaster to another. As advertised, hubris will be the death of me."

Aurie glowered in her direction. "Speaking of hubris. When are you going to start acting like a team in there? You keep disappearing at the important moments, and when things go to hell, you escape into the forest."

Pi's face warmed with embarrassment. She'd been exploring the area around the fort, trying to figure out what seemed wrong to her. "I really don't think the whole thing is set up like we think it is. And we're not getting anywhere doing what we're doing. The top teams are on wave nine, and we're back at five."

"I'm not sure why you don't think it's a fort. It's got walls and everything," said Aurie. "Try to work with us. You're always doing things on your own."

Pi was a big ball of tangled emotions inside. She hated going against the group, but they kept wanting to beat their heads against the wall.

"The contest is about strategy and tactics, and using the talents of the whole team. When are you going to see that, Pi? Or are you going to ignore everything again like you did with Radoslav and cause serious harm?" said Aurie.

Pi regretted telling her sister about the encounter with the Jade Queen, not because Radoslav had told her not to, but because Aurie kept bringing it up as an example of her failings. She'd only done it to prove to Aurie that Zayn wasn't any good. Priyanka had given the Ruby Queen an assassin spider as a way to start a war.

"At least I learned about what a liar Zayn was; otherwise, you'd probably still be mooning over his every word," said Pi, instantly regretting the tone, but Aurie seemed to accept it with heavy regrets.

"I thought he actually liked me until the very end when he told me it was only a game. Even then I didn't believe it," said Aurie.

"I still think it has to do with the wish spell," said Pi.

"It's got to be the prize at the end of the contest. That's

the only thing that makes sense, and the Cabal must have enough teams that are nearing the end to feel confident they're going to get it. Invictus even said *you'd wish you'd won* in the memory gem," said Aurie.

"What if he knew he was going to die when he made that?" said Pi, remembering the way his skin had been discolored, his hair matted. He'd been a living ruin.

"I don't know," said Aurie. "We'll never know since we're not going to win the contest."

"What about Nezumi?" asked Pi.

Aurie's face pinched to a point. "That's not fair."

"You brought up my trip to the land of the maetrie," said Pi.

"It's relevant."

Pi crossed her arms. "We can't just leave him and his family to the demon. You and I both know that our protections aren't working anymore. It's only a matter of time before he figures out where they are. Hell, the damn thing might decide we're interfering and come after us. We can't just wait for it to make its move."

Aurie threw her hands up. "Don't you think I've thought of that! I can't fix everything. Hell, I can't fix any of it. Violet's going to win the contest, the Cabal's going to figure out how to use the wish, the two of us can't beat that stupid demon."

"I'm so sorry, Aurie. I'm such a shit sister. I've been little help, causing new problems instead of solving some," said Pi.

Aurie climbed onto the couch. They shared a smile. The last few weeks had been hard, and it was only going to get harder.

"Too many problems, not enough solutions," said Aurie, shaking her head softly.

"What if we have solutions and don't realize it?" asked Pi, unformed thoughts coiling through her mind.

"Talk sense, sis," said Aurie.

Words tumbled from Pi's lips as fast as they formed. "Maybe we need some cross-training. Flex our muscles in different ways. You know doing the same thing over and over again and expecting different results is insanity. So let's try something different."

"It's a fort, Pi," said Aurie.

"Not that. Nezumi and the demon Grat. What if we took the Harpers against it? I'm sure this is something the six of us can handle," said Pi.

Aurie cringed. "I'm not sure I like the idea of putting them at risk. In the contest, we don't really die. If Grat kills us, we don't come back."

"Then why did you become a mage if you weren't willing to take risks?" said Pi.

"I know. I'm not disagreeing. But it's easier to sign yourself up for risk than to ask others," said Aurie.

"It's up to them if they want to do it," said Pi. "We can't force them, but I think it's important. We can't let the Cabal get the wish spell. Who knows what they would do with it."

"Become the head patron," said Aurie.

A moment passed between them as they looked each other in the eye. They both knew the idea had crossed the point of no return.

"Fine!" said Aurie. "Let's double down on our insanity and go out swinging."

"That's the spirit," said Pi.

"You contact the team," said Aurie. "I have some things to look into about our demon Grat that have been bothering me."

"I was hoping you'd contact them. They like you better," said Pi.

"What better way to learn some teamwork than to take a job you don't like?" said Aurie.

Pi growled and poked Aurie in the leg.

"I guess," said Pi with a wink.

As much as she hated that her sister was right, it gave her joy to be working with her. That was the thing she missed the most about not having a functioning family. Aurie was her sister, but their responsibilities kept them from spending as much time together as they'd like. Taking another run at the demon Grat, despite the horrible danger, would be great for more sisterly bonding. She just hoped it wouldn't also be the end if one of them got hurt.

26

The Harpers met outside the boarded-up clinic, the place that had once been called Enchanting Apparel. It'd been painful to nail the boards up, because it had felt like failure, but Aurie hoped to rectify that today.

"Thank you all for coming on short notice," she said. "I know everyone's got a lot to do with finals coming up."

Hannah rolled to a stop. Rigel and Raz leaned against the dragon fountain. Echo had found a ladybug and was letting it crawl back and forth across his hands. Only Pi seemed ready for what was to come, biting her lower lip with increasing ferocity.

"Anything to help," said Hannah, "though I don't understand what we're doing here."

The others voiced their agreement. Aurie was confused until she saw Pi's body language shift away. "Pi? What did you tell them?"

"I may have been vague on the details, but heavy on the cross-training bit," she said.

"Why are we here?" asked Raz, looking between the sisters. "I've got vocal lessons tomorrow morning early. I only came because it sounded important."

"Pi," growled Aurie.

She couldn't believe her sister. She'd given her one thing to do.

"Look, Aurie, they wouldn't have come for the clinic. As important as it is to you, and to me being your sister and all, the others needed more persuasion," said Pi.

Rigel shook his head. "Look. Not to bugger on about it, but we've got a lot on our plates. Bloody get to the point."

This wasn't going as planned. Aurie wanted to slink away and forget the whole thing. Why the hell was she doing this? She put her face in her hands.

"Wub-wub," said Pi. "Tell them about wub-wub."

Even Aurie looked at her sister as if she'd gone crazy. Then she remembered Annabelle's doll. Right.

"Yeah, tell us about wub-wub," said Raziyah, a fierce look in her eye.

"There's this family of..." Aurie almost said non-humans, but decided against it since she didn't know the prejudices of her friends. "This, well, poor family, they got attacked by Grat's minions, who's this pseudo-demon, forcing them from their home."

She indicated the three-story brick house on the other side of the street. The glass on the front door was still missing.

"When they tried to help us, Grat found out. Luckily, we got them away, and have been keeping them safe until we can figure out a way to stop this demon, or whatever he is. But it's not working anymore. It's going to figure out where they are, and when it does, I don't know. I just don't know," she said.

The team looked skeptical. She wasn't winning them over with her argument. Aurie decided that she had to tell the whole truth, then let them decide.

"It's bigger than Nezumi and his family. We need to win

the contest," she said.

"Yeah, we know," said Hannah. "I'd like a good grade in that class, and the prize sounds really cool, even if we don't know what it is."

"We know what it is, and that's why we have to win it," said Aurie. "The prize is a wish spell."

They exclaimed their surprise.

"Brilliant," said Rigel, eyes full of ideas.

"No, not brilliant," said Aurie. "Bad. Really bad. That wish spell in the wrong hands could be disastrous."

"If that's the prize for the contest," said Raziyah, "then why aren't we taking another go at the bugs?"

"Because the semester is almost over. We've only got one more shot in there. We've got to figure out how to work as a team without ruining our last chance," said Pi.

"Count me in," said Hannah. "Not because of the wish spell, but because I'd never forgive myself if something happened to either of you because I wasn't there." Then she pulled a pair of manacles from a back pocket. "These will come in handy. They're resistant to spell work."

"Why did you have those in your back pocket?" asked Aurie.

Hannah gave her a look, the one that reminded her that Hannah was far more adventurous than the rest of them.

"Right," said Aurie. "Moving on."

Rigel raised an eyebrow. "Wub-wub is a kid's doll?"

"The girl's name is Annabelle," said Pi.

"Count me in. I've got a younger sister. Couldn't imagine anything happening to her. You either," he added with a wink. "And I'd like a crack at the spell. I could be the next Frank Orpheum with it."

"Echo helps Aurie and Annabelle," said Ernie with a grin.

Raziyah, who at this point had been standing back with a

skeptical expression, put her hand on Echo's shoulder. "Echo, I don't think you know what you're getting into."

"Echo helps Aurie and Annabelle," he repeated.

Raziyah turned. "Aurie. It's great that you're trying to help these people, and I'm not sure about this wish thing, but you can't ask Echo. It's not right."

Aurie sighed. She felt the same way. She'd been debating with herself about allowing Echo to come along, but if she didn't then wouldn't that be making him different than the rest of them? He could handle himself so long as he had good direction.

"Echo help Aurie and Annabelle, just like Raz and Pi help Echo," he said.

The dark-skinned girl pushed her glasses up her nose. "Echo. You might die. This is dangerous." She looked at the others. "I can't let you do this. He can't make this decision himself. For god's sake, he repeats everything and plays with flowers during the contest. I'm sorry, Echo. I can't let you help."

As she tugged on his arm, Echo pulled away with a determined look on his face. As if another person inhabited him, he straightened and said, "Better to die in service to others than to live in fear of being yourself."

The words were a slap to Raziyah. She took a step back, almost looked like she was going to tumble onto her rear. Whatever fight she had in her faded. For a moment, Aurie didn't even recognize Echo. He had the same chubby face and vacant grin, but there was a hard glint in his eye. But as soon as she saw it, it was gone.

She didn't know what to think about the exchange. It was as if Raziyah feared Echo, which seemed ludicrous. The others sensed it as well, as uneasy glances were exchanged frequently. Was Echo who she thought he was? Based on her reaction, Raz had sensed it, too.

"We should get going," said Pi. "While it's not late yet, we don't want to get caught here in the dark. Bad things."

"If you don't want to do this, Raz, I totally understand," she said.

Raziyah couldn't meet her gaze. She had a look of a scolded child.

"Why are you doing this?" asked Raziyah. "Why do you care about Nezumi or this wish spell? Is this because you want it for yourself?"

A tightness formed in Aurie's chest. "If we don't help them, no one will. This isn't only about Nezumi and his family. This place here used to be filled with people, a vibrant district. The district is a symptom of the whole city's problems. Don't you see it? It's decaying piece by piece, street by street. But a city isn't made of buildings, or cobblestones, it's made of people, and if they don't stand up and stop what's happening, there won't be a city anymore. Especially if someone else gets the wish spell, someone who doesn't have the people's best interests in mind. So I'm standing up, and I'm asking you to stand up with me. If you don't want to, then fine. We'll do it on our own."

Raziyah side-eyed Echo and said softly, "I'll join you."

This only confused Aurie further. She needed the Harpers to work together. Teamwork was the only way they were going to get through it safely. She shared a glance with Pi, who had the same reservations, based on the frown haunting her lips as she looked at Echo. Maybe leaving him out of it was the safer course? But she needed everyone, and she'd made a big, stupid speech, so it wasn't like she could back out now.

"If we're doing this," said Raziyah, "can you at least tell us what we're up against? You said something about a demon."

"Pseudo-demon. Looks like one, but a salt circle didn't

hold it. Walked right out," said Pi.

"Maybe you didn't make the circle correctly," offered Hannah.

Pi raised an eyebrow. "Really?"

Hannah shook her head. "Right. Forget that. Not a demon. Check."

"So you know what it's not," said Raziyah. "That doesn't help that much."

"It had wings and other attributes of a demon, but other things bothered me," said Aurie. "Like why did it stay here after being summoned? Demons aren't usually happy homemakers. Usually, an escaped demon would rampage a while until the patrons put it down. Which means it's something else. Maybe a doppelganger, a kapre, or a rakshasa."

Raziyah shook her head. "Can't be a doppelganger if it had wings. They can't create appendages that aren't there. Same for the rakshasa. It's a shape-shifting thing, though you'd have to ask an animalian for confirmation."

"Kapres live in trees and aren't evil," said Hannah.

"How do you know?" asked Aurie.

Hannah reached down and pulled up her pant leg, revealing a tattoo of a bearded giant sitting in a grandfather oak.

"Well then," said Aurie. "Other ideas?"

"Tell us more about what you saw," said Raziyah.

Aurie explained the encounters with the wakers and the winged creature.

"Maybe it's an illusionist?" asked Hannah.

Rigel shook his head vehemently. "No way. That's world-class magery. No way to create those wakers, break windows, mimic the sounds and smells she described, especially on short notice. It would take a whole theater troop and weeks of planning. Which makes it bloody impossible."

"Winged vampire?" offered Raziyah. "Might explain the wakers. Could be weird thralls."

"He attacked us in broad daylight at his home," said Aurie.

"What about the maetrie? They're tricky bastards and they frequent the city," said Hannah.

Aurie looked to Pi, who shook her head softly. "No. Nothing like them."

"Maybe we're going about it all wrong. It's just weird to me that this creature has made its home in the Enochian district. What's so special about this place?" asked Aurie.

The silence stretched between them until Echo spoke. "Dragon is power."

Aurie was going to ask him to take the discussion seriously until she noticed him staring at the dragon fountain. No one else had taken heed of his words except Raziyah, who stared at him curiously. When they shared a look, Raz shrugged her shoulders.

"Can you repeat that?" asked Aurie.

"Dragon is power," he said.

"What do you mean?" she asked, getting chills regardless.

"Dragon, sphinx, mermaid, griffon," Echo said. "Dragon, sphinx, mermaid, griffon."

"I don't get it," said Pi.

Echo looked frustrated. "Dragon is power?"

"Like power how?" asked Aurie.

He looked constipated. "Wells of magic."

Rigel snapped his fingers. "The fountains! There are four of these in the city. A dragon fountain, the one here, and three others: sphinx, mermaid, and griffon. I remember it from the Hundred Halls website. It mentioned the fountains as a sightseeing tour, but wells of magic, I'm not sure about that."

"Shit," said Pi, staring sideways at the stone embedded with the poem. Aurie knew exactly what she was thinking.

Their parents had used the power in the area to construct a portal to the tomb in Egypt, the one they'd used to retrieve the Rod of Dominion. She wondered if the well of magic had something to do with the wish spell.

"Yeah," said Aurie. "He's right. There's a well of power below. We were exploring once and found some weird things. Thought it was residue from the city. Guess we were wrong."

"That's probably why those wakers are here," said Hannah.

"Doesn't explain the pseudo-demon," said Pi.

Raziyah was staring at her hands, squeezing them as if they ached. "Something wrong, Raz?"

She looked up and noticed everyone staring at her. "Got a bad feeling about this."

Aurie couldn't disagree. Something seemed out of whack, but time was running out to help Nezumi. If she didn't act now, he'd be screwed. There was no way Pi could protect him on her own, and it'd probably get her killed if she tried.

"Maybe we're not going to figure out what it is," said Aurie. "But whatever it is, the six of us can handle it."

"We know it has magic," said Pi. "That much we know."

Using an app on Hannah's phone that she had for making maps for her role-playing games, they sketched out the plan. Since they didn't know what Grat was, nor did they want to straight-up murder him, the goal was to knock him out so they could question him and find out how to make him leave. If it came to it, they would resort to deadly magics, but they preferred not to.

They decided to split the party and approach the house from the front and the back. Hannah argued against the tactic, claiming it always caused total party kills in her games, but the others accepted the plan.

Aurie took Echo and Hannah to the front, while Pi took Rigel and Raziyah to the back. Rigel would signal when they were in place with a bird whistle. He started to go on about what birds were found in the city, but they cut him off, since the demon wouldn't know either. He decided on a whippoorwill.

Hannah crouched behind the fence, while Aurie kept her hand on the gate and Echo crouched behind her. When they got to the door, Hannah would knock it down like a battering ram on her skates.

"When we go inside," she whispered to Echo, "you stay at the door to protect our escape."

She wasn't really worried about the escape, but didn't want him to get hurt. She didn't know if she'd be able to forgive herself.

After ten minutes of waiting, Aurie got nervous. It shouldn't have taken them that long to get into position. Hannah looked equally worried.

"Did we not hear it?" she asked Hannah in a hushed voice.

"Not sure."

Another ten minutes later, Aurie suspected something was wrong and crept towards the house to see if they'd gone inside already. She got halfway to the front door when a bird whistle rose above the house. It was the whippoorwill's song, but not by Rigel's lips, as he had a way of making a bird whistle sound like a summer day. By the time she realized this, it was too late. Hannah was already careening towards the front door, readying a spell to blast it wide open.

27

A tabby cat leapt down from a ledge, sprinting down the alleyway between the stagnant puddles. The feline gave them a parting meow before disappearing through a hole in a fence. Rigel wiped his damp forehead. His black hair glistened with sweat.

"You going to be okay?" asked Pi.

Rigel swallowed heavily. "I'll be fine. I get nervous before a performance."

Raziyah looked like she was about to remind him that it wasn't a performance, so Pi shook her off.

"If you're not up for this, there's no shame in staying back," said Pi.

He cleared his throat. "I'll be fine."

Pi wasn't sure she believed him.

The back of Grat's brick house had a wooden fence surrounding it. Pi opened the gate and stuck her head inside the backyard.

A tap on the shoulder brought her around.

"Did you hear that?" asked Raziyah, face pinched in concentration.

"No," said Pi.

Everyone was jumpy. The other two looked like she could play them like a violin. Pi was a little twitchy herself, but wasn't going to let them know it.

After a deep breath, Raziyah put a finger to her lips and crept up the alleyway. The nerdy stone singer moved as if she were getting constantly shocked by static electricity. She stopped at a passage between two houses, gave the sign to hold for a second, and stepped inside it.

Not seeing Raziyah made Pi nervous. If something happened, she wouldn't be able to help.

She motioned for Rigel to stay put and jogged to the location Raziyah had disappeared. Right before she got there, the black girl stepped out and shrugged, looking visibly relieved.

As they moved back to Rigel, Pi caught movement in the corner of her eye. Someone was watching them from the window of a nearby house. As they walked, Pi cast a spell, turning her palm into a flat mirror. Almost as soon as she directed the reflecting surface, the person disappeared, but not before she had identified the spy.

Zayn.

Everything seemed wrong.

Pi froze, which she knew had probably given away that she'd seen him.

Raziyah arched an eyebrow.

"Wait here," said Pi, and moved into the backyard of the house she'd seen Zayn in. If he was spying on them, it had grave implications for what was happening in the Enochian District. Pi wondered if this "demon" wasn't a plant from the Cabal. What if this area had to do with the wish spell? Maybe they needed it to make it work? Kind of like the portal needed the extra faez to reach all the way to Egypt. She paused, deciding between confronting Zayn and taking the other two back to Aurie's group to abort the plan.

Pi was on the back porch when she saw a man in a lime green Sundrop T-shirt ambling through the alleyway in a daze. By his slack expression and foot dragging pace, Pi knew it was one of the wakers that Aurie had told her about. She looked at the shining sun. Had Aurie been mistaken about their avoidance of daylight?

She spied another waker, a blonde woman in a peasant dress, coming from the other direction. She had scales on her arms and neck indicating she was a non-human. Raziyah and Rigel had noticed. They motioned towards her, asking what to do.

Zayn slipped out the front, moving into the next street. If she moved fast, she could catch him. Pi leapt over the railing and sprinted after him.

His eyes were wide when she appeared in the street. He cast a spell, but she was faster. The impact of the force bolt knocked him from his feet.

More wakers spilled onto the street, leaving their homes in twos and threes. The district wasn't as empty as Aurie thought.

"I'm not your enemy," said Zayn as he climbed to his feet. "You shouldn't have come here."

Before she could knock him back down, he motioned with his hand, blinding her. Pi feared the worst. When she opened her eyes, Zayn was gone.

She ran back towards the others when a whistle ripped through the air. Pi knew that it hadn't come from Rigel. An explosion from the front of the house urged her to run faster. More wakers entered the alleyway. Soon they'd be overrun.

Her heart leapt into her throat when she saw the body. Rigel lay on his stomach, a dark blotch spreading on his back.

Pi checked him to find no pulse. Wakers surrounded her on both sides.

She couldn't believe that he was dead, tugged on his shirt, trying to come to terms with it. *Why did we let them join us? It's all my fault.*

The wakers closed on her.

He had plans to join the summer theater tour. They'd even given him a spotlight performance based on *The Last Mage.* What about his mother? She'd lost her husband last year, and now her son? It wasn't right. It wasn't fair. Pi was shaking.

There was no sign of Raziyah. Had she been kidnapped, or fled whatever had killed Rigel?

Feeling like she had a target on her back, Pi searched around, expecting a giant bug like in the contest. But it was only more wakers.

She didn't want to leave Rigel, even though he was dead. Why did these things have to be coming after her? She wanted to scream but feared drawing more down upon her.

Before the wakers could grab her, she dodged around the slow-moving people toward the back of the house. A battle raged within.

Pi locked the gate behind her. As she ran up the concrete path past manicured bushes, she pulled a handful of explosive seeds from her pocket.

Something whizzed at her head from the side. Pi threw herself to the ground, barely avoiding a spinning blade. Only her verumancy-enhanced reflexes had saved her. She rolled onto her feet and threw two seeds at the fleeing figure. The explosions shattered windows.

Two more seeds were at her fingertips, but she didn't throw them when she realized it was Raziyah who'd attacked her. The diminutive black girl disappeared behind the house.

The feeling that they'd stepped into something much greater than they could handle nearly overwhelmed Pi. Rigel was dead. Raziyah had turned against them. Only fear for her sister got her to put one foot in front of the other toward the back door.

"Don't go in," said a familiar voice from behind her.

Raziyah stood at the back gate. It rattled from the wakers trying to push their way in. The alley was filled with wakers like floodwaters built up behind a dam.

"What are you doing?" asked Pi.

The way Raziyah held herself was like she was a different person. The meek math nerd that was bad at her hall's magic looked more like an MMA fighter about to step into the ring.

"I like you, Pythia. You and your sister both. So I'd rather not do what I had to do with Rigel. Leave now, and don't come back," she said.

A scream from inside the house—Hannah's it sounded like—almost made her turn and run inside, but she knew if she did, then Raziyah would kill her.

"Maybe I don't think you can," said Pi. "I've seen you in action. You can barely kill a bug on your own, let alone me."

This seemed to amuse Raziyah. She took off her glasses and threw them at a tree limb. They landed and spun around the limb like a horseshoe. "You have no idea how hard it is to be bad at something you're oh-so-good at. At least when I was doing stone singer work, the mediocrity was real. I'll give you one more chance and then I'm coming for you."

Before Pi could say anything, Raziyah's form shifted. It was like one of those videos that morphs one person into another, except this was real. Pi understood why Raziyah knew so much about doppelganger physiology. Raziyah was really Priyanka Sai, patron of the Academy of the Subtle Arts. And Pi was so, so utterly screwed.

234   Thomas K. Carpenter

"Face a patron of the deadliest hall as a second-year initiate? Sure, why not," said Pi to herself as a pep talk.

"I'm very sorry about this. I truly am," said Priyanka, producing twin blades in her fists. "Three. Two. One."

Pi raised her arm to launch the seeds when Priyanka blurred forward, almost too fast for the eye to see, almost too fast for thought. Options were limited at that point. Pi could almost feel the blades enter her chest, and knowing that, did the only thing she could. She exploded the seeds. All of them.

28

Grat was waiting for them when Hannah blew the door down. He looked like he'd woken from an all-night bender. Something was wrong with his wings. They'd been leathery and bat-like last time and this time they were more feathery.

To Hannah's credit, she was not deterred. Years of roller derby had taught her how to hit. Grat didn't seem to understand. Maybe he was expecting her to pull up.

She dropped a shoulder into his gut, throwing him across the room into the drywall. A chandelier in the entryway rattled from the impact.

A cheer lifted to Aurie's lips. "Go Hannah!"

Aurie ran in behind her.

Hannah threw a pair of manacles at the fallen demon. She spelled them onto his arms, clicking them into place. He lay on a broken vase.

"Got 'em!" yelled Hannah.

The demon clapped his hands together like a magician signaling a magic trick and the manacles fell off. Then Grat reached out like he was plucking something from Hannah's eyes, and the big girl went limp.

Aurie threw a force bolt, but Grat knocked it away. He'd used the Five Elements gestures, rather than summoning the energy elementally. If Grat was a demon then she was a talking goat. He was most likely human.

They dueled for a minute. Fire. Water. Elemental twists. Rock. Air-knife. Spirit-blast. She hit him hard, but he was quicker. He had fingers like a concert pianist.

They were at an impasse. Her raw skill versus his virtuosity. The house had taken a beating. The walls were blackened, steaming from being caught on fire then doused with waters from the underworld. Tiny air elementals swirled above their heads creating smoke vortexes, only to pop like bubbles at the next pass.

When Hannah grabbed her arm, interrupting her timing, the demon's force blast threw her into the wall. A knifelike ache formed in her side. She'd broken a rib.

Hannah loomed over her, the vacant mask of a waker on her face. An ear-rattling explosion in the backyard broke the dining room windows. The demon Grat moved behind Hannah.

He tried the same trick with the hand gesture towards her face. For a moment, Aurie felt a little sleepy and thought she heard voices whispering in her head, but they were distant enough she could ignore him.

He's trying to hypnotize me, she realized. And with that the rest of the pieces fell into place. The wakers. The reason Grat had walked out of the salt circle. Maybe even why the Enochian District was important.

"You're Frank Orpheum," she said, stopping him in his tracks.

She'd never dispelled an illusion before, but she had an idea, based on mendancy. They were first cousins, magically speaking. It was like knowing the exact thread to pull that would unravel a hastily made sweater.

The illusion fell away, revealing an older man in his rumpled bed clothes. She saw the resemblance to the Frank Orpheum she'd seen on TV shows or on the movies, but this one looked like a carved wooden version that had been left out in the sun too long.

He wasn't even that attractive. He had a thin mustache and a weaselly face. She could almost imagine him pressing his face against a window, peeping on other people's lives.

The disgust that reflected from her face enraged him. With a simple hand wave, he brought back a more handsome version of himself, the one she'd seen in the theater. He looked ready to strangle her.

This little distraction gave Aurie a chance to work a second spell. With a word, the anchor on the chandelier weakened. Aurie pulled it from the ceiling. Frank Orpheum dove out of the way before it crushed him.

Aurie climbed to her feet, grimacing with the pain in her side. She'd made it onto the first stair when a gut-punching explosion rocked the back of the house, blowing glass throughout the levels. Aurie hoped her sister was nowhere near that blast. Windows for a block had shattered. The back door had been knocked off its hinges. She ran up the stairs, taking two steps, then stopping for air. It hurt so much to breathe.

The streets were filled with hundreds of wakers. She knew what they were now. Frank Orpheum had hypnotized them like he had that stadium full of people a bunch of years ago as a stunt. He'd made them into zombies. It explained why the streets of the district hadn't looked totally deserted, why the glass in front of her clinic had been cleaned up. They probably came and went during the night, and didn't stir during the day.

She also knew what she'd seen on the first floor last time,

and had gotten a brief glimpse of again today. Orpheum had access to the Garden Network in the house.

Shit, she thought, *Echo is out front with the wakers.* There was nothing she could do about it now. She needed to get herself and the others out of here. They were completely outmatched against a patron of the halls.

Aurie ascended the second flight, reaching the third floor, and Hannah appeared. At first she thought Hannah had shaken the hypnotism, until she charged Aurie.

"Slick," she said, convincing the floor that it was made of grease, and stepped out of the way.

Hannah careened towards the window. Too fast. Her friend went through it. Limping after, she found Hannah lying on the roof of the two-story building next door.

A wailing cry came from the front. The wakers had captured Echo and like a group of ants, carried him towards the house. Where were the others? Rigel, Raziyah, and her sister? They should have entered the house by now.

Aurie stuck her head out the shattered window, boots crunching on broken glass, and spied a motionless figure lying in a small crater. It was her sister.

"No!"

Awoken faez swirled around in her in a rage. The broken bones in her side knitted themselves with a thought. She would not be stopped. Frank Orpheum would pay for this. Pi was everything to her, the only thing in the world.

Aurie was on her way down the second flight when she saw someone coming up. At first she thought it was a waker. Then she saw the familiar face minus her glasses. Raziyah looked like she'd been through a war zone. Her right eye was swollen, lip blooded, and she had a limp. It looked like she'd survived the explosion that had killed her sister. Raziyah looked on the verge of tears.

"Aurie," she said, her face breaking in a way that told Aurie to fear the worst.

Aurie hesitated. How had Raz gotten past Orpheum? She disbelieved any illusions, and her friend remained. It wasn't a trick.

"Where's Orpheum?" she asked, trembling.

"I didn't see him," said Raziyah. "But your sister, I'm sorry. She's..."

Raziyah held out her arms. The whole world shifted around Aurie, and she accepted the embrace rather than collapse on her knees. If she hadn't seen Frank Orpheum, then maybe he'd fled through the Garden Network portal, and there was nothing she could do now.

The next question never made it to her lips. The blade went into her chest, piercing her heart with a cold efficiency. The pain was surprising. It was like her soul had been dunked in ice.

Raziyah had an expression of sorrow, which only confused Aurie further until she saw the blade slip out of her chest, covered in rich, dark blood.

The form of Raziyah shifted into Priyanka Sai. She was a doppelganger. There had been no illusion to dispel.

Words failed, swept away by a river of darkness that rose up. Faez dissipated like a dream dispelled by reality. *This is how it ends*? Aurie clutched at Priyanka, who gently set her against the wall. A gurgle formed in her throat, followed by a bubble of blood on her lips. Then cold came, death unending, until she was no more.

29

The explosion had shattered every window within a block. Zayn looked down upon the fallen figure, knowing without a doubt that she was dead. The other one, his patron, didn't move for a few moments either.

Zayn had mixed emotions as he waited. If Priyanka was dead, then he was free, but would never be able to practice his magic again. On the other hand, if she wasn't, then almost nothing had changed for him.

The dark haired woman stirred. Zayn considered slipping down there and putting a dagger into her back while she was disoriented, but decided against it. For one, even in her weakened state, Priyanka could still take him, and two, he wasn't about to murder someone in cold blood, even if that's what he'd been trained to do.

He watched her stumble to the crater and check Pythia's pulse. The soft shake of her head told him what he needed to know. She was dead. Zayn tried not to let that bother him. He was supposed to be detached from his feelings. Five years in the hall should have erased that from him, but the tugging went deep.

Zayn was only partially surprised by the sadness displayed in Priyanka's hunched shoulders. His patron had shown him kindness when no one else had. It was just a shame she'd chosen to side with the Cabal.

When Priyanka looked in his direction, he barely got himself hidden again. He didn't think she'd seen him, but it was close. Even after nearly getting blown up, Priyanka had the senses of a demon cat. It didn't help that he was linked to her. Only his other link confused things and allowed him to oppose her without her knowledge.

Inside the house, a battle of elements raged. Aurie was battling Frank Orpheum. Zayn wasn't surprised that she was holding her own against him. The dramatics patron wasn't used to head-to-head battles, preferring subterfuge as his main weapon, which was why he'd teamed up with Priyanka to find the wish spell. But Aurie was the strongest mage he'd ever met.

Around the time his patron went to the back door, the battle ended, and a minute later, the big blond girl on rollerblades went through the third-floor window.

Zayn moved through the houses, which wasn't hard since the wakers had flooded into the street. Orpheum had kept the whole population of the district subdued with his hypnotism trick. Zayn climbed onto the second-story roof, making it up the vertical incline as easily as walking across a room. Hannah was alive, but unconscious. He lifted her and carried her into a nearby building, hiding her in an abandoned house.

If he could get inside, maybe he could get Aurie out too. He shouldn't be so stupid as to risk it, but he'd been the one to get them into this mess.

Through the downstairs window, Zayn spied Priyanka and Orpheum talking. They had the kid Echo. It was strange to think that Invictus had put the wish spell inside that kid.

Messed him up pretty good to have that much magic swirling around inside of him. Zayn didn't have the starry-eyed ideals about Invictus that other people did. The head patron had done some pretty shady stuff, and dooming this poor soul into carrying his pet spell was as shitty as it got. Almost like making him a slave to the magic.

He wasn't sure how they were going to get the spell out of poor Echo, but that wasn't Zayn's concern at this point. Aurie was still inside the house. If he could get her out, then maybe he could salvage something.

Climbing the wall was trivial after a bit of shape shifting. Not even Priyanka could detect him if he focused.

Back in his human form, Zayn nearly broke when he found her.

Slumped against a wall, Aurelia Silverthorne stared into vacant space, the awful lines of betrayal on her face. He knew it as soon as he saw that open-mouthed gape.

Blood had pooled around her. Zayn almost couldn't believe it. He'd seen death before. Known it from his very hand. But this was someone he'd cared about, maybe even loved.

It'd never been his intention to fall for her. He'd only gotten them involved to spite Priyanka. He'd hoped they would figure out what the Cabal was after and inform the Arcanium patron, not get involved themselves. But he hadn't counted on her ambitions.

The night on the Spire came back to him. Lying with her as the storm tickled their skin with electricity, moving together, cries of passion on their lips. Now, dead. *What have I done?* That moment had been the happiest he'd ever been in his short life.

He wanted to march downstairs and confront her. *Do you know who you murdered?* he'd say. *Aurie was kind, curious, brilliant. She was fierce, protective of her friends, understanding of her enemies. She was the best of us. And you killed her.*

But he knew he wouldn't because in a way, he'd killed her too.

Zayn wiped the tears from his face, stared at them like traitors. He hadn't cried for real in years. *Is this what I've become? I'm no better than Priyanka with all her deceptions. If I hadn't mentioned the book, or fixed the sorting contest to get both Aurie and Pi into the group, then this would have never happened.*

He closed her eyes with his fingertips, lifted her mouth shut. She was so soft. As beautiful as a sleeping angel. He crept back to the window. They were all dead, or would soon be. Even Hannah wouldn't escape once they'd pried the wish out of Echo. Because once they had, he knew Priyanka's intention. She would use it to take control of the Hundred Halls, place herself as the head patron. Nothing would escape her notice after that. Zayn fled.

30

The world was one big throbbing nerve end lost on a stormy sea. Pi groaned inside the crater. Any attempt to open her eyes was met with soul-crushing vertigo. The verumancy spells she'd cast before the assault on the house had protected her from the worst of the blast, but it hadn't been able to shield her brain from the concussive blow.

She wondered if this was what running backs felt like when they got hit by a linebacker. If it was anything close, she thought they were stupid for continuing to do it. She felt like a child, and each movement reinforced her weakness.

The ringing in her ears made the world seem distant. She climbed to the edge of the hole, fingers digging into the packed earth. The smell of gunpowder was strong.

She held on as the buildings seesawed, closing her eyes when the vertigo got too bad.

"You almost got me with that," said a voice from near the house.

It was Priyanka Sai.

"Pretty ballsy to blow yourself up to get me. I shouldn't be surprised after seeing you in action in the contest. You're brilliant and unpredictable. I wish I had you in my hall," she said.

Spent faez made Pi's skin tingle. The worst of the vertigo disappeared, but Pi thought if she tried to move quickly or cast a spell, she'd end up vomiting.

Priyanka helped her out of the crater and pushed her into the house. Echo was sobbing on a chair, while Frank Orpheum stood over him.

"Messy, but it's done," said Priyanka. "Now for the important part."

To Pi's surprise, Priyanka approached Echo. His hands were jammed between his quivering knees. She placed a long fingernail under his chin, made him lift his head.

"You know who I am, right?" she asked.

He didn't want to answer at first but she dug her fingernail into his neck.

"Yes," he said weakly.

"You know what I do?"

He closed his eyes and nodded. A tear formed at the corner of his eye.

"It's okay, Echo. I'm not going to do that to you. You know, I remember you when you were a boy living in Invictus' apartments. You loved to tend his flowers, get your hands dirty in the soil. When I would visit, you would tell me about the flowers and their scientific names. Even as a seven-year-old boy you could wax on about the *tagetes erecta* or *canna generalis*. You were as sweet as you were intelligent. It's awful what he did to you."

The revelation that Echo had been Invictus' assistant was not as surprising as it should have been. It explained why he was on the school rolls without ever revealing his house. But Pi didn't understand the direction of the conversation.

"This isn't the way I imagined this would happen," said

Priyanka. "The plan had been to befriend you, make you understand that I cared. But you knew who I was the whole time, didn't you?"

Echo nodded slowly.

Priyanka cocked a grin, glanced at Pi. "He's smarter than you think. Saw through my deception."

"What do you want?" asked Pi.

Priyanka chuckled, shared a smile with Orpheum. "That's right. You don't know."

"I know about the wish spell," said Pi. "But I don't how Echo fits into it."

"You're *looking* at the wish spell," said Orpheum.

"Echo?" asked Pi, receiving a nod.

"A spell is an algorithm to solve a magical problem with faez as the supplied energy. A wish spell is the ultimate conundrum and no spell could plan for every contingency. Invictus solved that issue by placing the spell inside of a human child so the mind and the spell could work as one," said Priyanka.

"Oh dear god," said Pi.

Echo's inability to interact or focus, his near helplessness. It wasn't because he was weak, it was because he was too powerful.

"You see it now," said Priyanka.

"What will you do with it?" asked Pi.

"The only thing that matters," she replied. "Head patron."

"You bitch," said Pi.

Priyanka smirked. "Better me than one of the others. That's why Frank and I conspired. Do you really want Bannon Creed to have that position? Or Celesse or that jackass at Coterie? The role of head patron might as well be emperor of Earth for all the power that it enjoys. Every patron is beholden to you."

"But you're one of the Cabal."

"Cabal," she spat. "It's a word. A name to frighten people, because fear is useful. Not enjoyable, but useful."

Pi stole a glance at the outside. Where was her sister? Where was Hannah? She hoped they'd gone for help once they realized what they were up against.

Priyanka stared at her with real empathy. "I see that look in your eye. You're wondering where Aurie or the others are at. They're not coming. They're all dead."

Pi went numb. She was already recovering from the concussion, but hearing that her sister was dead only pushed her back down a deep hole. It wasn't supposed to be like this. Aurie was the only family she had left.

"Once I found you had a pulse, I knew what had to be done. Echo likes you more since you were the one to save him from those gang members. Though it was supposed to be Aurie, but I wasn't willing to throw away a lot of preparation just because the wrong sister was available," said Priyanka, advancing on her. "It was never supposed to be this way. Our plan was to befriend him and put him in a situation that using the wish was the only thing that would save the city. A useful thing having the master of illusions on your side. Now we'll have to do it the hard way. I'm very sorry, Pi. Until Echo agrees to work with us, you're going to be in a considerable amount of pain."

Pi was expecting the blade, but Priyanka put a spell on her. At first, her skin grew warm, then it got hotter, until her body felt like it'd been dipped in lava. She resisted screaming at first, because she knew that once she did, it would never stop. Pi expected the skin on her hands to peel off from the fire. There was nothing but pain. Nothing but pain. Pain.

31

There were forty-seven different shades of blue in the *ipomoea purpurea* growing in the planter's box outside the house. Echo traced the boundaries between the shades with his eyes. They formed spirals like a galaxy.

That was the way the world worked. The patterns repeated themselves. Galaxies and flowers. Leaves and rivers. Even people.

Echo watched Aurie run into the house after Hannah. There would be a battle. He could see it in the patterns. It always ended this way.

People were like volcanoes. They pushed together, building pressure, fighting to be on top. The eruption was inevitable. Sometimes it was clean and orderly, a lava ejection straight out the top, fired like a gun, leaving the mountainside intact. Other times, the explosion ripped the hillside away, turning everything into ash and fire.

Was this the big explosion? A super-eruption? The one that would change the world? Would the ash cloud blot out the sun for a few months and change the weather patterns? Or would there be an explosion but the pressure would remain?

People spilled from the houses. Aurie had called them wakers. But that wasn't right. They were asleep, tricked into living their lives in opposition to the sun. Like the negative in the photo.

Blue. Slate. Sky. Navy. Teal. Cobalt.

The color was soothing. He could bed down in the color blue. It reminded Echo of the days when his Opa was still alive. They'd seen him as a towering figure, a man to be feared and for some, worshiped. To Echo, he was the color of the sky on a sunny day when big, puffy clouds reigned.

Peacock. Teal. Aegean. Berry. Sapphire. Arctic.

The wakers grabbed his arms, his legs. Lifted him up, but he wasn't done with the colors yet. He repeated them quickly, before he forgot. He always forgot what he was doing.

Denim. Admiral. Stone. Spruce. Azure. Indigo. Lapis. Cerulean. Ocean.

The wakers carried Echo into the house like a tide washing to shore.

He felt the patterns tug and pull around him. A thread snapped—Rigel, no!—and others thinned.

Sometimes Echo could find himself in the patterns. Those were the good days, when he could remember when people were talking to him, use his words like he should, like Opa asked him to. Today wasn't a good day. Today the patterns crashed around him, seized his thoughts in their tortured webs.

He felt the gift inside him, moving like a pupa inside a cocoon. That's what Opa had called it, a gift. It'd never felt like a gift to Echo. Before the gift, he'd been able to think, to remember, to keep the patterns at bay.

But Opa had been scared. Echo didn't know that Opa could get scared, but he was. His skin was cracked and broken, eyes bloodshot—oh to see that pattern in those eyes—Echo had felt his need as if it were his own.

Echo had agreed to take the gift, though even he knew he was too young to understand. How does one understand the pattern without truly understanding it? That was the paradox. It was the need that Echo had understood, nothing else. If Opa asked, the man who had saved him, taught him, fed him on a sky full of blue, then he would say yes, he could take the gift, even if the gift would be the end of him.

What would it be? What would it become? The gift wriggled and wiggled inside him. The patterns swayed and sang. He knew the gift wasn't for him. It couldn't be. Using the gift in that way was like dividing by zero. He would have to use it on someone else.

The Woman Who Was Everyone. The R in Harpers. She wanted something. She wanted to control the pattern. To be the pattern. The liar wanted it too, but he knew he would never survive against the others and clung to her.

She'd been kind to him. Back before the gift. Opa had liked her. They liked each other. She had hard eyes, but kind. Like a surgeon with a scalpel. When the cancer was inside of you, it had to be cut out.

But The Woman Who Was Everyone was wrong. The gift didn't give control of the pattern. That was somewhere else, something else. Opa knew the patterns better than Echo, had seen in them in his spells, his divinations. Knew what was coming and had been afraid. Many possibilities, many deaths.

When Aurie's thread was cut, Echo knew it was wrong. She was integral to the pattern. There was going to be a volcanic eruption, but if she wasn't a part of it, then the pressure would build until the whole mountain exploded, knocking down everything from one end of the world to the other.

Pi was screaming.

The Woman Who Was Everyone wanted the gift. Echo would give the gift. It was the only way to save the pattern.

She would be disappointed, angry, but eventually she would have to choose.

The magic spilled out of him in a torrent. There weren't forty-seven shades of blue in the flower, but a hundred million, and every one of them spelled out the name Aurelia Silverthorne.

32

The world was one blinding color of blue.

Aurie shuddered awake—no, not awake, that was something else—this was different. It felt like someone had flicked a switch, turning her on. There was no groggy climb out of the depths of sleep, only an existence that started with that singular moment.

Aurie was aware that she had died twelve minutes ago. It was a fact of her existence. She remembered the cold metal entering her heart, the horrifying slide into oblivion.

People were talking downstairs. Without considering the consequences, Aurie went to investigate.

Pi was slouched against the wall, head between her legs. Sweat dripped from her arms, her hair glistened.

Echo lay on his side. Aurie didn't know if he was alive or not. Priyanka didn't seem to know either as she'd knelt by his side and was shaking him lightly while Frank Orpheum looked on.

They didn't know what Echo had done. Aurie knew it, now that she'd seen him.

"It's over," said Aurie, startling the three of them.

Pi burst into tears the moment she looked up—happy, delirious, exhausted, what-the-fuck tears.

"He used the wish to bring me back, whatever that means," she said, the second part to herself. *What was I? Dead? In limbo?* These were thoughts she wanted to contemplate, but the needs of the immediate brought her back. She was, as she recalled, speaking to two patrons, one of whom had killed her only a short while ago. This seemed like something she didn't want to happen again.

But first things first. Aurie moved past them both, knelt beside Echo, and checked for a pulse. It was there faintly. Aurie didn't know if he would survive the unraveling of the spell. He'd carried it within him for so long that it'd grown roots into the essence of his being.

"I killed you," said Priyanka Sai, unbelieving, then looking to the theater patron. "I killed her."

"You clearly didn't do a good enough job," said Aurie.

"What's going to keep me from finishing it? The three of you are no use to us now," said Priyanka.

Aurie had no doubt that the patron of assassins meant it, yet she wasn't afraid. Why was that? The answer bubbled up from her thoughts. Oh, yes.

"Because I know you don't mean it," said Aurie. "You could kill me when it was a means to an end. I was a sacrifice on the altar of your ambition, but to kill for no reason, that's not your way. You're not an indiscriminate killer. Not a sociopath."

Blades appeared in Priyanka's fists. She twirled them expertly. "You don't know me well enough."

"Actually, I do, Raz," said Aurie. "And not just because of the Harpers. Invictus put a little of himself in that spell, so I know what he thought of you. He didn't think of you as a killer. You have that ability, but it's not who you are."

It was also because of what Zayn had said about his patron, but she wasn't going to reveal that.

"You're wrong," said Priyanka. "You're a danger because you know that we tried to usurp control of the Halls without the rest of the Cabal. If that gets back to them, the pair of us are finished."

Eldritch flame appeared on her twin daggers. As it was, the three of them didn't stand a chance. Echo was near death, Pi looked like she'd been stuck in a jungle cage for a week, and Aurie had recently been deceased. She wasn't going to win with force.

"Yet, I'm not worried," said Aurie, searching for a reason. When the words came to her lips, she almost felt like she was casting a spell. "Don't you wonder why Echo saved me? Why did Invictus create the wish in the first place? It wasn't for himself, or he would have saved himself when the Cabal killed him. I don't know why he saved me, but don't you think it was for a good reason? Wasn't he the greatest diviner the world had ever known? You know that his biggest fear was that magic would destroy the world. That was why he created the Hundred Halls. Kill me if you think you must, but know that you may be dooming yourself."

The ghostly flame on her blades went out as her arms dropped to her side.

Aurie wanted desperately to collapse onto the floor, but she called on the last of her reserves, spelled strength into her limbs, and lifted Echo's near-lifeless body from the floor. Pi struggled to her feet like a newborn foal.

"Get us to Golden Willow," said Aurie. "I know there's a Garden Network here."

Neither patron made a motion towards the other room.

"Don't worry," said Semyon, stepping into the room and giving Aurie a curious glance. It was clear by the look on his face that he'd thought she was dead. "I'll take you."

Aurie was confused until Pi mouthed a name: Zayn. He must have contacted Semyon. If Priyanka found out, he'd be dead.

"You got my message," said Aurie, hoping to throw the trail.

To his credit, Semyon nodded agreeably, not giving the truth away.

As Aurie carried Echo out of the room, Semyon spoke to the other two patrons.

"We are going to destroy ourselves, and the city with it, if we keep doing this," said Semyon.

Frank Orpheum frowned. "Would you rather Bannon Creed get control of the Halls? We might not be your first choice, but we're better than the others."

"This can't last forever, Semyon," said Priyanka. "The city is falling apart without Invictus, and he left us no obvious way to replace him. As far as anyone knows, he's left the method hidden for a reason, and that reason is that we're to find it, and whoever finds it has earned the right to claim the position of head patron."

Aurie knew in her gut that this was the truth. He had hidden the method of ascendancy, but it hadn't been the wish spell.

"You're on the losing side, Semyon," said Priyanka. "Think about it from our point of view. If you win, then life will go as it did with Invictus. But if Bannon, or Celesse, or Malden get control, then anyone that opposed them will be dealt with swiftly. So you see the choice is quite clear."

"Have some spine, Pri," said Semyon, shaking his head. "There was a time you once showed some. Goodbye."

The four of them went through the Garden Network to Golden Willow. She carried Echo into the emergency room. Dr.

Fairlight happened to be the doctor on duty, and immediately took him from her.

"What's wrong?" asked Dr. Fairlight.

"A powerful spell was put inside him when he was young," said Aurie. "But it's gone now. I think his soul doesn't know what to do without it."

"I know what we can do," said Dr. Fairlight as they wheeled Echo away. "A friend of yours was brought here a little while ago. She looked like she'd fallen."

"Hannah?"

"Does she always wear skates?" asked Dr. Fairlight.

"Always."

Aurie made Pi sit in the waiting room, while Semyon went with Dr. Fairlight to make sure Echo was going to be okay.

"You look like hell, sis," said Aurie.

"I feel worse," she said, tears welling up in her eyes. "Rigel's dead. Priyanka killed him."

Aurie alternated between rage and sorrow. She didn't know what to do with her hands, made fists out of them, held them against her mouth.

"I didn't know," said Aurie. "If I'd only known."

"If you'd attacked her, she would have killed you. I saw her in action. She's a human blender," said Pi. "What about all that crap you said about Invictus wanting you alive? Like he'd had a prophecy about you or something?"

"All lies," said Aurie. "I knew some things about her from Zayn. I made the rest up."

"Jesus, Aurie. You're getting freaky good with this lying stuff," said Pi, half in adoration, half in concern.

"I'm a little worried about it myself," she admitted.

Pi looked away, wiped away tears. "Rigel's poor mother. It's not fair. He'd made the summer tour, was going to live his dreams. We should have never invited them."

Aurie clutched her sister tightly. "I know, Pi. I know. It's all my fault."

"Our fault, you mean," said Pi.

"Does it matter that it was important? Keeping Priyanka and Frank from the wish spell?" asked Aurie.

"It doesn't feel like it right now," said Pi. "I feel like a giant pile of dog shit. We got our friend killed."

"He knew what he was risking," said Aurie. "And it was important, even if it sucks. If we hadn't gone, then they would have gotten the wish out of Echo, and then killed him to hide the evidence. Someone was dying either way."

Pi sunk against the side of the chair, gaze faraway. "I wish I could see it that way."

Aurie climbed onto the chairs and held Pi, who clung to her as if they were six years old again. "Why does this have to be so fucking hard?"

"The important things are never easy," said Aurie, squeezing tightly. "*Dooset daram.*"

"Fuck death," said Pi, bringing stares from a family on the other side of the waiting room, "and fuck the Cabal. Rigel should be alive."

Aurie couldn't disagree. She held onto her sister for a long time. She didn't want to let go, but eventually they had to. It felt like something had changed in them both. Something they'd never get back. In that moment, she wanted more than she had in many years to be able to call her parents.

33

Without a doubt, it was the saddest contest room in the Spire, Pi thought. Hannah was sitting on a bar stool—sitting, no skates, boots, not even fidgeting—with an uneaten bar of chocolate in her fist. Aurie sat against the wall, legs splayed out before her, gaze vacant.

Echo was there too, except he didn't seem like Echo. He was focused, sitting quietly like an A student patiently working through a problem in his head that was painful to consider. He was still chubby, wearing the same tan slacks and gray T-shirt that he typically wore, but the keenness of his gaze transformed him into someone Pi hardly knew.

The scoreboard blinked, indicating a team had finished their final attempt. When the day was over, the team with the highest score—which at the moment was Violet's team—would earn the prize.

"What is wrong with you people?" Pi gestured towards Hannah. "You're not even wearing skates?"

"What's the point?" asked Hannah. "Rigel's dead, and Raz is...god, I can't even wrap my head around it. There's only four of us. We don't have a group of experts helping us with our strategies like the other teams. We never made it past wave five with the whole team, and now you want us to commit suicide by giant bug? Count me out."

"What about you, Aurie? Are you giving up, too?" asked Pi.

Aurie stared at the scoreboard. "It's not that I'm giving up. I just don't see the point. Can't we go watch a play in Rigel's memory or something?"

"Echo?"

He carried with him an invisible weight. It wasn't hard for Pi to see that he felt guilty for Rigel's death too. He also had to be coming to grips with not having that spell inside his head. She had no idea how that had affected him. He appeared as a man freed from prison after a long sentence who, faced with the overwhelming new reality, could not come to grips with it. Pi wondered what kind of man Invictus was that he would do that to a child.

"I'd prefer Ernie," he said cautiously, as if he weren't sure what words would come out of his mouth, "and I don't know. I'm trying to sort out who I am."

Aurie slapped her hand against the floor. "Face it, sis. The reason we wanted to win the contest so bad was because we thought the wish spell was at the end of it. Without that, there's not much point. We're going to get a decent grade, nothing special, but I'm not up for dying again with nothing on the line."

Hannah spoke up. "You know I would have appreciated knowing about that wish business. I thought I was your friend."

"I'm sorry, Hannah. We didn't want to get you involved," said Pi.

"You got me involved with what was supposed to be a simple demon banishing," countered Hannah.

Pi had no answer.

"Why do you want to do it?" asked Ernie.

When she looked at Aurie, she almost broke into tears. Pi paced around the room while they watched, clamping down on her fears before they overwhelmed her.

"Because Rigel's dead, that's why. And we lost our friend Raz. Yeah, I know, she wasn't really our friend, but I feel like Raz died too. I hate the idea of just rolling over and doing nothing. I'd rather go down fighting, even if it doesn't mean that much. I don't know if that's something Rigel would have wanted us to do, but dammit, it's something we should do. Even if we only have a tiny chance of winning, and I think we have a bigger chance than we think, we owe it to ourselves to try and knock Violet and her posse off the top of the leaderboard. Wouldn't that be worth it? Come on, Ernie. Remember what she did to you at the beginning of the year? Or all the hell she's put you through, Aurie?"

When Pi looked Hannah's way, she added, "I think she's a major twit."

"It doesn't matter if we want to win," said Aurie. "We need a plan that gives us a chance. I don't think we'd make it past wave three with the four of us, let alone make it to the queen."

"What if I know a way we don't have to fight through the waves?" asked Pi with a grin.

The hopeful glances were all the encouragement she needed. Even if it didn't work, just taking a chance, doing something rather than sitting around and moping, was worth it.

"Are you going to tell us?" asked Aurie.

"Only if you promise that you're willing to try, even if it's a little unconventional," said Pi.

"I'm in," said Ernie, "if only to keep me from having to think about who I really am for a short while."

Hannah scrunched up her face. "Fine. Unconventional. I'll make an attempt without my skates. I swear you two are relentless about them."

"No," said Pi. "I want you in your skates. They're part of the plan."

"They are?" asked Hannah, her face lighting up.

Aurie sighed. "I'm getting the strong feeling that I'm not going to be given a choice."

"There's always a choice." Pi smiled.

Aurie raised an eyebrow. "And hear about it for the rest of my life? Hell, no. I'll take a pair of mandibles chewing off my face compared to that any day."

"Love you too," said Pi.

"So tell us the plan," said Hannah.

Pi slipped out of her backpack and threw it onto the couch.

"Jesus, what's in there, dead bodies?" asked Aurie.

"Books," said Pi. "Pull 'em out and start eating."

Hannah and Ernie gave her a horrified stare.

"They've been magically binded to transfer knowledge," explained Pi. "It's one of the things they teach us in Arcanium."

Hannah shook her head. "You guys are so weird."

"That reminds me," said Pi. "What hall are you actually in, Ernie? We've been wondering all year, and you avoided our questions without answering."

"I...I don't really have one," he said. "I was bound to Invictus at a young age."

"Could that mean that he's still alive? I mean, it's not like you're frothing at the mouth with faez madness," said Aurie.

"He's definitely dead," said Ernie. "I didn't see it, but I felt it the moment it happened. It was like having a shard of ice shoved in your gut. It was the worst."

"Wait. We can't have you continue. You're unprotected from faez madness," said Pi.

"It's okay," he said. "Having the wish spell sort of hardened me against that. Mostly, anyway."

While they dined on the books, washing them down with energy drinks and chocolate, Pi challenged the rest of the Harpers with a question.

"Why are we defending the fort?" she asked.

Everyone shrugged and made noncommittal noises. She felt like a high school teacher in front of a reticent class.

"Because the bugs are attacking us?" Hannah asked skeptically.

"Sure, but why else?" asked Pi.

Ernie gestured. "It's a classic tower defense game with multiple waves of enemies that get successively more challenging."

Everyone nodded in agreement, but Pi was smiling. It was the exact point she was hoping someone would make.

"What if that's what we're supposed to think? We're all born and raised on games. So what do we do when we see a challenge? We figure out what game it's similar to so we can utilize those strategies," said Pi.

"If it's not a tower defense game, then what kind of game is it?" asked Aurie.

"It's not a game at all," said Pi. "The book you just ate is called *Flora and Wildlife of the Fourth Quadrant of Human-Inhabitable Extra-Planar Spaces*. Concentrate on the part about Planet 8b.5."

One by one their eyes lit up as the knowledge came to the forefront of their awareness.

"Holy balls," said Hannah. "It's the bug planet."

"The technical name for that species is *Heinlein Kiranides*. They are the dominate life form on that planet. There's not a lot of research on them, but they have a similar breeding program to many Earth bugs like armyworms, or Japanese beetles. They lay their eggs in other locations than their nest."

"So the fort is just their breeding ground?" asked Hannah.

"And we're camped on top of their eggs. No wonder they keep attacking us," said Aurie.

"The flowers!" exclaimed Ernie.

Pi grinned. "You got it. They repel the bugs, which is why they plant them in the breeding areas to keep other colonies at bay. The so-called fort walls aren't rock, but hardened saliva from the bugs to keep the ground-based predators from burrowing in and eating the eggs."

"We're practically inviting them to attack us," said Aurie.

"Yep."

"So what are we going to do, sis?" asked Aurie with a suspicious tone.

"We're going to split the party," said Pi.

The three of them responded in unison. "You never split the party."

"We're going to split the party," she said again with a shrug.

"Didn't we learn that lesson already?" asked Aurie.

The reminder of Rigel's death brought the mood down, but Pi forged ahead. She wasn't done mourning him, would probably never get over it, but they had to do this.

"Sometimes you have to do things differently, even if they don't seem right at first," said Pi.

Aurie shook her head skeptically. "I don't know. Splitting the party is bad. We're already down two."

"What is it that you always tell me—when the going gets tough, the tough study harder? I've done my homework, I've studied harder. Once we get into the fort, we're going to kill the initial bugs, but then get out without messing with any of the young bugs in the ground. We'll need to grab the flowers off the bushes before we go, but that shouldn't be too hard.

If we haven't killed the eggs or the young bugs, I don't think they'll be in a frenzy to kill us. Then we can find the queen's home and take her out."

"Do you know where it is?" asked Ernie.

Pi sighed. "No. I've tried to find it, but no luck so far. That's one of the reasons I made the books. I thought we might be able to figure it out on the way."

"What was all that about splitting the party?" asked Aurie.

"The bugs aren't going to stay away forever. Eventually we'll need a distraction." Pi looked at Hannah.

"Me?"

"Once the bugs find us, and they will, I want you to drop your flowers and lead them away. It'll give us more time," said Pi.

Hannah frowned. "That's your plan?"

"If it doesn't work, what's the worst that can happen?" said Pi.

"I become a bug shish kabob," said Hannah.

"And reappear here," said Pi. "No risk, no reward."

"I'm still in," said Hannah. "I just think splitting the party is stupid."

"Anything else?" asked Aurie.

"That's it."

"Well it sounds better than anything we came up with before," said Aurie. "I guess wanting to do things differently sometimes works out."

"Is that an apology?" asked Pi.

Aurie raised an eyebrow. "I'm proud of you, sis."

"Don't be proud, let's win this thing!"

Loaded up on enchantments, they moved into the portal room. There was an energy in the air, bouncing between them with secret smiles and knowing glances. Excitement was welling up inside Pi. This was a chance to prove something to herself and to her sister. The prizes at the end of the contest were nothing to sneeze at either. Despite the likely possibility that she would get murdered by an oversized insect with a cutting fetish, she was glowing.

"See you on the other side," said Aurie as the portal activated.

"For Rigel," said Pi.

They repeated it as a team. "For Rigel."

Together, they touched the obsidian stone.

34

Something felt different to Aurie almost immediately, but she didn't have time to contemplate with the bug bearing down on her.

Using a solar spear, a variation on the fire spear in which she convinced the spell it was using energy from the sun, Aurie annihilated the bug into ash. One of the benefits of failing repeatedly in the contest had been refining their abilities and tactics.

The others easily took care of their bugs. Even with only four left on the team, the initial portal fight was trivial.

"Nobody move away from the cube," said Pi. "We don't want to trigger any of the adolescent bugs."

"How do we get the flowers?" asked Hannah. "There are bugs in the ground on three sides around them."

Ernie raised his hand. "I can get them."

"Great," said Pi. "Just be careful."

While Ernie focused internally as if he were meditating, Aurie watched her sister. She'd never looked more radiant, as if she were an angel of battle in her element. It was strange to think how different they were. Aurie preferred working within the given structures, making them better, even incrementally, while her sister trampled over the system to get her way. At the moment, their two styles had complemented each other wonderfully. Aurie hoped there wouldn't be a day that their different methods would cause a rift.

"Whoa," said Hannah.

Ernie hadn't moved, but the plants were growing rapidly. The branches snaked out and upward, leaves bursting from limbs as the plant strained to reach them. After a minute, a flowery arch connected with the obsidian portal and the purple flowers knitted themselves into crowns.

Ernie plucked them off and handed them to each person. He had a pleased look.

"I tended his gardens in the Spire," said Ernie proudly.

"We should get moving. I'm not sure if the waves will start since we didn't kill any eggs, but let's not give them a chance," said Pi.

"Before we go," said Aurie. "Did anyone else feel that spark of electricity when we first arrived? I'd never felt that before."

Based on the nods, it appeared everyone else had too, but no one had an explanation, so they continued with the plan.

In a single file line, they followed a torturous path out of the fort that avoided the sleeping adolescent bugs. Once they were on the far side of the secreted walls, Pi led them into the trees.

They kept to a line, Pi in front since she'd spent the most time in the jungle, Ernie next, then Aurie. Hannah stayed in back. Skating over the earth as if it were hardwood flooring, Hannah made loops to make sure no bugs were sneaking up on them.

But nothing attacked and the team made it to the crest of the nearby hill.

"Aurie. Can you climb up and find out if the bugs have attacked the fort? It might give us an idea if we're being followed," said Pi.

Aurie enchanted her hands and feet with the dexterity of a monkey and scurried into the canopy before the rest of the team could exclaim.

The view took her breath away. She'd always lived in cities and had never gotten a chance to explore the wilderness. It was weird to think they'd been coming to this place once a week for nine months, but this was the first time she'd actually noticed her surroundings.

Aurie almost forgot why she'd climbed up, until she looked back into the valley to the fort. It was empty.

With a grin on her lips, Aurie made her way down. She kissed her sister on the forehead as soon as she could.

"Thank you," said Aurie.

Pi got a suspicious look. "What?"

"For this. I'm glad you got us to try one last time. The view was spectacular," said Aurie.

Pi rolled her eyes. "You're so weird."

Her sister had brushed the compliment off, but the blush in her cheeks was unmistakable.

"Any sign of the bugs while I was up there?" she asked.

Hannah had finished a circuit of the hilltop. "Nothing directly. A few times I thought something was watching me from the corner of my eye, but I couldn't catch it. Might be the unfamiliar territory. I'm used to standing on the wall waiting for the next wave."

Ernie scratched at his arms. "I feel it too. I feel like something's been removed from my skin. Like I was varnished before, but now I'm exposed raw wood."

The experience was mutual. Aurie resisted the urge to itch, or she didn't think she'd stop.

"Where do we go from here?" asked Hannah.

"I don't know," said Pi. "That's why I had the books made. I thought they might help us figure out where the queen is located. It's a real shame the scholars that wrote it didn't figure that out. Probably too busy avoiding being murdered."

Aurie focused on the book inside her head. Having the knowledge without the experiences to implant it there was a lot like surfing the internet about a subject. A lot of time was lost trying to figure out where it was located. Typically, the scholars in Arcanium meditated on the information to mind map it before they tried to call upon the details. But the Harpers didn't have time for that.

"It might help if we knew what they eat," said Ernie.

"Omnivores," said Hannah. "Though I don't see anything besides plants around here."

Everyone looked around. "I haven't seen a single critter, like a squirrel or anything like that. The book details some mammal-like creatures, but they're mostly subterranean or very good at hiding."

"The bugs are a super predator," said Aurie, almost as a surprise. The knowledge bubbled up without warning, which made her feel like someone else was speaking. "They've wiped out their food sources, so they eat mostly plants and fungus to survive unless they're locked in a grand battle between colonies. But that doesn't happen too often."

"I bet they live in a cave system," said Pi.

"Augh," said Hannah. "No caves please."

"Did you see any areas that look like they could have caves?" asked Ernie.

"Let me check," said Aurie, making her way back up the tree system.

The second time in the canopy Aurie forced herself to pay attention to the details, rather than getting lost on the majesty of her surroundings. A cliff on a distant hillside seemed like the only place that could have a cave, though she supposed any opening in the ground could lead to one. It was their best shot.

Before she went back down, Aurie checked on the fort. This time, it was crawling with bugs as if it were an ant farm upended. Scouts were heading into the trees, some in their direction.

She went back down as fast as she could. Everyone sensed the concern on her face.

"The bugs are out," said Aurie. "We'd better get moving."

"Did you see a cave?" asked Hannah.

"Possibly," said Aurie. "Only one way to find out."

"Better than hanging out here waiting for them to find us," said Pi.

They moved out immediately at a hurried pace. Yet, the sense of adventure was still there, which was probably why Aurie felt strange.

The foliage grew denser, leaves slapping at Aurie as she followed her sister. The air was thick and earthy, stronger as they moved towards the other hill. Beads of sweat formed on Aurie's forehead, which she wiped off from time to time.

As they entered the next valley, Hannah yelped. They circled around her as she held her arm. Blood ran through her fingers.

"I caught a thorn. Ripped my arm right open," said Hannah, grimacing. "It hurts, a lot."

"I can fix that," said Aurie.

Closing the wound didn't take long. Hannah looked uneasy as she knocked the crusty blood from the faint pink line where the thorn had cut her.

"That's weird," she said, poking the scar.

"What?" asked Aurie.

"I had lots of cuts and bruises from our earlier attempts, but they never left a scar. It hurt a hell of a lot more this time," said Hannah.

"Maybe they upped the realism for the final try," said Pi.

"Yeah, I guess," said Hannah, though she didn't believe it by the look on her face.

"Oh no," said Ernie, eyes wide with fright.

"What's wrong?" asked Pi.

"Before, when I was, you know, lost in the wish spell, I could easily be distracted by the slightest thing, the shimmering wings of a dragonfly, the shape of a clump of dirt, the colors of a flower. Sometimes, I would get lost examining a spell. You probably haven't noticed it, but when we portal here, there's a protective spell that keeps us from actually dying here. It's clever, powerful magic that was placed on the portal stones. When we get sent to this plane of existence, we get sent back to the same starting point. Time. Place. Everything. But since you can't actually travel through time, it's a sort of weird pseudo reality that allows you to experience it briefly without impacting it."

"I always wondered why the bugs were in the exact same spot each time we came back," said Hannah.

"So what's wrong? Did we get sent to the wrong time or place?" asked Pi.

"No," said Ernie, face etched with worry. "We got sent to the same bug fort we get sent every time. The only difference is that this time is for real. There's no protective spell to save us from death. If we die, we're dead for good."

The reality sunk in. It felt like being slowly lowered into a grave that you'd dug yourself.

"We can't even go back to the fort. It's crawling with bugs," said Pi, nearly to tears. "I'm so sorry, guys. I've killed us."

"We're not dead yet," said Aurie. "And you didn't do it. I

bet I know who it was."

"Priyanka Sai," said Pi immediately. "That bitch."

Hannah sucked in a breath. "I bet that's who I keep seeing out of the corner of my eye. I swear someone's been following us, but I thought it was nerves."

"I don't think Priyanka is our big concern right now," said Ernie.

"Of course she is," said Pi. "You didn't see her move. She could kill us all in the blink of an eye. I only survived last time because of luck."

"No," said Ernie, pointing behind them. "The bugs have found us!"

The hillside glittered with hundreds of glistening mandibles. The angular bugs came careening through the trees. Chitinous death surrounded them on three sides.

The Harpers fled into the valley towards the cliff. Their head start was eaten up by the quicker bugs, probably drawn on by the excitement of a fleshy meal. Aurie wondered if they had memories of the previous battles, and knowing finally that this was for real, could barely contain their salivation.

Darts rained down from above, shredding the foliage and impacting into the trunks, narrowly missing them. The ground burst open before Aurie. A burrowing bug lay in wait. Aurie threw a solar spear into its maw and ran through the curtain of ash.

Their headlong rush came to an end when they reached a crevasse. The gash in the earth was at least a hundred feet wide and stretched into the distance in both directions. Looking into the darkness, Aurie heard more chittering bugs beneath them, climbing over themselves, toothy maws ready. They would have to make their stand here.

The Harpers, even minus two of their number, were not without defenses. In the fights at the fort, the bugs came in strategically, testing their skills in a variety of ways. In an open valley with kills in sight, the bugs attacked with mindless ferocity which left them exposed to counterattack.

The four of them rained death upon the bugs. Aurie launched hailstorms of solar spears, destroying the darters from a distance. Ernie brought the forest to life, and vines wrapped themselves around the insects, ripping them to pieces like leafy krakens. Hannah turned into a human battering ram, which kept the attacking bugs off balance as she flew into their midst, knocking them away like bowling pins before circling around to hit the next group. Pi had brought her explosive seeds. The bugs were turned to mush whenever she hit, which was nearly every time, guided by her magic. The Harpers functioned like a well-oiled bug killing machine.

After what seemed like an hour but had probably only been the span of a few minutes, there was a lull in the fight as they had destroyed the first few waves of bugs. More were coming down the hillside, but the gap gave them a minute to get a breather.

"We need to get across this hole," said Pi. "If we can get to the other side, we have a chance. Then maybe we can circle back around and use the portal to get back home."

"We can't jump that far, even if we use verumancy," said Aurie.

"I wasn't thinking about verumancy," said Pi.

Aurie knew that look in her sister's eyes. "No. No way. It's too far, and there's nothing to work with. I can't lie a bridge into existence."

"What if I can extend some vines across the gap? Could we walk across those?" asked Ernie.

The pit was too deep and too wide. The bottom of it had to be crawling with bugs.

"I don't know," said Aurie.

She didn't want to drop them. She'd never tried something this difficult. Even in the practice room, the conditions had been set up for her to succeed. She was exhausted from the fight, the running, and the fear of getting shredded.

Pi grabbed her by the shoulder. "You have to. It's our only shot to escape."

They didn't give her the chance to refuse. Ernie waved his hands, and vines climbed through the air towards the other side.

"We'll keep 'em off you while you build the bridge," said Hannah, skating back into the forest.

Pi weighed her bag of explosive seeds. It looked like she had used up about half of them. "These are no good if we're dead."

While explosions went on behind her, Aurie focused on the vines, picturing a bridge in her head. She imagined the foundation deep into the ground, the beams crossing the wide gap held up by invisible girders. By the time the vines had touched the far side, she had the spell of mendacity ready, and let it flow out her lips.

She took the first step herself. The leafy vines provided a walking space about a foot wide. Aurie didn't look to see if anyone was following her. She kept describing the bridge: how strong it was, how many earthquakes it had survived, that it was the first bridge ever created, made by the gods, and that it would exist for all time.

She talked about great marble pillars lifting up from the depths, carved into titans that held the bridge above their heads. She told the story of how the beams were forged in a volcano, hammered into shape by Hephaestus himself.

Aurie was vaguely aware of the shouts behind her. The others had followed her across the abyss, keeping the way clear of bugs with their terrible magics.

When she was halfway across, she had a moment of awareness, as if she were a cartoon character who'd run off the edge of a cliff and had realized they were not on solid ground anymore, which was the only thing required to turn gravity back on.

The vine bridge dipped lower. The spell started to unravel. Aurie imagined the four of them falling into a sea of mandibles and stabbing chitinous feet. This was the danger of mendancy. If you couldn't believe the lie anymore, it was doomed to fail.

But she kept it up and, rather than thinking about the consequences, focused on the description of the bridge and how it had survived ancient calamities.

When they were about twenty feet away from the far edge, Aurie started to believe that they were going to make it. She focused on the lie even more, the flood of faez like a raging river.

When she saw him, the surprise nearly popped the bubble of her magic. She held on, but stopped, bringing their progress across the crevasse to a halt.

Frank Orpheum stood at the threshold of where the bridge and the ground met. He wore the expression of a villain as if he were portraying one for his greatest role.

"You robbed me of my victory," said Frank Orpheum. "I was so close to what Invictus would never let me have in all those years."

Though it took a supreme force of will, Aurie glanced behind her to see bugs crossing the bridge behind them. Her friends were wearing out. Pi looked almost out of seeds.

Aurie didn't bother asking. She knew what he wanted. Could see it on his face, but he said it anyway.

"I could make them love me. All of them. They would build shrines for me, make a religion out of my every breath. I have the power, but this damn binding keeps me from unleashing it. Invictus tricked me all those years ago. I didn't kill him, but I was glad when he was dead," he said.

Through gritted teeth, Aurie said, "You weren't going to get that anyway. The wish spell couldn't be used for that. Ernie said so."

"You're so limited in your thinking. I wasn't going to let Priyanka use the wish. She wasn't even aware that she was working for me. I'd hypnotized her many years ago. It helped that she'd always had a crush on me," said Orpheum.

Aurie couldn't hold it much longer. She needed one of the others to knock him aside, but she was in the way. They were teetering on a thin bridge.

"It's too bad you won't make it back," he said. "You showed such promise with your falsehoods. I know Invictus didn't make you his special snowflake. That was all a lie. But I need you to die here so no one will know. It's just a shame I couldn't do this from the other side. I really don't like bugs."

Aurie was ready to sprint across the space when he dazzled her with a bit of hypnotism. She was mostly immune to his charms, but the momentary distraction destroyed the lie of the bridge. Her mendancy failed. The vines collapsed, dragging the four of them into the abyss.

35

Pi remembered climbing a tree behind their neighborhood when she was seven years old. It was a tall pine that stretched above the maples in the small grove.

She'd wanted to climb it because she saw the boys taking turns seeing how high they could go; the bravest boy stopped about two-thirds of the way from the top, because the tree was less ridged up there.

Pi knew that because she was smaller than the others, she would be able to climb higher, but cognizant of the risk, made preparations in the form of a harness of bungee cords that allowed her to stay connected to the tree should her hands slip. The bungee cords made her look like she was wearing a thrift store steampunk outfit, especially with the goggles that kept the pine needles from poking her in the eye.

While the other kids, including her sister, Aurie, were playing on the swing sets and jungle gyms, Pi climbed the tall pine. The bark was full of sap, and halfway up her fingers were sticking together, but she kept climbing. When she crossed the highest point that the boys had gone, a wellspring of pride made her tingly with excitement. But she wasn't done yet, and making careful handholds, reapplying her bungee-cord harness at each point, she reached the tippy-top of the tree. She was so high that her weight bent the tree and it swayed in the wind. Pi stayed up there for an hour while the others, oblivious to her feat, ran around the playground.

While Pi had been afraid of falling the whole way up, not once during her climb had she allowed that fear to silence her thoughts.

So when the bridge collapsed beneath them, Pi yelled at Ernie, "Grab us!"

Then Pi threw one of the last of her explosive seeds at Frank Orpheum. She didn't aim at him, because he surely had enchantments to protect himself. Instead she exploded the seed directly behind him. The concussive force threw him over the edge.

The vines wrapped around her midsection, redirecting her plummet towards the wall. The impact jarred her shoulders and cut up her hands, but she was alive. The four Harpers hung by vines on the crevasse wall.

"I can't hold much longer," said Ernie. "There's nothing to grip onto up there."

The vines slipped downward. Pi tried to grab the wall, but her hands were numb from the impact.

Before she could get another word out, the vines released them. Her scream was swallowed by the fall. She hit the ground a moment later. Hannah fell next to her, the skates slamming into her leg.

They'd landed on a ledge halfway down the crevasse. Everyone groaned around her, but otherwise seemed alive.

"Nice save, Ernie," she said.

"From the frying pan into the fire," said Hannah.

Pi peered over the edge. A faint bioluminescence revealed the bottom another forty feet below them. The silence was promising.

"We should climb out," said Aurie.

"No," countered Pi. "I think we have an opportunity. The bugs have spilled out of the caves to hunt. Falling down here probably saved us. There's no way we were going to get back to the portal at the fort. This place is probably mostly empty. We can take a few bugs at a time easily. If we find the queen, the portal should be nearby."

"I don't want to fight the queen," said Hannah.

"We don't have to," said Pi. "We only need to reach the portal. I'm sure we can figure out how to do that."

Aurie gave her a worried look. "What about Frank Orpheum? He did something that slowed his fall. I'm sure he survived. He's down here somewhere too."

"Let's not run into him then," said Pi.

Ernie had been exploring the little cave connected to the ledge. "Hey, there's a passage back here. Looks like it goes down towards the other areas."

"Let's get going. We have to reach the portal before the other bugs realize we're not up top and come home," said Pi.

As they went into the passage, their eyes adjusted to the dim light created by fungus.

When they reached the main passage, Aurie asked, "Which way?"

"Down, I think. The queen is usually at the bottom of the nest," said Pi.

The caves were brutally quiet. Occasionally, the echoes of chittering bugs moving somewhere nearby reached them, forcing them to take defensive postures. But after the noises receded, they realized the bugs had been in a different passage.

Pi heard other things too: water dripping, the controlled breathing of her companions, occasional foot scuffs, and unidentified noises that made the darkness more oppressive.

When they reached a crossroads that had multiple bridges of hardened saliva reaching across an empty space, guarded by a trio of enormous brute bugs, they huddled up to form a plan. The bridges went both up and down, leading into a network of passages.

"We can go straight down from here," said Pi.

"We just have to get past those brutes," said Hannah. "They have massively thick plates of armor. They look like tanks."

"We need to kill them quickly. So they can't warn the others," said Aurie.

"Kill them fast enough and they can't do a thing," added Ernie.

Pi held her hand out, showing two seeds remaining. "I was hoping to use these to help us get past the queen."

"Save them," said Aurie. "Too loud. I can take one with a solar spear."

"I could knock one off the bridge," said Hannah.

Pi and Ernie looked at each other. "I'm sure if we hit the last one with fire spears we can take it down."

When they were ready, Hannah strode onto the bridge, churning her legs to achieve a high speed in a short time. With the multiple layers of enchantments, she was up to ramming speed within a few strides.

Once the brute bugs noticed Hannah, the other Harpers stepped out of the darkness and readied their spears. They launched them at the bugs, two spears outshone by the third, which flew higher and harder through the empty space.

Before the brute bugs could react, Hannah was upon the first, slamming into it. The massive bug slipped over the edge, angular legs scraping at the bridge.

The spears hit together. Aurie's solar spear vaporized the body of a bug, a set of legs remaining like a crab leg buffet.

Pi and Ernie's fire spears impacted the third, but failed to do more than scorch the outer armor.

"Shit," said Pi, readying a second spear.

But Aurie was faster, and as the bug raced away to warn the others, the second solar spear took it in the front, turning its head to ash.

"That was close," said Aurie.

A loud rattling sound went off. Far above them, a second trio of bugs rattled a chandelier of bones. The noises echoed throughout the complex.

"Run!" said Pi. "We have to get to the queen before they all arrive!"

They went down the ramp, skidding around corners, being careful not to fall over the sides. The bugs didn't believe in safety guarding it seemed.

When they reached the bottom, it was easier to see because the luminescent fungus covered everything and a faint mist hovered above the ground, collecting the ghostly light.

"It's like an underground graveyard," said Hannah.

No one could disagree. There was only one way to go, so they took it.

They stumbled onto a couple of bugs moving toward them, but destroyed them before anyone was in danger.

After a short passage, the way opened up into a massive chamber. A sea of squishy-looking yellow-brown eggs the size of basketballs covered the front half of the chamber, the mist floating between them, swirling from unseen breezes. Softer bugs moved amid the eggs. They lacked the armor of the others. An egg near the wall opened with a sickening suction sound. A creature the size of a large lobster climbed out of the egg into the arms of the soft nursery insect.

"This is worse than an underground graveyard," said Hannah. "This looks like—"

"Don't even say it. Don't. Even. Say it," said Aurie.

Beyond the eggs was an oppressive gloom. Pi's skin felt prickly just looking in that direction.

"The portal is back there," said Ernie. "I can feel it."

"So is the queen," said Pi.

They all nodded.

"Should we worry about those bugs over there?" asked Hannah, referring to the soft-skinned bugs.

"No," said Pi, "and be careful not to damage any eggs. The less we can enrage the queen, the better off we'll be."

Stepping between the eggs made Pi's skin crawl. She kept expecting one to explode open and a bug to latch onto her leg, or run up her face.

As they made their way through the eggs, the view of the queen became clear. The monstrous insectoid was hunched over a pile of refuse, stuffing rotting plant material and other foul things into a maw that was the thing of nightmares. Her dread turned into full-fledged horror when she realized the queen was sitting on the portal.

No one knew what to do. They just stood there within fifty feet of their escape.

"We're screwed," said Hannah.

Movement out of the corner of her eye prompted Pi to throw the final two seeds. Frank Orpheum was moving through the eggs towards them. She never had a chance to make them explode as he mesmerized her with a wave of his hand.

The rest of the Harpers were entranced too, even Aurie, who had resisted his charms thus far. She was fighting against it as if she were being held by invisible chains.

"I can't hypnotize you," he said to Aurie. "But you're not immune to bug poison. I found one of the dead darters you killed and took one of its little poison barbs. It was a simple thing to poison you."

The queen shifted its enormous weight. It seemed to be realizing that they had entered the chamber.

"Yes," said Frank Orpheum. "The queen is stirring. Soon she will lumber over here and despite your efforts to resist, you will start destroying eggs, which will only draw her down upon you. While she snuffs out your little lives, I will reach the portal and escape this nightmare unharmed."

Frank turned his head towards the entrance. Bugs were arriving. Even if he didn't bring the queen down on them, the others would kill them. Only their fear of injuring eggs kept them from streaming into the room. The first bugs took tentative steps into the room, moving carefully around the eggs.

"I'm very sorry," said Frank Orpheum. "Our time together is at an end."

He waved his hand and Hannah stooped down. She wrestled an egg from the floor. Creamy goo coated her arms as she lifted it above her head.

The queen lurched forward, drawn by the threat to her brood. With tears in her eyes, Hannah threw the egg to splatter against the ground, and a half-formed insect spilled out against the ground.

The queen mashed her mandibles together, the cacophony of sound almost deafening in the small space. She made ponderous steps towards them, dragging her bulk across the floor while the four of them made no move, frozen in place by charms and poison.

Pi fought against the spell, but could not move her arms or legs. There would be no getting away from the queen. When she was almost upon them, Pi took one last look at Frank Orpheum, who crept around the other way.

Remembering the unexploded seeds, Pi concentrated, hoping she could trigger them through his hypnotism. When the first seed exploded on the other side of Frank, throwing egg slime in all directions, everyone froze. The queen turned her enormous head towards Orpheum, suddenly aware that he was there.

Using the distraction, Pi exploded the second seed, which was only a few feet behind the theater patron. This enraged the queen. Frank Orpheum started running the other way around, hoping to slip past to the portal, but she was faster.

He waved his hand and created the illusion of a soft-skinned nursery bug overtop of himself. Pi couldn't tell the difference, and had to look a second time, only knowing it was Frank Orpheum by his location.

But the bugs were immune to illusions. Rigel Yamaguchi had taught them that.

The queen rose above Frank Orpheum and brought her bulk down upon him, turning him into mulch. With him dead, the charms evaporated. Hannah threw Aurie over her shoulder in a fireman's carry.

They hurried towards the portal as bugs from the entrance dashed after. After climbing over refuse and bug offal, they reached the cube of obsidian, collectively placed their hands against the cool surface, and activated it.

The last thing Pi saw before she was teleported back into her home realm was a sea of bugs climbing over themselves to annihilate her.

36

The sheer whiteness of the portal room was soothing in ways Aurie had never considered. Cradled in Hannah's arms as poison coursed through her veins, Aurie relished the simplicity of the blank room.

Using a simple spell, Pi was able to cleanse the poison from her veins, allowing her to stand on her own.

No one spoke for a while. They sat in the room, careful not to touch the portal even though they knew it was dormant, quietly reflecting on how near they'd been to death.

Hannah stood up and announced, "I need chocolate." They followed her back to the waiting room.

Ernie was digging through the refrigerator when Pi said, "Uhm, hey guys. Check out the scoreboard."

The first thing Aurie noticed was that none of the scores were blinking, which meant everyone had finished their final attempt. Then she searched the bottom half of the lists for the Harpers' score. It didn't occur to her to look at the top until she heard Hannah laughing.

There, at the top, one spot above The Indigo Sisters, with a score of 125,781, were the Harpers.

"We won?" asked Aurie, not because she was completely surprised, but because she was still recovering from the horror of escaping the queen. Since they hadn't killed her, Aurie had assumed they hadn't won.

When the scoreboard split in half, it startled the whole group. They shared nervous laughter as the wall became a passage.

With shrugs and clutching cold energy potions, the four of them trod forward. They walked for a good two minutes down a featureless hallway. Aurie kept checking behind them to make sure the door hadn't closed. She knew it'd take a while to get over the whole bug thing.

A stone archway signaled the end of the passage. In a small room, a chest the size of a steamer trunk waited for them.

"Should we check for traps first?" asked Hannah with a grin.

"I think we're okay on this one," said Aurie. "You do the honors, Pi. You deserve it."

When the lid flipped open, the small room glistened in the reflections of gold. Overwhelming gold. Coins, a pile of them, filled the space. There were other items in the huge chest, but Aurie could only really see the gold.

"Holy balls," uttered Hannah. "I can buy a lot of gaming books with that."

"You can buy *all* the gaming books with that," said Pi.

With the revelations of sudden wealth behind them, the Harpers examined the items. There were six magical trinkets inside the trunk: a stylish black leather jacket, a music box, a fancy screwdriver, a necklace made of seashells, a pair of bracelets, and a runed knife.

Pi pulled the leather jacket out, looking hopefully at the others. "Can I has?"

After everyone nodded, Pi slipped it on. At first, Aurie

had thought it too big, but it seemed to conform to her form. Pi walked away, examining the inner pockets, eyes alight with wonder.

Hannah went right for the screwdriver. As she yanked it out, she said, "It's a Universal Tool. I can build anything with it."

Ernie poked at the music box, then the bracelets before settling on the runed knife. Once his fingers touched it, his face lit up. He tucked it into his belt without a word.

After a little experimentation, Aurie determined that the bracelets provided magical protections to a variety of dangers. They seemed to be the most normal of trinkets when compared to the others, though they made up for it in strength of enchantment.

The seashell necklace initially proved impervious to her investigations until she put it on and asked Pi if she noticed anything different about her. Pi had been on the other side of the room and immediately spun around.

"I totally heard you speak inside my head," said Pi.

Aurie tried it again, this time mumbling subvocally, "There's a bug behind you."

When Pi reflexively glanced backwards, she knew it had worked.

"Not funny, sis."

Aurie put the necklace back and tried the music box. It was ornate with a winding handle on the back. She flipped it open to find a dancing faerie wearing a leafy crown. After a couple of spins of the handle, the tiny doll danced while ethereal music filled the air.

The notes were played on instruments Aurie had never heard before. She was so entranced that she didn't notice the song was over until the silence crept back in.

"That was magical," said Ernie.

Everyone looked at their limbs as if they were different after listening.

"I feel better now," said Pi. "My hands don't hurt from slamming into the cliff."

Hannah pulled back her sleeve. "The scar from the thorn is almost gone."

Aurie hugged the music box. "I think this will be perfect for the clinic."

When it came to the final two items, Aurie thought there would be a big debate, but Ernie and Hannah said they had no interest in them. So Aurie took the necklace while Pi took the bracelets.

"We'll split the gold five ways," said Aurie after the trinkets were given out.

"Five?" asked Hannah.

"Rigel's mom should get a share. It's only fair," said Aurie.

Everyone nodded in agreement. It wouldn't bring back her son, but it would at least give her a measure of comfort.

After collecting their gold, they left the Spire. Aurie and Pi went straight to the bank. There was a bit of controversy when they showed up with a bucket full of gold coins, but eventually the Hundred Halls was contacted. The bank manager had thought the coins stolen, but once that was cleared up, Aurie and Pi were treated like royalty.

With the gold in the bank, they headed back to Arcanium.

"What are you going to do with yours?" asked Aurie.

"Pay for tuition, obviously," said Pi. "But after that, I'm not sure. It wasn't as much as I thought, but it means we're not poor anymore. What about you?"

"The clinic," said Aurie. "With Frank Orpheum gone, the district has a chance of rebounding."

Pi had a funny look on her face.

"What?" Aurie asked.

"You remember what Frank Orpheum said about Priyanka?" asked Pi.

"Yeah," said Aurie. "He'd hypnotized her."

"What does that mean? You know, since she was Raz," said Pi.

Aurie frowned. "I don't know. Maybe nothing."

"What about Zayn?" asked Pi.

"Who knows? He's graduating in a week. He was never really that forthcoming about anything outside of here. I have no idea what he's going to do. As far as I'm concerned, I'll never see him again," said Aurie, remembering the last time they'd spoken.

They walked toward the Red Line train station. Aurie carried the music box under her arm. It was quiet in the city, and the nightmare of the bug planet was fading behind them. Besides, they had finals to study for. A student's work was never done.

37

The clinic bustled with activity. Since Aurie had opened it two weeks ago, the number of patients had increased each day. Eventually, she'd have to modify the old dress shop. She was using the changing stations along the wall as the visiting rooms, but they didn't give as much privacy as she would like.

She'd just finished speaking with the parents of a little girl with pigtails and aquamarine scales across her body who had contracted a fungus on her lower legs. Aurie had taken samples and promised them a solution in a few days.

As they left, Aurie made notes about the fungus. Pi could make her a book on the subject to eat. Her sister had been busy working for Radoslav, though in the downtimes, she made edible books for Aurie. There were so many things she didn't know, but she was learning every day. The only problem was that medical texts on non-humans were rather sparse. They were clearly an underserved minority, a problem she hoped to fix.

She was about to call on the next patient when Hannah tapped her on the shoulder. Hannah had been helping out with the running of the clinic since business had picked up.

"There's someone here to see you out front," said Hannah.

"Have them take a number," said Aurie.

Hannah had a cagey expression. "You probably want to take this one. You're caught up anyway. The rest of them just need a minute under the music box."

Hope bloomed in her chest as she thought about who the visitor might be. The little bell on the door rang when it closed behind her. That hope evaporated when she saw him.

"Nezumi," she said, trying not to sound disappointed. "It's good to see you."

He gave her a short bow. "Nezumi happy to see you, Aurie-mage."

"You look well," said Aurie, noting his clean clothing. "How is Annabelle?"

His black eyes lit up. "Annabelle have good strong tail. Sharp teeth like her mother. Grow up strong. Now that wakers gone, Nezumi move family back home."

"Great," said Aurie sheepishly. It'd been her fault they'd had to move. She was glad it had worked out. "Stop by anytime."

Nezumi pressed his hands together, face pinched with thought. "Nezumi feel bad about Aurie-mage's friend."

Frank Orpheum's mass hypnotism had left the district's residents with holes in their memories, but enough remembered the day of the battle that it had become common knowledge.

"Thank you, Nezumi," said Aurie with a heaviness on her heart.

Even though Frank Orpheum had gotten his just deserts in the end, it didn't erase the pain she felt about losing a friend, especially when it'd been her decision to involve him. Thinking about it only made her more dedicated to the clinic.

The little man stepped forward, his coarse eyebrows waggling. "Nezumi ask favor?"

"What is it?" asked Aurie.

"It would be Nezumi's honor if you would have dinner with family tomorrow night. As thank you," he said.

Images of unsavory meals went through her head. She must have done a poor job of hiding her expression because Nezumi chuckled.

"Worry not, Aurie-mage. Wife Christa is head chef at Le Petite Bistro," he said with a giggle.

"Wonderful," she said, relieved. "I'll be there."

Nezumi looked away, mumbled to himself, then sighed.

"Please ask sister-mage to join. But only if not threaten Nezumi or family," he said.

Aurie stifled laughter behind her cupped hand. "Yes. I'll bring Pi. Don't worry. She's much nicer than she seems."

Nezumi said his goodbyes and went across the square to his brick house.

Aurie was about to go back inside when she sensed someone watching her. A figure in a dark hoodie leaned against the dragon fountain. Plumes of water sprayed out of the dragon's mouth, sending streamers of mist into the wind.

Aurie squinted away the sun and approached. Her skin felt tingly and her thoughts scrambled.

"Zayn," she said softly as he pulled back his hoodie.

A moment of pain crossed his gaze as he looked at her. "Aurie."

"Congratulations on graduating," she said.

He bit his lower lip. "You know the last time I saw you, you were dead. I didn't learn the truth until I read an article in the *Herald of the Halls* about your win."

"I'm so sorry," she said, stepping forward to touch him, but feeling a barrier between them. She ached to hold him, kiss him. "I didn't think about that. That you wouldn't know that I was alive."

"It's okay. I deserved it. I was the one that got you mixed up in Priyanka's schemes. It wasn't an accident that you and your sister ended up in a group with Raziyah," he said.

"That's right," said Aurie, remembering the sorting contest. "I always wondered how we both ended up in the same one."

"When I saw you and your friends with Ernie, I knew you would be the best hope for him," he said.

"What about Rigel?" she asked.

"He got unlucky," said Zayn.

"Why? Why were you risking yourself? If Priyanka found out she would have killed you," she said.

"She would have," he said. "But for the same reason you were risking yourself. The only thing I didn't know was that Orpheum had hypnotized her. It's a good thing he's dead, or she'd make him die slowly for that."

When she made a face of not understanding, he added, "I talked to Pi earlier. That's how I knew where to find you. She told me everything. Though you two were the first people I thought of when I heard that he'd died."

His death had been immediately felt by his students and followers. The mourning went round the world. They were planning a Frank Orpheum Day in many countries, including the United States. Aurie had no plans to celebrate it.

"It's the first time a patron has died, well, since Invictus," said Zayn.

"I feel bad for all his students," she said.

The entertainment industry was a wreck. Without a patron to protect them from faez madness, production on new movies and TV shows had ground to a halt. Only the mundane plays and musicals were running on Broadway and at the Frank Orpheum theater. Mages from other halls had been recruited, but they weren't trained in illusions like he had been.

"Some of the older mages from his hall, the ones who

are hardened against faez, have taken a patronage role, but the number is tiny compared to the whole industry," he said. "They're just not strong enough to keep it going."

Every paper in the world was currently debating what to do. When Invictus had died, it'd mostly been a Hundred Halls problem, since the patrons had lived long enough not to need his protection any longer. Though it meant no new halls could open until a head patron was reinstated.

When Orpheum had died, that orphaned a large population of mages that a massive industry had been built upon. Governments around the world were debating the impact.

"How's Priyanka?" asked Aurie.

"It's a good thing classes are over. She's in a foul mood," he said.

"What's she really like?" asked Aurie, thinking about Raziyah. Despite her best efforts, Aurie missed the nerdy black girl.

He gave her a shrug. "I wish I could tell you for sure, but she doesn't really let people in close. The only things I do know is that she's brilliant at what she does, and she's a survivor. I want to believe that she's generally good, but she's practical enough to be brutal if she thinks it's important enough. Why do you ask?"

"I don't know. I spent a year hanging out with her. I'd like to believe that some of Raz was real, though I'm not foolish enough to get my hopes up. I also recognize that this whole thing with Invictus dead has to be coming to a head. The Cabal have too many plots and schemes for it not to. So I'm wondering if she's the enemy or not," said Aurie.

"Give her a reason to be on your side and she might be. Might," he said.

"What about you? What are you doing now that you've

graduated?" she asked hopefully.

"I'm headed home," he said. "I have things I have to take care of back there."

"Why? Why can't you stay?" she asked.

"You know when you found me in the closet, half naked, and I said I was a diabetic? That was a lie, sort of. I have to take regular injections, or I die."

"What? That's terrible. Is that an exotic disease or something?" she asked, brushing her fingertips across his arm.

"Not a disease. Think of it like my blood is poison, and I have to take the antidote to keep it from killing me. It's not exactly like that, but close enough," he said.

She wanted to crush him in her arms.

"So you see," he said, "I don't know if I'll be back. There's only one place to get the antidote, and that's back home. I was only allowed to come here to get training, and now that it's done..."

"Oh," she said softly.

He stepped forward and grabbed her hands, squeezing them tightly.

"What I said on the Spire," he started, but Aurie cut him off.

"I know. You didn't mean it," she said. "I knew it at the time, though it didn't hurt any less to hear it."

"I really like you," he said. "In ways that, given my circumstances, I shouldn't."

"Vague much?" she taunted.

"Sorry. I wish I could say more," he said.

"You don't need to," she said. "I can see it in your eyes, whenever you mention your home, that you have a lot to deal with. But if you ever need someone to talk to, I'll be here."

His eyes were watery, so she leaned in and kissed him.

He tasted like mint. She wrapped her arms around his neck. They kissed until some passerby whistled at them.

When Aurie pulled away, she felt drunk, knees wobbly.

"When do you have to leave?" she asked.

"Tomorrow morning, early. I'm taking a bus," he said.

"Good."

"Good?" he asked.

"That means you can spend the night with me," she said, grinning.

"Really?" he asked, excited. "Where?"

"Meet me at the usual place."

He nodded hungrily.

She glanced at the sky. It was the sort of blue that hung over a mountain range.

"I think there might be a storm tonight," she said.

He looked skeptically at the sky.

"If not, we'll make one," she said, pulling him back in for another kiss.

§§§

Find out what happens next
with book three of The Hundred Halls

ALCHEMY
OF
SOULS

February 2017

Also by Thomas K. Carpenter

ALEXANDRIAN SAGA
Fires of Alexandria
Heirs of Alexandria
Legacy of Alexandria
Warmachines of Alexandria
Empire of Alexandria
Voyage of Alexandria
Goddess of Alexandria

THE DIGITAL SEA TRILOGY
The Digital Sea
The Godhead Machine
Neochrome Aurora

GAMERS TRILOGY
GAMERS
FRAGS
CODERS

THE DASHKOVA MEMOIRS
Revolutionary Magic
A Cauldron of Secrets
Birds of Prophecy
The Franklin Deception
Nightfell Games
The Queen of Dreams
Dragons of Siberia
Shadows of an Empire

THE HUNDRED HALLS
Trials of Magic
Web of Lies
Alchemy of Souls
Gathering of Shadows
City of Sorcery

ABOUT THE AUTHOR

Thomas K. Carpenter resides near St. Louis with his wife Rachel and their two children. When he's not busy writing his next book, he's playing soccer in the yard with his kids or getting beat by his wife at cards. He keeps a regular blog at www.thomaskcarpenter.com and you can follow him on twitter @thomaskcarpente. If you want to learn when his next novel will be hitting the shelves and get free stories and occasional other goodies, please sign up for his mailing list by going to: http://tinyurl.com/thomaskcarpenter. Your email address will never be shared and you can unsubscribe at any time.

17139477R00183

Printed in Poland
by Amazon Fulfillment
Poland Sp. z o.o., Wrocław